He Turned My Mourning Into Joy

He Turned My Mourning Into Joy

A Novel

Lynette Chambers
IOL Publishing

This book is lovingly dedicated to my precious friends
Gilbert and *Joyce Ward*

You have inspired me,
believed in me,
and been there when I needed you the most.
Thank you.

Acknowledgements

THERE ARE MANY people who have helped in my writing endeavors. You each know who you are, thank you.

To my family and friends who have shown me special love and encouragement as I've grown as a writer, I appreciate you more than you might know.

I would also like to thank my Beta Reader Group: This is a special group of women who come from all walks of life. They have challenged me, encouraged me, lifted me up in prayer, and believed in me when I didn't believe in myself. Their invaluable help with proof reading, giving suggestions, prayerful input, and godly wisdom have made this book better than I ever imagined. Without them, I might have given up finishing it long ago.

To my editor, Belinda Forgy, a simple thank you is not enough. May the Lord bless you abundantly for all the hours spent pouring over my drafts, for giving wisdom and input where needed, and for caring enough to challenge me when something could be made better. Without your encouragement and support, this book may never have come to fruition.

And of course to my husband; Jim is my iron that sharpens iron. He pushes me harder than anyone else would dare, and yet he believes in me more than any other. Thank you for all of your help and for your faith in me.

Most of all, I want to thank the Lord for all that He has done in my life. I pray that He will bless this work, accept it as my humble offering and use it for His good purpose in the lives of others.

In His Grace and Mercy,
Lynette Chambers

Daddy?

I'M TAKEN SO aback at how aged he's become
　　The relaxed clothes
　　　　and shorter hair,
　　　　　　so different from when at home.
Then... that sweet smile and outstretched hand
Brings back to my heart a hope.
He at least, I think, knows me, "Daddy's baby."
But, as I hug and greet him without the warm response, the reality of life
prevails.
He no longer sees me as
　　　"his baby,"
I'm just an interruption in his confused routine.
He can no longer connect the memories that stagger through his jumbled
mind.
　　　So,
How do I say good-bye to Daddy, he's here, is sitting in this chair?
What do I do?
How do I cope?
Play the part? Nod and smile?
Is Daddy here, or has he gone?
I grieve! I grieve! He's gone! He's gone.
Yet, here he sits and walks and sees . . .
The TRUTH is all to which I shall cling . . .
　　　. . . of Daddy following our Heavenly Father . . .
　　　. . . of him teaching me to do the same.
To this I cling.
Knowing that someday this moment will pass - much better times will
remain!

　　　　　　　　　　　　　　　　　　　~ L. B. Farris

This poem was written by a dear friend, *L. B. Farris*, as she walked with
her beloved father through the maze that is Alzheimer's. Thank you for
sharing this deepest part of your heart with me and my readers.

Trust in the Lord with all thine heart; and lean not unto thine own understanding.
In all thy ways acknowledge him and he shall direct thy paths.
Proverbs 3:5-6

CHAPTER 1

SUZANNE PARKER WONDERED where the years had gone. It seemed only yesterday when she stood at the altar of the little country church saying her vows to a groom she hardly knew.

She had been a blushing young bride with the whole world ahead of her. He had been a distinguished older gentleman who promised her the world on a platter.

Settling herself for the flight from Dallas to Little Rock, she leaned back in the seat beside her daughter and closed her eyes. She relaxed, knowing that Autumn would entertain herself with her iPod and music of choice during the flight. Truly glad that Autumn was the easiest of children to be with, Suzanne smiled softly to herself. She was blessed with three beautiful children, two sons and a daughter. God had heard the desire of her heart.

Suzanne was tired to her very bones. The past year had taken more out of her than she could ever have imagined. The future looked less bright than she let on to others outside of their immediate family circle. She found herself wondering why things had gone so wrong.

Daniel and she had always had an almost perfect life. Nothing had prepared her for the sorrow of losing her husband before his time. But losing him she surely was, one agonizing day after the other.

Turning her head toward the window and opening her eyes, Suzanne stared out at the azure blue sky, watching a white fluffy cloud drift a few hundred feet away. Blinking to keep the tears from falling, she swallowed hard; pushing back the sorrow with all of her might. Her throat ached with tears held too long, a reflection of the aching of her heart. Now, however, was not the time to give in. It would never do to fall apart with a plane full of strangers looking on.

Leaving Daniel in the long-term care facility while she went back to her hometown to help her mother with some issues, ripped her heart out. And yet, there was little she could do for him; other than sit by his side, reading, praying and hoping for an occasional glimpse of the man she had once known. This had been her life for months now. Only the Lord knew when the anguish would end.

Spying a huge thundercloud forming in the far distance, she watched as bolts of lightning flickered against the bruised blackness of the cloud. Unable to hear the thunder, she was sure it was rumbling across the heavens in unison with the building storm.

"*It's rather like my life,*" she thought. "*Darkness and turmoil building and there is no way to stop the storm from coming. I must simply wait it out and trust that the Lord will see me through.*"

Restless now, she pulled her Kindle out of her bag. Turning it on, she opened it to the Bible section. It always helped to read the Word when her emotions seemed to be spiraling out of control. How many times over the years had she turned to God's Word for solace, wisdom, and understanding. It was her lifeline.

Glancing over at her daughter, she was relieved to see that she was fast asleep. The stress was taking its toll on them all. Autumn was the most exuberant of girls and could find the good in almost anything, yet having so many changes in her young life was overwhelming right now.

She adored her father and was as scared of losing him as Suzanne herself was. This was one of the reasons Suzanne had agreed to make the trip to her hometown to help with some things her mother needed. Both she and Autumn needed a break from the relentless pressures put upon them day after day.

Suzanne was sure that in an emergency she could depend on either of her sons to be there for their father within a moment of time. For that she was more than thankful. They, too, were grasping at trying to understand what was ahead. But they were strong young men and Suzanne had few fears for their ability to cope.

Turning back to her Bible, she turned to Jeremiah 29:11 and read, "*For I know the thoughts that I think toward you, saith the Lord, thoughts of peace, and not of evil, to give you an expected end. Then shall ye call upon me, and ye shall go and pray unto me, and I will hearken unto you. And ye shall seek me, and find me, when ye shall search for me with all your heart.*"

Closing the Kindle and leaning her head back once again, Suzanne meditated on these words for a long while, dissecting them as she had often taught others to do when teaching classes at their church.

"Lord, Father God," she prayed silently, "*I have prayed for you to heal my husband, and yet it seems you have other plans for his life. It would seem that you are determined to take him home with you. If this is true, then I ask that you do so quickly; and that you spare him the humiliation of this terrible disease. Father, I know that you will give us all the strength to get through the loss. Right now, Father, I am so weak and so weary. Hear my prayer, please! Give me your strength. Whatever the expected end is that you have in store for me and my family, I pray that you will lead and guide us to that end. I pray that nothing other than your complete will may be done in our lives. I love you, heavenly Father, and I trust you to the very depths of my being. Thank you for the assurance that you are still in control. Amen.*"

Letting go of all the worries, all the fears, Suzanne Brummell Parker slipped off into a calm sleep, never waking until the plane touched down and it was time to depart. The flight attendant stopped by to offer refreshment, but seeing the sleeping woman with dark circles under her eyes, she thought better of it and went on her way.

She wondered briefly what ordeal might cause such sorrow to be etched on the relaxed features of the mother and daughter. Oh the stories that could be told of passengers on her flights, if only there was time to capture them.

Descending into the Little Rock airport, the giant bird made a rather uneventful landing. Waking a little more refreshed than before and ready to face the future, Suzanne and Autumn made their way to the baggage area where their mother and grandmother awaited them.

Velma Brummell greeted her daughter and granddaughter with a warm hug. Exclaiming as every grandmother has for generations, she marveled at how tall Autumn was growing.

Giving her daughter a quick onceover, she made a funny little snort and said, "Well, Suzanne, I've seen you looking better! I'm thinking a few days of rest and relaxation may be just what the doctor ordered."

Suzanne simply smiled at her mother, knowing that she meant well. Velma was known for her blunt way of putting things, but one never doubted her love for her family and friends.

The next few days flew by in a flurry of events. Suzanne gave in to the pleas of her daughter and agreed to accompany Autumn and her niece, Brenda, along with her own sister, Karen, to the annual Fall Festival. This was held each year at the school where she had grown up. It would be fun, she decided, to see a few friends and to let Autumn experience the rather old-fashioned time of fun and games.

And so it was that she found herself standing in the noisy old gymnasium after so many years; watching people mill around. Some were laughing and talking, others simply taking it all in.

Surprise crossed her face as she recognized the tall man walking toward her through the far door. He was the last person she had anticipated seeing here this night.

C H A P T E R   2

A WAVE OF unexpected emotion swept over Suzanne. She had not laid eyes on him in nearly twenty-five years, had hardly thought of him in almost that length of time. Her life had been full and rewarding, and she rarely dwelt on those days so far in her past. Now, here he was, watching her from across the length of the pockmarked basketball court.

The old sandstone gymnasium was full of busy, noisy families, with children laughing and yelling as they played games for nickel and dime prizes. The Evening Shadows annual Fall Festival was already in full swing. Booths of every kind were hawking their wares. Schoolgirls were selling last minute raffle tickets for a beautiful quilt, handmade by one of the grandmothers. For a moment, the happy sounds were deafening as they echoed through the large gym.

Her eyes connected and tangled with his. Time was suddenly suspended. Suzanne felt as if she was drowning in the sensations washing over her. Everything was so much the same, yet, so very different.

In the space of a few seconds, her mind flew across the years. It was once again homecoming night of their senior year in high school and Peter Clifton was escorting her across the gym floor. She floated beside him in her soft golden chiffon gown. The crimson cape fell in satin folds from her slender shoulders to her ankles. Her sun-streaked golden hair spilled down her back in a cascade of satiny ripples. It was a night when dreams could come true.

Even now, all these years later, she remembered the feelings of that magical, yet uncertain night. Her heart had pounded relentlessly against her ribs. She was nearly breathless as they approached the center court. Suzanne remembered holding onto Peter's muscular arm with a butterfly touch. The sensation of being special was new and heady and exciting.

It had long been the custom of Evening Shadows High School for the homecoming couple to walk slowly from the sideline to center court. Once there, the queen would receive a kiss from the escort she had selected for this special evening and he would present her to the excited crowd by handing her a dozen long-stemmed white roses. As the school flower, they were a high badge of honor. Really though, it was the kiss that was anticipated by one and all.

Each year it varied as to how the kiss was given, and how it was received. Some years the homecoming couple was already engaged and everyone expected them to put on a good show. Then again, some years it might be a pair who had been best friends all through school but everyone knew that they would never be a couple. Regardless, a lot of teasing and catcalls could always be heard from the bleachers as they made their way slowly down the court.

To be sure, Peter and Suzanne were hardly the usual couple. She was the ultimate introvert and he an outstanding star basketball player – a strange pair indeed. Suzanne Brummell didn't have a special guy in her life.

In fact, she had rarely even spoken to any of the boys in her class other than to ask about a class assignment or to respond to a question. On the other hand, Peter could have dated any girl he wanted, and was often seen in the presence of first one girl and then another throughout the years.

It was a long story. Between her minister father being very strict, and the long distance into town, it was nearly impossible to have a steady dating relationship. Added to that, Suzanne was so shy and unsure of herself that even if she had been allowed to date, it was very unlikely that anyone would have asked her.

At least, that was what she had thought before almost the entire senior basketball team selected her as their Homecoming Queen. That came as a complete surprise. To this day, she sometimes found herself wondering if it had been a joke and perhaps she'd never quite gotten the punch line.

Suzanne remembered how very difficult it had been for her to get up the courage to ask Peter to be her escort for that special night. In fact, she was not certain even now how she had gotten up the nerve to ask him. It had all seemed to transpire in a golden glow.

She did remember Peter's best friend, Sol, coming to her and saying that Peter would like to be her escort. Sol even volunteered to let Peter know she had chosen him, if she wanted. He was actually rather cute in his approach.

However, she had told him, "Thanks, but no thanks."

She then indicated sweetly that if Peter Clifton were to be her escort for the special evening she would ask him herself.

She had almost convinced herself that Peter would refuse to be her escort, and she almost gave in to allowing Sol to ask on her behalf. However, rather than hide behind Sol, she finally got up the nerve to approach Peter. To Suzanne's great surprise, he agreed. Almost before she realized it, there they were at center court on that wonderful night.

She remembered, too, her astonishment on that long ago afternoon, during the pre-game pep rally when her name was called out. Her surprise was complete when she realized that almost the entire school was excited that she was to be their Homecoming Queen. Her... little old Suzanne Brummell. If there had been a railroad track in their area, she would have most definitely been from the wrong side. For some reason, she was the chosen one, for this particular night at least.

Suzanne worried that with four brothers and sisters, and the lack of money for extras, she wouldn't have anything appropriate to wear. Her daddy pastored the smallest church in town, and his salary was pitiful, to say the least. Often he gave more away to those in need than he ever made. If it hadn't been for the farm that her mother had inherited, they likely would have starved to death over the years. Even though she and her mama were both very good with the sewing machine, there simply wasn't the money to buy material for a fancy dress.

However, her two best friends had put their heads together and found the lovely dress she had worn. It was a loaner, but even that didn't matter as the soft chiffon drifted around her.

The anxiety had skyrocketed as they drew closer to mid-court. She remembered thinking, "*What if Peter doesn't give me the 'kiss' that everyone expects the queen to receive?*"

It would be the most embarrassing moment of her life if he simply ignored protocol and chose not to kiss her. She would be the laughing-stock of the whole school. In fact, she had overheard someone saying in the girls dressing room that the guys on the team were making good-natured bets. Apparently they, too, were all wondering whether Peter would follow through with the kiss.

He had not disappointed them, or her. Pulling her close, he'd brushed a kiss over her blushing cheek. Whispering in her ear, with a wicked twinkle in his green eyes, and a low chuckle that only she could hear, Peter said, "Let's give 'em a show, Suzie."

Grasping her upper arms in his strong hands, he pulled her closer still and kissed her squarely on her soft lips. She gasped in surprise, while he chuckled once again and said softly, as the crowd roared their approval, "Don't worry, Suzie, I'll still respect you in the morning."

Peter was the first boy ever to call her Suzie. Usually that pet name was reserved for her immediate family. Somehow, it seemed right, coming from his lips.

Now, standing there in a daze of remembrance in the noisy gymnasium these many years later, Suzanne suddenly realized that Peter Clifton was once again speaking to her. He had crossed the room while she was deep in thought, reliving that incredible night and all that led up to it. Now, he was touching her lightly on the arm to get her attention. She looked up, her eyes locking with his, and realized he was asking her a question.

Mentally shaking herself, she listened as he asked her what she was doing back here in his gym after all this time. Gazing wide-eyed up at him with a surprised smile, she asked in return, "What do you mean by 'your gym'? It is as much mine as yours!"

"Oh no," he replied, "you went away and left it and I've had to stay here all these years to make sure that nothing happened to destroy all the memories it holds."

"Memories," Suzanne murmured with a bemused smile on her lips, "I didn't know you guys kept up with things like that."

"But of course, we do," Peter replied softly, "especially when they include someone as lovely and as special as you are."

"If I didn't know better," Suzanne laughed softly, "I'd think you were flirting with me!"

With a definite challenge in his hazel green eyes, he smiled down at her without saying a word. Those same eyes rested momentarily on her slightly parted lips. Then, tearing his eyes away and abruptly changing the subject, Peter asked why she was in town.

Suzanne replied, "My daughter and I came to help Mama take care of some things around the farm and I am assisting her with some legal matters. Then she will go back to Dallas with us for a few weeks."

Peter gazed down at Suzanne for another long moment before touching her arm; he then asked if she would step outside with him.

"Let's go out where it's less noisy so that we can talk and catch up on a few dozen years of happenings," he drawled.

Suzanne glanced around the crowded gym to see if she could find her family. She and Autumn, had come to the festival with Suzanne's older sister, Karen, and her daughter, Brenda.

What would the girls think if they saw her going outside in the evening shadows with a tall, good-looking man? Or worse, what if Karen came back from the restroom and couldn't find her? She would be very upset. Yet, Suzanne really wanted to speak for just a few minutes with Peter, catching up on old times – after all, there was nothing wrong with talking to an old friend.

"Karen will try to make something of it, but then she is always trying to find something wrong with whatever I do. Just because I am married to a minister and have lived most of my life in the proverbial fish bowl," Suzanne thought in a tiny spurt of rebellion, *"it doesn't mean I can't talk to an old friend; even if he is an extremely good-looking fellow!"*

Responding to Peter with a quick, yet uncertain smile, Suzanne shrugged and said, "Sure, I would love to visit for a moment or two."

As they stepped out into the cool evening, Suzanne wondered if Peter had also thought about that night of so many years ago which was still so special to her heart.

Peter seated her on the big granite rock that hundreds of students from years gone by had written their names on, and she thought of all the years in between their homecoming night and now. For the most part, they had been good years. She and her husband Daniel had been happy. They had traveled, raised three children together, and had pastored a successful church for many of those years. When it came right down to it, she knew that she would not change a thing in the life the Lord had blessed her with over these many years with Daniel.

Yet, there was sometimes a feeling of something missing, some longing she had never been quite able to put her finger on. She supposed it was mainly due to the fact that she had missed living in her hometown and being around the ones she had grown up with. Or, perhaps it was that the last few years had been exceptionally difficult.

As kids, she and her sisters used to laugh and say, "Life is tough and then you die!"

"Maybe that's really the way it is," she thought. *"It certainly seems that way for my poor, sweet Daniel. He seems to have more difficulty to deal with than anyone I know."*

Suzanne thought of all the years her husband had spent working so hard to become recognized as a leader in their denomination. She remembered the honors he was awarded and accolades he'd received from his peers. In addition, there were all the times he had given up family times and sharing special things with her and their children. It seemed he always had to work on a project, a writing deadline, or to prepare the next Sunday's sermon.

Somehow he always seemed to come out on top, had always made it come together. Yet, when all was said and done, even he could not seem to overcome this awful, final challenge: the unspeakable horror called Alzheimer's.

CHAPTER 3

Peter was again asking her a question. Suzanne realized she had been in that far off place she often visited of late; the zone she went into of remembering those times with Daniel in his struggle for recognition and acceptance. Remembering the years of hard work and sacrifice the whole family had undergone as he reached to attain the goals that had seemed so important. These things were vital to who Daniel was as a person.

Lately, she found herself trying, perhaps by some half-forgotten thought, to understand all the turmoil that was happening in their lives now. Why had they worked so hard all those years, for it to only come to this? Why would God allow Daniel to suffer as he was? There had to be a bigger plan, a purpose to it all. This illness, and the effect on their lives, was devastating.

It was different from their years of ministry and hard work. Those were difficult in so many ways, too, and yet, they were rewarding in and of themselves. This -- this was different. It was more than the constant striving, trying to understand where the Lord was taking them; and for what purpose. With this illness and the all-encompassing exhaustion, it often felt as if they were all dying one day at a time, right along with her beloved Daniel.

"When does a person ever find peace, and a simpler way of life, or is there any such thing?" Suzanne wondered.

Mentally shaking herself, she realized that she was being rude. Looking up at Peter, she asked him to please repeat what he had said. He responded gently that he only wanted to know if she was all right.

"You seem upset all of a sudden."

"I'm fine," she replied, "things just felt a little strange for a moment."

Squelching a shiver, she reached out her hand toward him beseechingly, asking him to forgive her for not paying attention.

With a small laugh she said, "I feel like someone just walked over my grave, that's all. I'm sure you must have felt that feeling before!"

"Are you cold?" he asked. "But, of course, you are. I am silly for suggesting coming out here in this night air."

"No," Suzanne insisted, "I really am not cold; just a bit disoriented with a deluge of old memories."

Still, Peter shrugged out of his leather jacket and insisted that she put it on. He proceeded to wrap it warmly around her shoulders as if she were made of porcelain. Looking at her intently, he suddenly asked if she was embarrassed to be seen with him.

Wide-eyed with surprise, she replied, "Of course not! Why would I be embarrassed to be with you of all people?"

"Well, I didn't know if you were worrying that someone might tell your husband that you were talking in private with me, or what. You suddenly seemed to draw away. I thought perhaps you wished you had not come outside with me."

"Oh, no," Suzanne replied quickly, "you don't understand. It's not like that at all. You see," she said with a little half laugh, half sob, "Daniel likely wouldn't know if someone did tell him. He has been very ill for the past year with Alzheimer's, and rarely even recognizes me anymore. Besides, Daniel and I have a relationship built on trust."

"Peter, Daniel is in a long-term care facility now, at least when he is not in the hospital. We go there to visit and care for him. I've stayed with him for days on end for the past months, even when he doesn't remember me being his wife. Almost daily, he asks my name, wanting to know repeatedly who I am and why I am there. I have to admit, it is very hard at times to stay and watch what is happening to him. It is so difficult to watch him falter and fade before my very eyes."

Peter instantly became very contrite and reached for Suzanne's hand.

"I'm so sorry, I didn't know. From all that I've heard about you and Daniel over the years you've seemed so happy. Anytime anyone mentioned you, they mostly spoke of your travels all around the world and of the incredible things you and Daniel were doing. You know how people in small towns are; they love to talk about anything of interest! Especially since you and Daniel were always in the limelight, and with his being such an outstanding writer and speaker. I suppose what I am trying to say is that you both have provided folk around here with an inside view to the bigger world that is out there."

As he saw the look of puzzlement on Suzanne's face, Peter sheepishly continued, "Let's just say that you always give them lots of fodder to feed on!"

"Seriously," Peter went on, "the last I'd heard, I'd understood that Daniel was being considered as a candidate for the Pulitzer Prize for one of his translations of a far Eastern literary writing, or something. However, with all of that, I'd not heard that he was sick."

"Well," Suzanne said softly, "we weren't sure what the problem was until about a year ago. However, he had been ill for some time before that. We thought it was stress related, because we were always on the go, and rarely took time for rest or real vacations. In fact, I don't know if Daniel even understands the meaning of the word rest. He has always been one of the most driven men you will ever meet. Anyway, as the symptoms progressed, the children and I were forced to deal with the fact that he'd become worse; and that this is, in fact, a very serious, and potentially fatal illness."

Continuing on, she said, "Daniel's publisher has asked us to keep it quiet as long as possible, or at least until his latest book is published and the award ceremony is over. He is concerned that it might unfavorably affect the sales of the book if the public realizes that Daniel is so seriously ill. I honestly don't think it would hurt the sales at all. In fact, I think it might make people even more anxious to get the book since it is very possibly the last one he will ever write. But, we are under quite an obligation to do as they ask, and I would do nothing to ever exploit Daniel in this illness."

"Daniel isn't that old is he?" Peter inquired gently.

"Not really," Suzanne responded. "He is fourteen years older than me. However, this illness doesn't always recognize age, or even intelligence levels. Oh, to be sure, it is considered an old people's illness. However, as in Daniel's case, it came on earlier than we'd realized, shortly after he turned fifty and has progressed very quickly."

With a deep sigh, Suzanne continued, "It is a very sad thing to watch this happen to anyone, but especially to someone as brilliant as Daniel. There are days that I just have to get away rather than watch his frustration as he tries to remember who he is and what it is he's supposed to do next. It seems that at times he does remember working on his writing projects. So often, however, when he attempts to start working on something, the idea simply slips away from him. Many times, he sits in front of his computer with tears rolling down his face in frustration. It breaks my heart as I can see the anguish he is experiencing at what is happening to him. Sometimes I just have to leave and catch a fresh breath of air."

Drawing a deep breath, Suzanne continued, "More than once, I have been accused of running away and not caring, but that is the farthest thing from the truth! I simply can't stand to see him hurting so and not be able to do anything about it."

Reaching out, Peter touched her shoulder gently. Murmuring softly, he inquired, "Did Daniel get the recognition and acclaim for his work while he could still realize what was going on?"

"Thankfully, yes, somewhat," Suzanne replied. "He did realize the accomplishment of this book being completed, but the process usually takes a year or more to come to fruition, so he has not actually received the award yet. It looks like he will miss that part. However, he did know that he had been nominated and accepted for it. Actually, he has been invited to make an acceptance speech before the Writers Guild in April this next year. It is scheduled to take place the day before his birthday; he will turn fifty-nine that day. However, knowing that he will not be able to attend, short of a miracle, I have petitioned for our oldest son, Adam, to be allowed to appear on behalf of his father. He will accept the award and offer the speech in Daniel's stead."

"It is very difficult for us to accept that Daniel cannot be there," Suzanne continued softly. "This is something he has worked his entire life to accomplish, and now he doesn't even get to experience the joy and fulfillment of that goal coming to completion. Added to that, is the situation with our church. Daniel was forced to resign not quite two years ago now. He just could not keep up with the demands of the position. He began making serious mistakes in administrative decisions and was unable to deal with day-to-day issues. The leadership team eventually came to us and suggested that we step down. Of course, they were more than kind and provided Daniel with a very generous retirement package."

Eyes awash with unshed tears, she added, "Regardless, there is not enough money in the world to replace the sense of fulfillment which Daniel felt with being the pastor of our church. I will never forget that night. He came home a broken and desperate man. It literally ripped my heart out."

Taking Suzanne's chin in his hand, Peter reached out with his lean, solid thumb and gently wiped away a single tear as it trickled slowly down her cheek. Then he reached for her, and without even thinking about it, she was in his arms, surrounded by the solid, warm embrace of a strong, caring man for the first time in more months than she cared to remember.

She smelled the aroma of his cologne and realized that he still wore the same spicy scent as he had on that homecoming night so many years before. Gently, she rested her head on his shoulder and relaxed in the comfort of simply being held by a friend, with no expectations and without any strings attached. It felt right, somehow.

CHAPTER 4

SUZANNE LEANED INTO Peter's embrace for a brief moment, savoring the warmth and the feeling of safety that emanated from him. Even as she hesitated there for a moment longer, she realized that there was no way she could take advantage of the kindness being offered her in even that simple embrace. It suddenly felt uncomfortable for her to take advantage of a friend in this manner; to perhaps give him false hope of something that could not be.

Just as she was pulling away and beginning a shaky apology for her moment of weakness, she heard the sound of a gasp. Turning, she saw her sister, Karen, charging toward them from inside the door of the gymnasium.

Tilting her head back and staring up at the millions of stars overhead. Suzanne took a deep breath and then expelled it slowly; waiting for the storm that she was sure was fixing to break.

Karen, who was clearly furious with her, grabbed Suzanne by the arm and began yelling at her, screaming that she was a hateful, self-centered person.

She shouted, "Here your poor, sick husband is stuck away in a hospital room and you are already making your move with the next man you expect to take his place. You are disgusting and I am ashamed to call you my sister."

She went on and on, until several people passing by on their way into the gymnasium, stopped to stare, trying to figure out what on earth was going on.

Peter stepped over to Karen and, putting his hand out to touch her shoulder, attempted to calm her down. He tried to explain to the distraught woman that she had clearly misinterpreted what she saw happening, but she refused to listen.

Rather than try to understand, Karen turned and snarled at him, telling him how he should be ashamed for trying to take advantage of someone like Daniel.

"And even more," she spewed, "you are exploiting my sister who is obviously in a terrible, hurtful situation."

"But," she said with an ugly smile, making absolutely no sense, "that does not excuse Suzanne for throwing herself at you. I always knew she never really loved Daniel the way he deserved to be loved!"

Breaking away, she immediately began to cry with great shaking sobs as she ran jerkily toward her black BMW parked next to the school lunch building. She yelled back over her shoulder that Suzanne could get her own ride home.

"I am deeply ashamed of you and I am leaving! I don't care how you will get home. Have your friend take you for all I care! You make me sick, sick, sick!"

Watching her sister pull away in a spurt of gravel, Suzanne stood with her hand resting lightly on the old rock where she had been seated just a short while before. With head bowed, feeling as if a ton of bricks had fallen on her. She was the very picture of forlornness. Slowly she turned and looked imploringly up at Peter. She simply held out her hands, palms up in a gesture of surrender, as she shrugged.

"What can I say? I am so sorry for subjecting you to that scene. Karen has been very distraught ever since we informed the family of the true nature of Daniel's illness. She and Daniel have been very close over the years. I even teased him occasionally that I thought my big sister was more than a little in love with him, but he always called me a silly goose. He'd respond to me in that delightful Scottish brogue of his, saying that I was perhaps just a wee bit jealous of his friendship with Karen."

Drawing a deep breath, Suzanne continued, "Well, I guess I wasn't so silly after all! She clearly had deeper feelings for Daniel than even I realized. I am so sad for her, for you, and for Daniel. Oh, goodness, I am just sad for it all! I should never have stepped outside with you. Had I remained inside with the girls this would not have come about."

Peter refused to accept Suzanne's apology and told her to stop worrying about him, and about Karen. He reminded her that there was nothing wrong with what they had been doing.

Growling softly, he said somewhat defensively, "I simply put my arms around you and hugged an old friend who is hurting, for Pete's sake!"

"I know," replied Suzanne, "but you have to understand, living with Daniel over the years was rather like living under a very bright spotlight much of the time. One learns quickly that they can never show their emotions, nor allow their feelings to be too obvious, because there is always someone watching. While we have always loved being in the ministry, Daniel and I learned early on that people can at times be the most vicious creatures on earth. Especially if there is even a hint of scandal about a minister's family."

"Honestly," Suzanne continued in her frustration, "sometimes even if there is no scandal, they will create rumors and make hurtful comments just to have something to talk about! It's quite often like living in the proverbial fishbowl, uncomfortable to say the least."

Completing her vent, Suzanne stood helplessly with shoulders slumped for a moment longer before whispering sadly, "Peter, what I am saying is, that as the wife of a prominent church leader, I have learned to never allow anyone to find reason for even a hint of scandal. I was completely aware of that when I chose to step out here to talk with you for a few moments. I should have allowed wisdom to rule my heart and simply stayed inside waiting for my family."

Sighing, Suzanne continued a bit more heatedly, "At the very least, I certainly should never have let it go so far as to return your embrace. I do admit though, it is sweet of you to care, and I felt comforted for a moment at least. I treasure your gesture of friendship more than you can know."

With a tiny catch in her voice, Suzanne softly admitted, "It has been very difficult to carry this burden alone for so long."

Then, putting up her hand as if to ward off his comforting touch, she hurried to say, "Now don't get me wrong, my children and my mother have been wonderful. My sons, Adam and Jamie, as well as my daughter, Autumn, have been so compassionate and careful of me. The children have spent hours at a time with their father to allow me a chance to escape for a few moments to regroup. Mama has come and stayed with us, and has cooked meals and cleaned house for me, when I was so exhausted from caring for Daniel that I could do nothing more than collapse on the couch. Their strength has gotten me through the worst of times."

"And now," she whispered, "to know that you are here as my friend, is amazing. It is wonderful to know the genuine, caring concern of an old friend, even if for a fleeting moment. Thank you for giving me that moment."

Peter reached out mutely for Suzanne, but she held him off with an outstretched hand.

"Peter," Suzanne continued, "I never even considered running into you tonight. Having all of this come about was certainly not intentional. I am so embarrassed by Karen's reaction, but in some ways, she is right. I have no right to seek comfort from another man with my husband lying ill in a hospital bed."

Laying her hand gently on his arm, she whispered, "Please forgive me for making you a spectacle before the town's people and your friends. I will be gone in a few days, but you must live on under their scrutiny."

Finally, unable to take her emotionally beating herself up any longer, Peter reached over and placed his hand over hers, squeezing it gently.

"Suzanne," he said, "nothing you could ever do would embarrass me. You are a wonderful friend and a lovely lady. My heart goes out to you in your pain. If anyone should be embarrassed, it should be me for taking you in my arms and setting you up for condemnation. And Karen should be held responsible for completely misreading a situation that she butted into and did not take time to evaluate before spouting off."

However," he continued with a lopsided grin, "you don't need to worry, Suzie, I'll still respect you in the morning!"

Suddenly, they were both laughing together; a long lost memory shared. Suzanne looked up at Peter through unbelievably long, thick lashes and murmured achingly, "Do you know how long it has been since I have had anything to really laugh about?"

Then, with an intense look crossing her face, Suzanne asked, "Peter, may I ask you one question before I go find the girls and get us a ride home?"

With just a touch of laughter left in his voice, he replied, "Suzanne, you could ask me for the moon right now and I would probably try to reach high enough to pluck it from the heavens for you! Ask away!"

Just then, Autumn and Brenda came flying up. Autumn grabbed Suzanne around the waist, swinging her around in a whirlwind of love and emotion.

"Mom," she exclaimed, "where did Aunt Karen go? We saw her leave and she seemed as if she was very angry! What did you do now to get her so incredibly upset?"

Digging her heels into the gravel to stop the momentum of Autumn's excitement, Suzanne scolded her affectionately, "Autumn, remember your manners."

Looking at Brenda and Autumn with a smile, she said, "Girls, let me introduce you to one of my old school friends. This is Mr. Peter Clifton. Peter, this is my daughter, Autumn, and her cousin, Brenda. They are sometimes a little wild and crazy, but overall are really very nice people!"

Peter acknowledged both girls with a handshake and a smile, and asked if they were having fun at the festival. Brenda grinned hugely and replied that the festival was a lot more fun than sitting in History class with him. She then proceeded to explain to Autumn and Suzanne that Mr. Clifton was her History teacher.

Smiling with deep dimples and a sparkle in her sherry brown eyes, she said, "He sure seems to be a lot more fun and exciting after school hours than during! You better be careful, Aunt Suzanne, he might just sweep you off your feet!"

"Brenda," Suzanne reacted, "please don't say things like that. You are embarrassing me. Besides, we have had more than enough drama with your mother tonight to need any more for quite a while."

"Now, to answer your question, Autumn," Suzanne said, "I may as well tell you before you hear her version. Your Aunt Karen came upon Mr. Clifton and me talking. I had been telling him about your father's illness. Just then, Peter reached out and gave me a hug of comfort, as is often shared between two old friends. That's when Karen came through the door and saw us in what she thought was an inappropriate embrace. She became very angry. After saying a few hateful words, she left before we could convince her that what she thought she saw and what had actually happened were two totally different things."

Turning to her niece with a look of apology, Suzanne continued, "Brenda, please, understand; I am not trying to make you uncomfortable by discussing your mother. However, Karen really should have gotten the facts straight before she reacted the way she did."

"Don't worry, Aunt Suzanne, I understand," Brenda replied. "Mom is always acting first and thinking later. It must be that red hair of hers! Besides, everyone who knows you knows that you would never do anything wrong. Why, my goodness, you have been married to Uncle Daniel for simply forever!"

"Thanks, Brenda. I think." Suzanne smiled.

Continuing, she said, "Well, girls, I forgot and left my cell phone in my jacket at home, but I wasn't worried about it since Karen was driving us here and back. I suppose one of you should use your phone to call your grandmother and see if she can come pick us up. After all, it is getting close to the stroke of midnight and we all know what happens to lovely young ladies then!"

Watching the three of them with a smile on his lips, Peter spoke up and said he would be glad to see them home.

"After all," he noted, "it really isn't that much out of my way, and it was technically my fault for you losing your ride home. If I hadn't embraced you, then Karen would not have gotten mad, and you all would have been able to ride home with her!"

Suzanne thanked him laughingly, but said she thought she had done enough damage to his reputation already for one evening, and certainly to her own. She replied that she did appreciate his offer, but that they had better find their own way home.

Leaning toward him, she softly murmured, "Why, with the way rumors fly in a small town, if you actually took us home it would probably be all over the county by morning that a wildfire affair had started!"

With eyes filled with laughter, she took his hand in both of hers and bid him goodbye. She then turned to see if Autumn was calling her grandmother. The girls had started on ahead of her and were yelling back that they would call their grandmother, but first they needed to go to the restroom. They shouted that they would be right back to wait with Suzanne.

Peter called to Suzanne to wait up. He strode over to where she was already standing on the first step of the gymnasium stoop. Looking at her with a question on his face and a raised eyebrow, he inquired, "Suzanne, you never did get to ask me your question."

Looking a bit confused and more than a little embarrassed, she replied, "Oh, Peter, it is not important now, perhaps another time. It was just a thought I had, but it can certainly wait."

"Here," she suddenly exclaimed, "I still have your coat! I am so sorry. I certainly did not mean to take it with me!"

Shrugging out of the warm leather, she handed it back to him. Immediately, she felt the chill of the night air. Deep within she realized it was more than that. It was the loss of the warm jacket with a hint of

Peter's cologne about it that made her feel bereft. But even more, it was the thought of losing the comfort of a friend in her time of need.

Mentally shaking her head, she silently reminded herself that this was not the time, nor the place, to start mooning over an old beau, not that Peter had ever actually been that. As much as she would have loved to have been his special girl all those years ago, reality was that it hadn't been meant to be. Now, she had a life to live and a husband to take care of.

Holding the coat, Peter touched Suzanne's arm briefly. "May I see you again?" he asked.

Looking up at him, surprised, she replied, "Peter, I don't think that would be wise under the circumstances. I mean, really, we have caused quite a stir tonight already!"

"Please?" he insisted. "How long will you be in town?"

She reiterated again that they were just there for a couple of days to take care of some business matters for her mother. They would then take her back home with them to help with Daniel as he was being sent home for a period of what the hospital called home comfort time.

Suzanne explained that this was designed to put the patient back in his home surroundings on a regular basis to, hopefully, help him have a measure of normalcy in his life; in spite of the waste of the disease.

Nodding understandingly, Peter insisted that there must be some way that they could see each other, even if just for a few moments, before she left again to go back to Dallas.

After a few seconds of thought, Suzanne reluctantly agreed to meet him the next afternoon for coffee, but only for a few minutes.

Peter said that he could get away for an hour or so in the afternoon, after he finished at a teacher's workshop. He wanted to meet at the coffee shop downtown called Miss Pitty Pat's Cafe.

"Surely we can talk over a cappuccino, or a sandwich, without anyone being able to make anything of it," Peter said.

After a moment or so of uncertainty, Suzanne confirmed that she would meet him, but insisted that she would bring the girls along just to ensure that it would not look to anyone as if she was meeting him inappropriately.

In a very serious tone, and a deeply saddened look in her eyes, she reminded him that she had a reputation to keep, especially now that Daniel was so very ill. Knowing he might not truly realize her situation, Suzanne spoke earnestly to him.

"Peter, you may not quite understand my position. I would never wish to do anything that might bring even a hint of shame to Daniel's name, nor to our marriage. I know we were somewhat joking around earlier about the whole fishbowl thing, but the truth of the matter is that I am always careful to protect what Daniel and I have together. I love my husband more than anything."

"That said, yes, I will meet with you for little bit tomorrow, but just so that you will know that I am not a rude person, nor do I hold any anger toward you for this awkward situation tonight."

Peter immediately agreed to her bringing the girls along. "In fact," he said, "I should have thought of that myself."

"After all," he chuckled, "that 'spotlight' might come on and we certainly would not want to be caught under it in another compromising situation!"

"Of course, as a gentleman, I must insist on paying for our food," Peter stated in a no nonsense tone, with a straightforward look at Suzanne.

She smiled, and agreed to that.

Just then, the girls came bouncing outside, calling out to Suzanne.

Autumn pointed out Suzanne's mom coming to their rescue in her beat up old station wagon. Velma had been in town grabbing a few groceries and was able to run right over to pick them up.

On pure impulse, Suzanne reached up and gave Peter a quick, warm hug right there in front of everyone. She breathed a word of thanks into his ear for his compassion and concern, and then turned and hurried to the car as if she was embarrassed at her own actions.

Completely taken off guard by her unexpected behavior, Peter stood there dumbfounded and watched them drive away without saying another word. He felt like a whirlwind had just blown over him.

He knew he would be up long hours this night, waiting to meet with Suzanne and the girls come tomorrow. He could still feel the warmth of her sweet breath on his neck as she whispered her soft thanks before pulling swiftly away.

"*No doubt about it*," he thought, "*it will be a long, long night.*"

CHAPTER 5

AFTER WATCHING SUZANNE and the girls drive away with Velma, Peter walked slowly over to his old beat up Jeep Cherokee. Seeing Suzanne tonight had brought back a flood of emotions he had thought long buried.

He sat in his truck for several minutes before turning the ignition on, thinking back over the past twenty-five or so years. Right after high school, he had gone away to college, never dreaming that Suzanne would suddenly decide to get married while he was away.

He remembered the long nights of studying. Many times the only thing that kept him going was thinking of ways he would approach Suzanne on his next trip home. His plan was to at some point tell her how he felt about her.

He had loved her for almost as long as he could remember; even before the night of the homecoming event. Somehow, though, he could never seem to find a way to let her know how he felt.

Although he hid it well, he had always been almost painfully shy, in spite of the fact that he was one of the smartest kids in the class and considered an outstanding basketball player. It seemed when something mattered the most, that is when he just froze up completely.

Oh, he was popular to be sure, and the girls all made over him. He never doubted that he could date any of them he wanted. Yet, to ask Suzanne Brummell to go out with him was more than he could imagine doing.

He had been out with many girls over the years, but that was different. It was easy to ask someone to a movie or dance when there was no
emotional attachment involved.

Even now, Peter could still remember the feel of Suzanne's hand on
his arm that night as they had walked across the freshly buffed floor of
the basketball court. Although she wore long white gloves covering her
dainty fingers, he'd felt as if a fire were branding him for life as her hand
rested lightly upon his arm.

And the kiss. . . ah, that much debated kiss. It seemed such a little
thing in reflection, but he could still remember the confusion he'd felt
over whether to give her the expected and much anticipated kiss. All the
guys on the basketball team had teased him unmercifully for days on end.
He'd suspected they were laying bets on whether he would go through
with it. Sure enough, they were.

He had not wanted to defile the emotions he felt for Suzanne by giving
in to the peer pressure. Yet, he realized that if he didn't kiss her, then her
feelings were sure to be hurt and she would think that he didn't care. In
reality, however, he cared way too much.

Remembering how he'd managed to fulfill the expectations of the
crowd, without unduly embarrassing Suzanne, brought a smile to his lips.

That had been a night filled with wonder and excitement. It was
too bad he had not carried it beyond the moment, and claimed Suzanne
Brummell as his own. With all his heart he wished he had asked her to be
his steady girlfriend, and eventually put a ring on her finger. But there was
no going back, and life had taken a different turn. He wondered sometimes, even now, if she ever thought about and remembered that night.

It was at the beginning of his second college semester that he had
heard from a friend that Suzanne was getting married. He could still
remember the shock that had rocked his whole system at the news. He
felt like the world had fallen out from under him and that life would never
be the same again.

"*Surely it can't be true,*" he'd thought. "*How could this have happened? And why?*"

He remembered leaving class for the rest of the day and wandering around the small college town for hours. Later, he couldn't remember where he actually went. Somehow, he finally wound up back at the dorm, exhausted from the emotional turmoil he was experiencing.

One part of him wanted to get in his old truck and drive the two hours back home to confront Suzanne with the hundred and one questions of why, and how, she could do this to him. Then the rational side of his brain would remind him that she didn't even know that he loved her. How could he know or even think she would want to see him? Besides, what could he offer her?

At nineteen years old, with only a half year of college completed, he knew his dad would never consider letting him get serious enough about anyone for marriage and all that it would entail. His parents had worked hard to guide him in the direction his life should take.

It had been droned into him since childhood that education was the key to life and only those with a degree would succeed. How could he risk everything, particularly his relationship with his father, to go to a girl and lay his heart on the line? Especially when, as far as he knew, she barely even realized that he existed, and certainly wasn't in love with him. Deep down, he knew he was losing her forever. He remembered feeling as if the demons of darkness were pulling his mind apart. Every argument seemed to have an answer that led him everywhere but back to Suzanne.

For several hours he lay on his dorm bunk in the dark, trying to get a perspective on it all. He finally called his dad to get his input on the problem. After all, he reasoned, his dad knew Suzanne fairly well since he had been their high school Principal. Maybe he could help unravel the puzzle somehow.

Peter remembered how, after telling his father what he had learned of the upcoming marriage of the girl he loved, his father had said nothing. A long silence lasted on the phone, seeming to stretch for eternity.

Finally, after what seemed like forever, his dad had replied, "Suzanne Brummell is a fine girl, Son, but is she really the girl for you right now? You have your goals all set, your classes are coming along fine and your mom and I are so proud of the direction you are headed in."

Then with a slight hesitation in his voice, he went on to say, "Son, there is one thing I think I should tell you. Your mom was in the dress shop last week and overheard a couple of the ladies insinuating that apparently Suzanne is, how can I say this gently? She is said to be, well, in the family way."

Peter immediately burst out with a denial that this was impossible. "It is a lie, Suzanne would never do something like that."

His father replied, "Son, I wouldn't hurt you for the world, but these things do happen and let's face it, the wedding did come up very suddenly."

Stunned by the possibility, Peter slowly hung up the phone. Only after doing so, did he realize that he had forgotten to say goodbye to his father.

Even now, as he sat in his truck some twenty-five years later, he could remember the pain he had felt that night. Once again he felt the betrayal of lost innocence and the feeling of hope gone forever sweep over him.

Peter remembered going through the next few weeks of school in a daze, trying to get started into winter semester while feeling like his whole world had been knocked off balance. Somehow, he had always thought Suzanne would be there, waiting for him when he was ready to go to her and proclaim his love. She was his, in his heart at least.

"*How did she meet this guy?*" he wondered on more than one occasion.

He soon found out that the man Suzanne was to marry was from out of town and was quite a lot older than Suzanne. Apparently, they had met at some party and the courtship had moved forward with a speed that defied belief. For the life of him, Peter could not believe she would just up and marry a complete stranger.

This was a girl who had rarely dated and was very shy. Oh, she was beautiful, and had a lovely personality once you got to know her, but to fall in love with a complete stranger at the drop of a hat? What could have happened? And what was even more confusing; was she really having a baby? If so, how did it happen? Had the guy forced himself on her and then coerced her into marriage? Was the vicious rumor even true? There were so many questions and so few answers. He had heard, too, that the man was quite well set financially.

"Surely that alone would not have swayed the girl I know and love," Peter had groaned in his misery.

After much agony, Peter decided that he would go to the wedding. He'd found out that it had been announced in the local paper and almost everyone in town would be there. He argued to himself that at least then he could determine, once and for all, if Suzanne really seemed happy, or if it appeared that she was being pushed into something against her will. If so, he declared in the impetuousness of youth, he would challenge the ceremony and drag her away, even if it created the biggest scene this town had ever seen.

Sitting in the crowded pew that late Sunday afternoon, watching the girl he loved with all of his heart walk down the aisle, Peter felt as if a part of himself was literally dying. He held onto the edge of the old, worn out church pew with white knuckled fingers as the turmoil raged within. It took all of his willpower to keep from running to the front of the church and falling on his knees before God and everyone, begging Suzanne to please not make this huge mistake.

Watching her closely, he searched for signs of a possible pregnancy. From all he could see, she was the same sweet, gentle, pure girl he had always loved from afar. He searched for any sign of distress as she spoke her vows to the man beside her. However, she had a gentle glow about her that spoke of a calm assurance and well-being. It was all so utterly confusing to his bruised heart and mind.

He remembered hearing the murmur as the minister performed the ceremony. His mind rebelled at the giving and taking of the vows. The scene was burned into his brain as Suzanne and the groom replied, affirming their love and sealing his fate.

Realizing all of a sudden that the congregation had risen, he was brought abruptly back to reality. The bride and groom were walking down the aisle together as man and wife. She was smiling up at the handsome older gentleman as if besotted.

Peter was stunned. It was over. His dream of love died a violent death right before his eyes. The girl he loved now belonged to another.

His upbringing and commitment to his father's plan for him had won out. He had lost all that was truly important to him.

With an awful, terribly empty, gut-wrenching feeling, Peter pushed and shoved against people he'd known all his life. He barely recognized anyone as he tried to get out of the church as fast as he could. He found himself fighting against the crowd, like a salmon fighting upstream, trying to get out before anyone saw the unmanly tears that filled his eyes and threatened to flow.

All he could really remember of the rest of that terrible day was sitting under the old bridge down by the river, moaning and hurting like some wounded animal. He remembered clearly, wondering what all his efforts were going to be for from here on out. What was he going to do with the rest of his life... alone, alone, alone.

Later on, back in college, he had dated several girls over the next few years. At one point, shortly after Suzanne was married, he'd even considered engagement to one in particular, but when things started getting serious, he just couldn't follow through. His heart told him that to marry someone in retaliation was the worst of wrongs. Not only would it be unfair to the girl in question, it would ultimately destroy him as well.

"Funny thing," Peter thought, *"I can barely remember the girl's name now."*

It seemed no one had ever filled that deep longing in his heart the way just seeing and holding Suzanne, however briefly tonight, had done.

Peter thought about the day he had learned that Suzanne and Daniel had birthed their first child together; their son, Jamie. By then he had come to grips with the fact that he had lost his chance with Suzanne. However, the pain was still sharp as he heard from his mother, down to the smallest details, about the new baby boy.

Peter's mother, Nadine, had been at a wedding shower for one of the young women in the community. Velma was there too, and was excited to tell the group of ladies all about her new grandson. Of course, Nadine, came home and shared the information with him.

A part of him wanted to know the facts, all of them. Especially since it had been well over one year from the wedding date to when the child was born. He was glad that the old biddies had been wrong. Suzanne could not have been pregnant at her wedding, and for that he was glad.

However, another part of him wanted to stick his head in the sand and pretend that Suzanne was simply away visiting family and would be home any day. He wanted to hope that they could pick up where they left off in his dreams and form a life together. That was foolish, of course. Life was filled with disappointments, and he had long ago come to accept that his and Suzanne's life were on two separate tracks. Being the strong man that he was, Peter had struggled on, living one day at a time.

Slowly, as if coming out of a daze, Peter now realized that the parking lot was empty and he was still sitting there in his old Jeep. Feeling more than a little silly, he realized that even after all these years, Suzanne Brummell had the ability to make him lose track of time. She alone seemed able to induce daydreaming, and reduce him to feeling like a nineteen-year-old kid again.

Turning the key in his ignition, he began the drive back to his lovely log ranch house out on the back forty acres of his parent's property that he had built a few years ago. It was built from the remnant of his dreams and looked more as if it belonged in a magazine than to a humble high school teacher. He supposed that in the back of his mind he had always hoped to share it one day with the woman he loved.

"*Lord,*" he prayed, "*help me to keep my eyes on You and to know that all things work to the good of those who love You and are called according to Your purpose. I realize that I still have strong feelings for this woman, but it appears that once again the timing is all wrong. Help me to honor You in all that I say and do.*"

Peter glanced at his mom and dad's house as he drove by and saw that the lights were on in their bedroom. He knew they were probably reading together before dropping off to sleep. He was amazed that the old anger and hurt he had carried for so long against his parents was no longer there. It was a hard-earned victory; forgiving his father for advising him against having a relationship with Suzanne. One that had taken him years to get a handle on.

He now felt a deep sense of well-being as he thought about where God had brought him to over the years. Through the pain and suffering, he had grown and become a stronger man of God than he had ever believed possible.

Smiling at the goodness of his Savior, he pulled into his drive and turned the engine off. Peter sat for a few more quiet moments; resting in the peace that embraced him. The tall pines surrounding the cabin were stark black against the setting sun, swaying slightly in the evening breeze. Birds flitted here and there as they settled for the night. A small red fox ran across his side yard, hurrying to the den it had established out past the woodpile.

The scene before him filled him with joy and contentment; it always did. He loved this place that he had carved from nothing. It was a part of him. He was a part of it. The huge log and glass structure was a reflection of his life and his devotion to the Lord. It would be standing long after he was gone. The beautiful yard and surrounding forest was perfection. He would give anything to have someone special to share his home and his dreams with. For now, however, he was content to simply enjoy the home and life God had given him.

Although Peter's heart ached a little to know that once again he would be alone as night drew to a close, he was determined to stay the course. One thing that he had come to realize over time, in spite of everything, was that God truly does have everything planned out.

"His timing is always perfect," Peter said aloud as he opened the truck door and stepped out into the cool evening air.

CHAPTER 6

D RIVING TOWARD THE turnoff to her house, Velma asked Suzanne what had happened with Karen at the festival. Looking over at Suzanne with a concerned look on her face, she said that all she had understood from the girls' phone call was that Karen was upset and was yelling at Suzanne in front of people in the parking lot. Of course, then Karen had apparently left them all stranded, with Peter Clifton somehow the center of it all.

"Now that makes for a juicy morsel of gossip if there ever was one!" exclaimed Velma.

Suzanne patted her mother on the knee and said, "Bear with me, Mama dearest, I will explain it all once we are in the house and settled over a cup of your wonderful, hot blackberry tea. Trust me though, nothing truly terrible happened; and I haven't compromised poor Peter. Not too much anyway!"

Velma chuckled and replied that from what she had heard about Peter over the years, it would take an awful lot to compromise him.

"In fact," she said with a little wink at Suzanne, "maybe that would be the best thing that has happened to him in years! It seems like he has just gone from one bad situation to another, and yet he is one of the sweetest, kindest men around. It's rather unbelievable that some money grabbing she-woman hasn't snatched him up over the years! Now, I am really trying hard not to let my imagination run away with me and think something that would be better left unthought-of about the situation tonight."

"Seriously, Mama, why does Karen have to get so upset and jump to conclusions like that?" Suzanne asked.

Sighing, Velma replied, "Karen is just Karen. Sometimes we have to accept people as they are and love them in spite of themselves. You know that she always thought the sun rose and set over Daniel. In fact, forgive me for saying so, but I have often wondered if it might not have been better if Daniel had taken to Karen, rather than to you, Suzie; providing she had been free to marry. Of course, she wasn't free to consider it even if he would have wanted her, having married Bill Ivey already. But then, going through that debacle of a marriage with Bill was her choice. I've always thought she and Daniel might have been happier people had it been different and they had found each other early on. They seemed at times to have more in common than you and Daniel ever did!"

"There, now I have said it. I am sorry if that sounded judgmental or hateful in any way, but sometimes I couldn't help but wonder over the years why Daniel married you. It seemed at times he expected something out of you that you didn't have to give. Or, maybe, it was that he simply acted as if you never measured up to his expectations for you. I don't know. It used to make your Daddy madder than an old wet hen at how Daniel acted. He would fuss and fume for days after you and Daniel had gone home, wondering if Daniel treated you better when away than he did when here."

Suzanne didn't know what to say. She had never dreamed that her mother, or her daddy for that matter, thought anything of the sort, and she certainly had not entertained the idea that they held any ill feelings toward Daniel. In her mind, Daniel was the perfect spouse for her and was the man God had directed her to; their life was meant to be, without a doubt.

Sure, there were times when he could be stern and perhaps seem unreasonable, but she had simply considered that to be due to the age difference between them more than anything. It never overly concerned her that he would get frustrated with her or the children at times. For the most part, she had actually given his somewhat autocratic attitude very little thought, other than to try to do better to make him happy.

Remaining silent, Suzanne pondered the things her mother had rather unceremoniously shared with her. It was certainly a night of new disclosures.

As the car turned into the lane leading to the lovely old farmhouse where Velma had lived for the past fifty years, Brenda spoke up from the back seat, "Gram, you know Mom really struggles with some deep emotional problems. Besides, she takes so many prescription drugs that at times she is like a walking zombie. At other times she is just right out wild acting! Tonight was just an example of what my brother and I deal with all the time. We love Mom, but she really needs to get help! I guess we all need to pray for her."

Velma brought the old green station wagon to a stop at the end of the long, tree-lined driveway and turned to face the girls in the back seat.

She gently said to them, "I am so glad you know that prayer does help. So many times, I wonder where I went wrong with my own children. It seems that all of them, except Suzie, absolutely take pleasure in flaunting their sinful lives in the face of God. I swear, it is enough to make a preacher man curse at times."

Chuckling a little at her own private joke, Velma continued, "I am so very grateful that the sins of the father, or the mother for that matter, are not visited upon the children! You girls are such an encouragement to me, and I am so very proud of the stand you have taken in your Christian walk. I pray every day that you will stand firm in your faith and will not let the things of this world sway you in any way."

Suzanne reached out to take Velma's hand. Turning slightly, she reached across the back seat and held onto Brenda's hand tightly; while Autumn took Brenda's other hand and snuggled up close to her cousin. Together the four of them said a prayer for Karen, and for Daniel, and the rest of the family.

There was a feeling of the sweet presence of the Lord in the old worn out vehicle as they each one wiped tears from their cheeks. For several moments they sat, resting quietly in His presence at the end of the long day.

As the prayer and quiet time ended, Suzanne reached out and hugged her mom. She then sweetly scolded Autumn and Brenda, telling them it was way past their bedtime and they surely would turn into big, fat, orange pumpkins if they didn't get right upstairs, brush their teeth and get into bed.

Laughing, they all jumped out of the car and scurried into the house. Suzanne saw the girls settled in for the night. She hugged each of them tightly as she tucked the worn old quilts under their chins, and kissed each of them on the tip of their nose. She couldn't help feeling so blessed to have such a sweet, kind daughter, and a lovable and incorrigible niece.

Even at fifteen, they were still very naive and precious, all the while trying to appear quite grownup. She would never regret that she had sheltered her daughter as much as was humanly possible from the harsher things of life. Autumn was a lovely girl, and would grow to be a kind and caring young woman, without a doubt.

Leaving the room quietly, as their eyelids drifted slowly shut in the peaceful sleep that only the young seem to enjoy, Suzanne went down the stairs and wandered into the cozy old kitchen. She sank gracefully down in the ladder-back chair at the place she had sat all those long years ago when living at home with her mom and dad.

There was a steaming cup of blackberry tea already at her place. Velma had prepared it for her, along with a plate of homemade cookies. These just happened to be her favorite kind; chocolate oatmeal raisin with a hint of coconut in their depths.

Resting her elbow on the table, and putting her forehead in her hand, she closed her eyes and sighed deeply. Then, peeking up at her mother, Suzanne smiled a tired little smile.

"Come on," Velma said, "out with it. What on earth happened between you and Karen tonight, or between you and Peter for that matter?"

While sipping her tea and nibbling on the yummy cookie that Velma had baked just for her, Suzanne explained about seeing Peter again after all those years.

She told her mother about the instant connection and compassion she had felt with him; especially when telling him about Daniel and all that they were going through with his illness. Then she explained about Karen's incredibly embarrassing reaction when she saw her in Peter's embrace.

"Honestly, Mama," Suzanne said, "having Peter actually take me in his arms tonight was the farthest thing from my mind. We were simply outside talking and I was telling him about Daniel, and it just happened."

Looking confused, and a little sad, Suzanne said, "You do know that I love Daniel. I will always love him deeply. It is all just so danged hard. We know, that short of an absolute miracle, he isn't going to get well. In fact, the doctor just told me this past week that Daniel is in the final stages of the disease, and will most likely go downhill very quickly from here. I don't want to see that happen. I haven't even told the children that yet. I just feel like there should be something more that we can do, something that could fix the problem!"

Taking another sip of her tea, Suzanne continued, "More than anything, I certainly don't want anyone to get the opinion that I am looking for another relationship. That would be the ultimate disrespect to Daniel and to our love."

"How long does the doctor anticipate before Daniel takes that direction?" Velma asked as she reached across the table and placed her worn, wrinkled hand over Suzanne's.

"He wouldn't give an absolute, but probably within the next few months at best. Possibly even sooner," Suzanne replied.

"Oh, Mama," she cried, "how can I bear it? How does one watch the person they have spent more than half their life with just waste away and die? Where does God figure into all of this pain? I have tried so hard to believe for a miracle but it just hasn't happened. How can this be God's will; especially for a man like Daniel who has worked so hard and served the Lord to the very best of his ability all these years?"

Velma looked gently at her daughter. She saw her pain reflected on her face and realized she was hurting deeply. Praying for words to heal and to help she knew there was no easy fix to this terrible dilemma. Reaching out her careworn fingers, she gently pushed the hair off Suzanne's forehead and whispered to her.

"Suzie, don't let this illness, as awful as it is, come between you and the Lord. You know that in doing that you would break Daniel's heart if he knew, to say nothing of breaking our Lord's heart too. Remember what Psalm 30:5 says about 'joy coming in the morning.'"

"I certainly don't know why God is allowing Daniel and you, and the kids too, to suffer so, but I do know that He is still in control! We can't start doubting God at this point in the game. Besides, if He truly has our best interest at heart, and He does, He also knows exactly what the future holds and what each of us needs as we walk this walk of faith in Him. He will never let us down. God is ever faithful!"

Pausing for a moment, Velma drew a deep breath and spoke again, "Perhaps God is taking Daniel's memories and his sense of commitment from him so that it will be easier for him to leave this earthly world. It is even possible that the Lord is preparing you to begin the grieving process a little early so that you and your children can begin the healing process with a little less pain than it might have been otherwise. I certainly don't know all the answers, but there must be a purpose for all of this, a reason that God is allowing all of us to go through this terrible, hard thing."

Quietly, Suzanne nodded. Then she stood up, put her hand on her lower back and leaned backward in a long, tired stretch. Running her slender fingers through her hair in a futile attempt to think clearly, she shook her head at Velma.

"I know all of that with my head, Mama, but my heart still rebels when I get up each morning and have to see the state Daniel is in. It hurts so much when I see my kids missing their dad. To say nothing of all the multitude of other things that must be dealt with because of this tragedy in our lives. At these times, I can only remind myself that the scripture says that God will not put more on us than we can bear. Well, some days, I have to wonder if He knows what my breaking point is!"

Sighing deeply, Suzanne finished her thoughts, "There certainly isn't much room for joy; in the morning, or at any other time. But don't worry, I am not losing my faith, I am just bone weary and wish that God would choose to either heal Daniel, or to take him on to be with Him. As terrible as that might sound to some people, that is truly where I am right now."

Giving her mom a hug and a kiss on the softly wrinkled and familiar cheek, Suzanne turned to go slowly up the stairs to her old childhood room under the eaves.

Velma sat tiredly back in her kitchen chair and sipped at her now lukewarm tea. Tears of sadness for her daughter slid freely down her cheeks as she closed her eyes and offered up a prayer for strength for Suzanne, and for them all. After a while she got up, rinsed out their cups, and turned off the kitchen light.

Velma ambled slowly down the long hallway to her quiet and lonely room. She knew well the loneliness Suzanne was experiencing and would experience even more in the days and months to come. Today was the tenth anniversary of losing her precious George after over forty years of marriage. It seemed the deep sense of loss never completely went away. Yet, somehow, the Lord always gave her the strength she needed just at the right moment.

"*Dear Lord,*" she prayed as she entered the haven of her room, "*please keep my girl safe and help her to carry this load you have brought her way. I, too, am struggling to understand the why's and what's, but I know that we can stand* firm in our belief in you, and that you will never fail us! Keep her from making mistakes of the heart that she would regret in years to come, Father. In Jesus' name I pray, amen."

Velma turned back the coverlet on the worn old bed she had slept in for more nights than she could count. Before climbing into the warm sanctuary, she sank to her knees and spent several more long moments silently pouring her heart out to the One who hears and cares.

With a deep sigh that was part sorrow and part joy, she climbed into her soft old bed and snuggled into the warm mattress.

Suddenly, with a feeling of unease, and a deep need to see her daughter and make sure Suzanne was all right, she threw aside the bed covers and hurried upstairs to check on her.

CHAPTER 7

As Suzanne climbed the stairs to her childhood room at the top of the old farmhouse, she thought, "*If I were any more tired, I would simply give up and let it all go, I am that weary.*"

Digging around in her suitcase, she pulled out a soft, comfy nightgown. Going into the bathroom, she turned on the light and leaned back against the door, all strength completely gone. Brushing her teeth and getting ready for bed seemed to take more energy than she had left.

She was so very worried about Daniel, about her children, and about what the next months would bring. How they would ever adjust to a life without Daniel there to guide and balance them all was more than she could even comprehend.

Yet, there was also a sense of quiet peace that kept welling up inside of her heart; making her smile every time she looked in the wavy old mirror over the pedestal sink. Just being back in her old home always brought such feelings of comfort and joy.

Seeing Peter had brought back warm memories, even though his caring concern had rather knocked her off balance momentarily. It was such a contradiction of what her life currently was that she was confused and somewhat afraid of her own emotions.

"*I wonder if everyone has memories that sometimes seem more real than the real things in life. Or am I just so tired that I am being silly?*"

Mentally shaking herself, Suzanne stepped to the sink. Looking at herself long and hard in the wavy mirror, she saw a woman she hardly knew.

"Lord," she prayed, "*keep me from straying from your perfect will, let me remember all the good things that you have brought to me over the years in my marriage with Daniel. Help me to never be unfaithful to him or to you, whether in my thoughts or in my person. And please, give me the strength to get through the days ahead, even if it's just one day at a time.*"

Donning her nightgown and going back into the bedroom, she settled herself into her old childhood bed. Glancing over to where the rose-colored bedside lamp glowed softly she saw a stack of books. As she sank back on her pillow with a sigh, she reached for her well-worn Bible and held it against her heart for a few moments.

It felt good to lie there and let the feelings wash over her in waves. It seemed she had been in a surreal state of anxiety for so long, really for several years now, particularly since Daniel was diagnosed with Alzheimer's. She had somehow become accustomed to living in an in-between place where she was neither fully living, nor quite dead; a place of mere existence, it would seem.

Even before he had been formally diagnosed with Alzheimer's, Daniel had become very difficult to live with. For well over a year before his diagnosis, there had been days, and sometimes weeks, when he would be so depressed that he would barely speak or communicate with anyone. He would sit in his robe and stare into nothingness for hours at a time with a look on his face that sometimes frightened Suzanne. It almost seemed as if he was seeking some great solution to a horrific and terrible problem; one she nor anyone else could possibly understand.

Then there were times when, for no apparent reason, he would erupt into fits of rage. It was usually something trivial that would set him off. In those times, he would overreact and begin to kick the dog or the furniture. Often, he would throw things, while yelling and cursing at whoever was unfortunate enough to be close to him. Then, with no warning, he would switch into high gear and want everyone to have a party with him; laughing and smiling and dancing around the room. All of this bizarre behavior was so out of character from the man she had married and loved for nearly twenty-five years.

For the last few years, life with Daniel had been like living on an emotional roller coaster. Suzanne felt as if she was living with someone so unlike the man she had loved and married that she sometimes wondered if she was dreaming. Or then again, perhaps they were all characters in a bad movie, rather than living a life of their own.

She had grown weary of never knowing from one minute to the next what his mood was going to be, or when it would change. They had visited doctor after doctor, trying to find a solution to his increasing problem. Nothing, and no one, seemed able to help. It was through all of this, and his inability to handle things at the church, that Daniel was asked to step down as the pastor.

That had been the final straw for the strong, amazing man. He knew enough to know then that he was never going to get beyond the horror of what was happening to him. It was shortly after that when the doctor gave them the dreadful news of his diagnosis.

Even the way it had been presented had been part and parcel of the awful nightmare. Suzanne had called the doctor's office the week before the appointment. She asked that they give her the diagnosis and whatever the prognosis before telling her husband. Hoping to spare him the shock of what she already anticipated had been her only desire. Instead of heeding her wishes, the doctor breezed into the office, took his seat and proceeded to bluntly tell Daniel that he had the dreaded Alzheimer's Disease and there was no cure.

She had watched as the light was finally and totally extinguished from her beloved's eyes. He had not been the same since. From that point on Suzanne watched as her husband gave up the battle to get well. An air of resignation fell over him like a mantle. Nothing she could do could dispel the gloom that had overtaken their lives.

Switching off the light, Suzanne lay in the soft, cool darkness. Her mind whirled, thinking of the last few lonely years spent trying to live with, love, and deal with the man she'd married. Trying to understand him and who he had become as he changed so very much had become an impossibility at times. Her thoughts flowed backward to the night when she and Daniel first met.

It had been so strange, and yet, somehow magical, the way they met. She had just turned nineteen years old and had been out of high school for a little over a year.

Although she had dreamed of being an airline flight attendant, she had not known whom to contact to follow this dream. College sounded interesting to her, but there had been no real consideration of it. Partly because she was needed at home to help with the younger children and to give her mom support in running the household. Also due to ignorance of how those things worked, and the lack of money to pay for an education, she had not seriously considered going to school.

Thinking back, she realized just how limited her life had really been in those days. Unless you were born into money, or had someone around you who knew the ways of the world, there wasn't much hope for pursuing a formal education. College hadn't seemed to be an option.

That winter, Suzanne had gone to visit her sister, Karen. Her mother had sent her to help after Karen's oldest son was born. One cold night, she had gone with Karen and her husband, Bill Ivey, to a party at his boss's home. It was New Year's Eve, and Bill had insisted that she go along rather than staying home with baby Anthony.

Suzanne had actually looked forward to a quiet evening at home alone, with a roaring fire and a good book, while the baby slept peacefully. However, Bill would have none of that. He insisted that his boss would be offended if she did not come along to the party that was being held for all employees and their families.

Suzanne knew that his real reason for insisting was that Bill was always looking for ways to climb the corporate ladder. For some reason, he considered Suzanne an asset with her gentle good looks and pleasant personality. At his insistence, she had gotten ready and had gone with them to the party. Sometimes it was easier to comply than fight with the man.

The baby was left with the sitter although Karen and Suzanne had both hated leaving the little one behind. The party was for adults only and a baby would have been most miserable in the midst of the noise and merry making by the party goers.

Even before they arrived, Bill was way over the level of being soused. His idea of having fun was to drink one beer after another, as quickly as possible. In doing so, he became a boring, obnoxious fool. Suzanne made herself a promise that she would never consider marrying a man who drank. She reasoned that there had to be a few men out there somewhere who didn't follow that line of thinking.

"*Surely to goodness*," she'd thought, "*there is a man for me who can enjoy life without being intoxicated to do so.*"

The party was everything she had expected and more; noisy, crazy and wild. Many of the people were well on their way to total intoxication before even arriving. The drinking and partying only became more pronounced as the night wore on.

Lying in the dark, Suzanne thought about the life that Karen and Bill had lived, right up until the wear and tear on their marriage had resulted in divorce. Karen had never been the same thereafter. She became a bitter, angry woman who resented anyone who happened to find happiness. It was sad to see her expectations of life demolished. Suzanne grieved for her sister; she certainly deserved better. It was one more reminder to be careful of the choices we make.

On that auspicious night, Suzanne slipped out of the main party area and quietly opened several doors leading down a long hallway. She peeked carefully inside each one until she finally found the library. A library was a room she loved wherever she went; to her a room filled with books always felt like home.

Slipping inside, she gently pulled the door closed behind her. Glancing around to ensure she was alone, she glided soundlessly across the heavy, deep green carpet. Reaching the books lining the mahogany bookshelves, Suzanne sighed deeply. Taking her time, she read over the book titles displayed in all their grandeur.

She knew that Karen would be frustrated if she realized that Suzanne had slipped away to read, but there were times when she just had to forget about what Karen would think or say. Suzanne had decided long ago that the entire world didn't revolve around Bill and Karen and their problems. If she let them, the two of them would drive her absolutely crazy.

She wished things could be better for her sister and brother-in-law, but for now, she just needed a small oasis of quiet and peace. If it could be found in this delightful library, then so be it. The fire beckoned and her weary heart sought the solace at hand.

Many of the books were bound in fine leather with gold leaf lettering on their spines. She recognized some that she had read over the years. Several seemed to call her name as she lightly allowed her fingertips to whisper over them. Those were the old friends, faithful and true.

Finally, selecting one which she had never read before, she snuggled into one of the huge overstuffed, leather chairs that seemed to be holding out their arms just for her. Settling in, she could hardly wait to find out what wonderful things might be hidden between the covers of the lovely old book.

The smell of the leather engulfed her and she glanced through the French doors to the left of the fireplace to see snowflakes drifting slowly to the ground. The fire popped and crackled, and made her wish she had a big bowl of popcorn to enjoy. Pulling a soft afghan across her knees, she released a deep sigh of contentment. It seemed as if heaven itself was giving her a respite.

"*Who cares about the silly old party going on down the hall,*" she giggled softly to herself. "*I would much rather be here, alone, reading what will surely soon join my list of old friends.*"

Holding the book in her hand, she marveled at the fact that such an old classic was still around. Reading had always been one of her foremost passions and she treasured the older books the most.

She could remember as a child often sneaking off when her chores were done, to hide away with a good book. Of course, she had to be careful because if her father caught her and thought she was sloughing off on her work, she would be punished and given more chores to do.

As much as he loved his children and always tried to care for them, he could not tolerate what he thought was a lazy attitude. In his world, reading anything but the Bible ranked right up there with lying in bed until noon. Reading what he deemed frivolous books, such as novels or adventure stories, was a waste of precious time; time that could be spent in ways that were more useful. It didn't keep Suzanne and her sisters from reading though; in fact, it seemed as if their father's restrictions spurred them on to read even more.

Any excuse would do. A rainy day, a long cold evening, and even sunny days when the breeze blew lightly through the treetops, were good excuses to read. Even now, Suzanne could enjoy a good book in about any setting. However, her favorite place was in a cozy library such as this, with a fire burning softly and the sound of embers popping from time to time. This was purely heaven to her soul.

CHAPTER 8

SUZANNE HAD BEEN sitting there, reading in the quiet glow of the firelight for about an hour. Suddenly, the tall grandfather clock across the room bonged out the half past eleven o'clock hour. Just then, as if on cue, the door to the library swung open.

A distinguished looking, dark haired gentleman, who appeared to be perhaps in his early to middle thirties, stepped into the room. Shutting the door quickly and quietly behind himself, and leaning back against it, he closed his eyes and exhaled a deep sigh. It was as if he too, felt great relief to be away from the noise of the other party-goers.

Suddenly, as if he knew he was being watched, he opened his eyes and glanced around the room, trying to find who could possibly be there. His eyes slid quickly past the quiet girl sitting demurely in the large leather chair beside the fireplace. Then, as if drawn by a magnet, his eyes flew back toward Suzanne and he jumped almost guiltily. He struggled to absorb the fact that this lovely creature was indeed sitting there watching him, as he watched her in turn. The warm glow of the fire cast an aura of mystery around her as she mischievously looked across the room at him.

With barely concealed laughter, she asked, "Excuse me, Sir, are you running *away* from someone, or running *to* someone?"

Pushing away from the door, he looked back at her as if in a daze and replied, "Only if you are the one I am running to! You are the most beautiful thing I have seen all evening. Come to think of it, the most gorgeous thing I have seen in a very long time!"

His accent intrigued her immediately. Sure that it was a Scottish burr she was hearing, Suzanne could barely wait to hear him say something else, anything.

Shocked at her own boldness, Suzanne responded, "Are you by any chance teasing with me? If so, I must beg your pardon, I don't even know who you are!"

Leaving the solid support of the heavy wooden door behind, he walked slowly across the room to where she was seated. Dropping down beside her on one immaculately clad knee, he took the hand that was lying on top of her book; slowly he lifted it to his lips. After a long, exceptionally breathtaking moment, he kissed the pulse of her wrist and then tenderly replaced it on her book.

"I don't know who you are either, beautiful lady," he said, looking deeply into her eyes, "but my name is Daniel Parker and I hope and pray that you are not married. You are the woman of my dreams and, as of this very moment, I plan to make you my wife."

Suzanne sat there stunned for a moment, wondering if this man was simply as drunk as a loon, or perhaps he was escaped from the mental ward. Never in her life had she experienced anything remotely like this; nor had she ever dreamed she would. Surely, he must be jesting. Yet, it was rather fun to be treated like a princess in a fairy tale.

"I could get used to this," Suzanne giggled silently to herself.

She absolutely loved that deep Scottish brogue. At least she thought it was Scottish, it couldn't be anything else as beautiful as it sounded. It made her toes curl just to have heard him speak those few words. She wanted to beg him to talk to her, just to hear the sound of his accent; it was like nothing she had ever heard.

She realized that he was dressed too nicely to be from the mental facility a few miles away. He didn't seem to have been drinking; at least there was no smell of the horrid liquor on his breath such as her brother-in-law imbibed.

As she sat there in amazement and some uncertainty, Suzanne didn't know whether to be flattered or frightened. After all, no one knew where she had slipped off to, and this man really could be fresh out of bedlam for all she knew. Even so, somehow, she felt safe with him.

While she hesitated, he gently pulled her hand to his lips again. Kissing her palm, slowly and tantalizingly, on the tender underside, he asked her if she was going to tell him her name or not.

"After all," he whispered in that husky voice, "it is customary to know the name of the person you intend to marry!"

"Sir!" Suzanne sputtered.

"Daniel," he quickly interrupted, "my dear, you really should call me Daniel, or Darling, or anything but 'Sir'. That is entirely too proper of a way to address your intended."

That incredible brogue caught Suzanne quite off guard.

Trying again, somewhat surprised that her befuddled mind retained his name, Suzanne replied, "Mr. Parker, first of all, I don't even know who you are. Secondly, I don't make it a habit of agreeing to marry men I have known for less than ten minutes!"

"Well, then we simply must remedy that, and as quickly as we may," he replied.

"As I have already told you, my name is Daniel Parker. I am thirty-four years old and I am a writer, philanthropist, and an ordained minister in good standing with the Presbyterian Church of America, PCA that is. I have been married once, in my youth. My wife, God rest her soul, was killed in a car crash eight years ago. I have one son, Adam. He is nine years old and is the spitting image of me at that age. I have a solid reputation and a more than modest financial future in my position as the pastor of a church and through my writing endeavors. I am a published author of some standing and hope to complete a translation of some exclusive literary writings within the next five or ten years. I completed my Master's Degree in Theology a year ago, and have just recently been accepted into a Doctoral program."

Pausing for a breath, Daniel continued, "Wow, I sound like a pompous... well, you know. I never quite realized how stodgy I must seem until I began describing my life to you. See, you have come into my life for the sole purpose of keeping me from being a total bore! Already you have opened my eyes to how I must appear to those around me."

The expression on his face was one of pure bemusement.

"One last thing," the clearly besotted man continued, "I have been offered the position of the Senior Pastor of one of the largest churches in our denomination. If I accept, my son and I will be moving to Dallas, Texas within the next few months. I sincerely hope you will be going with us."

As the large clock boomed out the three-quarter hour, Daniel said, "We have now known each other more than fifteen minutes and I still don't know your name! Put me out of my misery, please. Just whisper it to me softly, if you will. I think that I may die of regret should you somehow slip away from me with your name unrevealed. I would perhaps never know your sweet name and never be able to taste it upon my lips."

Opening her mouth to reply, Suzanne had a momentary feeling of déjà vu. Had she read this in a book at some moment long past? Was she dreaming? Her befuddled mind refused to grasp that she was in the here and now, and this adorable, adoring man was begging to know her name.

Just then, the library door slammed open. Suzanne's brother-in-law, Bill, came stumbling drunkenly into the room.

"Suzanne," he yelled, "come on out and have some fun,. It's almost midnight and Karen sent me to look for you! C'mon, we're having a party!"

Before she could respond, Bill flung his arm toward her, almost as if to grab her from across the width of the room. "C'mon, and bring your friend too, we're gonna drink a toast to the New Year."

His words were badly slurred, and Bill was barely keeping his balance. Suzanne didn't think she had ever been quite so embarrassed.

Daniel growled to her softly, as a look of intense satisfaction crossed his face, "Well, at least I found out your first name, but who is this drunken lout? Shall I knock him over the head and stuff him behind the sofa? Tell me quickly that he is not your husband, nor your intended."

Stifling a giggle, Suzanne explained, with a sparkle deep in her blue eyes, that he was her brother-in-law, Bill Ivey, "And, he does love his booze," she whispered softly.

Quickly, before Bill could make a scene, Suzanne told him that they would be right out.

"Please get me a glass of ginger ale and have it ready for the toast."

Mumbling that nobody with any brains drank ginger ale when they could have perfectly wonderful champagne, Bill turned and stumbled his way back down the hall toward the noise of the other partiers.

Daniel held out his hand to Suzanne to help her to her feet. As she rose gracefully, she gave him a tiny old-fashioned curtsy. Glancing directly into his warm brown eyes she murmured, "Suzanne Claire Brummell, so glad to meet you."

Daniel gazed at her with amusement in his own eyes and replied, "I think you are quite a tease, my pet."

"I love your name. Suzanne Claire, it reminds me of some delicious treat that is waiting to be sampled. An éclair shall we say?" His eyes sparkled with hidden delight.

"Well," she responded haughtily, "I really don't make it a habit to meet distinguished, older gentlemen on the sly!"

"*At least until now,*" she thought to herself.

"What you think of me is no concern of mine. My name is not éclair, it is Claire. I would appreciate your remembering that in the future."

As her amazingly blue eyes twinkled up at him, they took the sting out of her words. Daniel swept down from his height of six foot two inches and kissed her thoroughly on the soft, inviting lips smiling up at him.

"My, you do move fast!" Suzanne breathed softly, pulling quickly away.

"We had best get on to the party before Bill sends out a search and rescue team. Believe me, he is completely capable of doing that in spite of his current state of drunkenness."

Whirling around in a blend of vibrant colors, the soft fragrance she wore reminded the besotted man of moonbeams and apple blossoms.

She swept across the floor in grand style, saying, "Follow me, kind sir, and I will show you how to bring in the New Year with style!"

In the weeks that followed the party, she and Daniel enjoyed a whirlwind courtship. It was on Valentine's evening that he asked her to marry him. Daniel was traditional through and through. This was one of the endearing qualities about him that Suzanne came to love in the ensuing years of their marriage.

Daniel booked dinner at a lovely old restaurant. Suzanne was thrilled with the soft music, candlelight and snowy white tablecloths. It was so much more than what she was accustomed to, but it felt right somehow. She knew she would never forget the moment when he took her hand across the table and held it for a long moment. Looking deeply into her eyes, he told her of his love again.

"I thought I would never find another woman to love after Joanna died, but you are more than I'd even dreamed of."

Reaching into his jacket pocket, he pulled out a black velvet box. Opening it, Daniel revealed a quaint, old fashioned ring with a lovely setting of Amethyst surrounded by diamonds.

"This was my grandmother's wedding ring," he shared quietly. "It has been worn by her for the past sixty years. It was left to me at her passing the year after my first wife was killed. The stone represents the honor of Scotland. It would be my delight if you would honor me by accepting this ring as a pledge of our marriage."

As the words rolled off his tongue in the soft Scottish brogue, tears welled up in Suzanne's eyes. Looking at this tenderhearted man in the soft lighting, his dark hair reflecting the chandeliers overhead, Suzanne experienced such an overwhelming feeling of joy and happiness. In spite of the short time they had known each other, she knew deep in her heart that this was good and right.

"Yes," she whispered. "Yes, I will be your wife."

As he placed the ring on her finger, a man wearing a kilt and carrying a bagpipe stepped from behind a curtain in the dining room. Placing the instrument to his lips, he began to play the most hauntingly beautiful song Suzanne had ever heard. Begging Daniel to explain the lyrics, he replied.

"Actually, a Scotsman, Duncan MacIntyre, penned 'A Mhàiri Bhàn Òg' for his beautiful young bride as a special love song written to express his love for her. They lived a long life together, as I too intend to live with you. It is said that when she had grown older in years, someone challenged Duncan, saying his wife wasn't as lovely as his song indicated. He simply replied, 'You haven't seen her through my eyes.'"

"My darling Suzanne, I wish only that others could see you as I see you today and forever; my beautiful one."

The love in his eyes said more than words ever could.

Suzanne admired her lovely new ring in the candlelight as she absorbed the fact that she was going to marry a true Scotsman. She felt caught up in a fairy tale experience.

They finished their evening amid congratulations from everyone in the restaurant. It was an introduction for Suzanne of what life with Daniel Parker would be like.

Life was a whirlwind for them both over the next few weeks before marrying on a cold, windy day in early March. Their honeymoon was amazing with a trip to Daniel's beloved Scotland. His accent blossomed as he showed her around the highland home where he had been born. She fell in love with the shaggy little ponies and marveled at the beautiful mountains that seemed to fill the sky with their majesty.

They had visited several places during their month away, but the highlight was the castle where they stayed the last four nights of their honeymoon. The lovely old place was filled with Scottish history and the couple running it were as authentic as they come. It was a magical trip such as Suzanne had only imagined ever taking.

Their only regret was in not taking Adam with them. Daniel and Suzanne both continually remarked on all the things they would love to show him. Daniel assured her that they would come back many times over the years, bringing their children with them.

Their first few months of marriage had been filled with theaters and plays, trips to the opera, and dining such as she had never dreamed of experiencing. They had initially moved into the apartment where Daniel lived with his small son. It was more than adequate for the interim as they prepared for the move to Dallas. The church in Dallas had offered them the use of the parsonage, but Daniel and she agreed that they wanted their own home in which to raise their family.

Moving to Dallas and setting up housekeeping as the mother to nine-year-old Adam had been like a dream come true. They had purchased a lovely home in an older, established neighborhood with a pool and a kitchen that made Suzanne drool. Other than missing her big, noisy family, she had never been happier. The years passed swiftly in a colorful collage of experiences.

It was a joyful few years when their two children had been born. She had watched as Daniel cried tears at the birth of each. When their son, Jamie, was born, their joy was overwhelming. The fact that he was the spitting image of his mother was a source of great pride for Daniel.

His older son favored him more, although in mannerisms and personality he was more like Daniel's first wife, who was his birth mother. The fact that Adam was like his mother, was not necessarily a bad thing. It gave him a connection with her that he otherwise might not have had. Suzanne often marveled at God's amazing ways.

Daniel's Scottish brogue was thick, as he held their daughter for the first time, exclaiming over her delicate beauty. He had shared with

Suzanne that while he loved his boys, he had often dreamed of having a beautiful little girl to spoil and pamper.

When it was obvious that Autumn took after her mother, while having brown eyes like her father, they were all agreed that she was the perfect blend of the two parents. And while she was certainly pampered, she was the most unspoiled child imaginable. It was as if she had welcomed her journey into the world with the most open of spirits. Rarely was the beautiful girl seen without a smile on her face.

Adam, who was nearly twelve when Jamie was born, welcomed his younger brother with open arms and an open heart. When Autumn came along some years later, he was awed, as they all were, by the beauty of the little girl. Throughout the years he had only grown closer to Suzanne as they shared in their love of the children, and for his father.

Suzanne would forever be glad she had married Daniel. She had loved the whirlwind experience of being the wife of a minister in a large congregation. There was rarely a week that went by that they did not entertain guests from around the world. Or, just as often, Daniel was the one going somewhere to speak, and as the guests they were treated like royalty in those times.

Daniel was more and more sought after as he became an author. The associate pastor of their church was called on more and more often to fill the pulpit to allow Daniel time to meet his other obligations. The stress and strain of travel only seemed to energize the dedicated man. He pursued his dreams with a whole heart. Always allowing space in his heart and his life for the family he adored.

Of course, as the children grew older, life became full with their school activities and Suzanne stayed home more often than not. Nevertheless, she treasured the times when Daniel returned home from his latest trip, with glowing reports of his travels and gifts for all. He never ceased to amaze her in his sensitivity and love for his family.

Once, he had brought her and Autumn matching Kimono's from Japan; another time he brought the boys matching Western boots from

Wyoming. Ever the one to pay attention to detail, the gifts were always a perfect fit. She never quite knew who got the most enjoyment from these little gifts, the recipient or the giver. Likely it was a toss-up.

Knowing that those days were gone, and that Daniel would never again be the man he had once been, brought quick tears to Suzanne's eyes. She was immediately reminded of the place they had come to in their lives; a place of loneliness for both him and herself. A marriage, and yet lives lived apart in a manner such as they had never dreamed of happening.

Hearing a soft knock on her bedroom door, Suzanne blinked her eyes to push the tears away. She realized she had been lying there in her childhood room for quite some time, reliving that early time with Daniel. The knock came again and Velma peeked around the corner of the door.

"Are you asleep, Sweetheart?" she asked.

"No, Mama, I was just relaxing and remembering how I met Daniel. For some strange reason he has been on my mind more than usual all evening. I pray that everything is all right. I called the care facility earlier and checked on him. They said he was restless, but other than that much the same as when we left."

"Well, my dear, for the life of me I could not go to sleep without checking on you. I had said my prayers and gotten into bed and just lay there thinking and thinking about all that we are going through. It seemed as if my mind and heart were racing. So, I decided to come up and see if you are alright. I wanted to say good night again and let you know that I am praying for you as you get through these next weeks and months. Please know, Suzie, you are well loved. Goodnight now, Sweetheart, I'm sorry to have bothered you, but I needed to say I love you."

"G' night, Mama, I love you, too," Suzanne responded. As the door was softly closing behind her mother, Suzanne said, "Oh, Mama, I did remember that this is the anniversary of Daddy's death. You don't worry now, you will be with Daddy again someday. In the meantime, I am sure he is looking down on us all with love and concern. But I am sure glad that you are here with the kids and me. I don't know what we would do without you."

Smiling gently, Velma whispered goodnight as she closed the door and went back downstairs to her own room for a good night's rest. She, too, knew that George was waiting for her in heaven. But, her work down here on earth wasn't finished yet. Suzanne was right, there was still lots to pray about and to do before joining her love. Still, she missed him so much and looked so forward to the wonderful day of seeing him again in glory.

Once again in her room, ready for some much-needed rest, Velma relaxed as she realized that everything was truly in God's hands. Climbing back into her cozy bed, she smiled with contentment as she turned off the bedside lamp and pulled her soft comforter up to her chin. It was good to be home and in her own bed. She would miss its softness while staying with Suzanne in Dallas.

Just before drifting off, she seemed to hear her George speaking softly to her from the shadows. She could hear him reminding her in his deep, warm voice that all would be well and that we are never truly alone in this tough old world.

With a smile on her lips, Velma turned on her side and snuggled in to rest for a few hours before morning came and the journey called life began all over again.

CHAPTER 9

Early the next morning, Suzanne awoke slowly. She lay looking around the sweet old room where she had spent so many days and nights as a child and teenager. Wondering what the faded, rose covered walls would say if they could speak, she smiled softly.

Perhaps they could tell the tales of her heartbreaks, dreams of homecoming night, preparation for date nights with Daniel in those few fast months before their wedding. And last but not least, all the things she had wondered about on the night before her wedding.

"If only walls could talk," she smiled quietly to herself.

Remembering her daddy coming to talk with her was one of her favorite memories. He had climbed the creaky old stairs that evening, as she and her mother were admiring her wedding dress. It's flounces, sequins and pearls were a sight to behold. As he entered the room, quick tears filled his eyes. Lifting the beautiful white dress from the hook on the wall, he twirled it around, watching the flare of the skirt come to life.

Glancing at his daughter, he smiled crookedly. "Darlin', you are going to be the most beautiful bride a daddy ever gave away. I sure hope this fella appreciates the woman he is getting. There isn't another like her on the face of this earth."

Suzanne's mother had slipped downstairs, allowing her husband and daughter a few moments alone; the last they would have for a long while. Suzanne had always been his special darling and he'd spoiled her more than he should have. They talked and cried together as George reminded his daughter that she would always be his little girl. If ever there was anything she needed, he would be there for her. And he was, until the day he died.

Missing her father all over again, Suzanne decided she had lolled around in the bed long enough for one morning. If her daddy was here she knew he would be yelling up the stairs, telling her she was wasting daylight.

Realizing that she had a lot to do, Suzanne threw back the faded quilt and quickly swung her legs over the edge of the bed. She needed to get going and get ready for the day. Grabbing her housecoat, she quickly shuffled across the cold floor to the bathroom. Hurriedly, she ran a brush through her hair and tossed on a light coating of lipstick. Uneasy, Suzanne glanced anxiously in the mirror; something didn't feel right in her spirit. It was nothing she could put her finger on, but somehow she felt as if there was something that she should be praying about, and these feelings were rarely wrong.

Even as she made her bed and tidied up the room, she continued to feel a strong feeling to pray for Daniel in particular.

Stopping for a few minutes, she knelt by her bed and prayed, asking God to keep His hand on Daniel, and on her and the children. Still feeling a burden, she stayed quiet for a few more moments.

"Lord," she breathed, "*please keep Daniel safe today and put angels around him. Let him know in his heart that we love him and that in your timing this will all be made right.*"

Wiping the tears from her cheeks, Suzanne rose to her feet and smoothed the quilt down to erase the wrinkles caused by her distress. Hurrying down the creaky old stairs, she looked around the kitchen to see what could be found for breakfast for her and her mom. She knew that Autumn and Brenda would sleep in as long as allowed, and they would likely want cereal when they did get up.

She put a pot of hazelnut coffee on to brew. She opened the fridge and pulled out a carton of eggs, a stick of butter and milk. Then she hurried to the pantry for bread, vanilla, cinnamon, and sugar. Quickly and efficiently, Suzanne stirred up the fixings for French toast. Once the golden slices were ready to put on the plates, she covered the skillet with a lid to keep them warm.

Next, she set up a breakfast tray with white linen place mats and napkins and used her mother's lovely old heirloom napkin rings, which had been formed from her great-grandmother's wedding silver. Suzanne had always adored the quaint old spoons and forks as napkin holders.

She knew that her mother was planning to give them to Autumn on her wedding day. What a surprise that would be! Autumn had drooled over them since becoming old enough to understand about the finer things in life.

Grabbing a couple of little green juice glasses which Velma had gotten in the oatmeal boxes many years before, Suzanne poured two glasses of sparkling orange juice and set them on the tray. She added two small plates with a half grapefruit on each for both her mom and herself. Last, she added the toast and sprinkled it with a smattering of powdered sugar.

Before heading down the hallway to her mother's room, she stepped out the old screen door, down the stairs and over to her mother's English Rose bush growing up the side of the porch. Selecting a few beautiful flowers and a couple of half-open buds, she broke them off and took them back inside. Sniffing their fragrant aroma, she marveled at their beauty, even as late in the fall as it was. Moving quietly, she arranged the roses in a lovely glass vase she found in the upper cabinet and placed the flowers on the tray alongside the food.

Carrying the tray with the scrumptious looking food, she left the kitchen behind. The warm coffee fragrance wafted upward toward her as she carefully made her way down the shadowy hallway to Velma's room. Quietly pushing the bedroom door open, she glanced around the room. Immediately, she caught sight of the old library table her dad had bought at an auction many years before.

Setting the tray down on top of the table, she lovingly ran her hands across the wooden surface. Quick tears sprang to her eyes, as she remembered the hours of helping her father refinish the beautiful old piece. She remembered how he had lovingly sanded the boards. All the while he explained to her how to bring out the best in the wood tones and what finish would make it glow with a natural warmth. Sighing, she realized anew how much she missed her dad.

Hearing a stirring in the bed behind her, she turned around. Carefully blinking the possibility of tears away, with a bright smile, Suzanne sang out, "Good morning, sleepy head! It's time to rise and shine!"

"Well, my goodness," Velma exclaimed, sitting up and pushing a pillow up behind her shoulders. "What on earth is this?"

"Why, breakfast in bed, of course," smiled Suzanne. "All for my beautiful mother, the queen of my life!"

"Oh, Suzie," Velma smiled as Suzanne placed the tray with the beautifully arranged French toast and grapefruit before her.

"You should have slept in and caught up on your rest. But you know I do love being spoiled this way! And the roses, why they still have dew drops on them!"

"Well, Mama, if this is all it takes to spoil you, then, you are very easily spoiled. Besides, you are always taking care of others, so I thought it was about time someone treated you special!"

"Now," Suzanne said as she settled herself on the foot of Velma's bed with her own plate of food. "I might as well tell you now as later. I have agreed to meet Peter for coffee this afternoon at Miss Pitty Pat's Cafe. I didn't tell you last night as I didn't want to worry you and have you up all night."

As Velma's eyebrows rose, Suzanne reached over and patted her on her knee.

"Don't worry, Mama, I know what you are thinking. Believe me, it isn't what it seems. Peter just wants to visit for a few minutes, and I couldn't see any reason that it would hurt. Besides, I am taking the girls with me, so there should be no problem with people assuming that I am doing anything improper!"

"Well," Velma replied, "it isn't always easy to predetermine what people will think, but perhaps we shouldn't spend so much time worrying about that anyway. However, please don't let yourself get hurt. You are very vulnerable right now and the last thing you need is for people to start ugly rumors about you and Peter. Remember the awful things that were said when you married Daniel so quickly, what with all the old, town biddies saying you were pregnant and all. The next few months may be some of the most difficult of your life yet. You certainly don't need anything coming against you to make it harder to bear."

"Wow," Velma exclaimed, raising her hands in the air, "enough of my sermonizing, let's enjoy this wonderful breakfast and this beautiful morning that the Lord has given us."

Bowing her head, she prayed aloud, "Lord, thank you for the bountiful food you've provided, and Suzie has prepared for us. Please surround us with your presence and your peace as we go forward to be all that you would have us to be throughout this day. Amen."

Looking up with a smile, she immediately took a big bite of her French toast and declared it the best she had ever eaten.

Suzanne chewed a bite of French toast slowly to give herself time to think before replying to her mother's comments. As she swallowed the bite and then sipped at the cup of warm coffee, it dawned on her that she didn't have to defend herself to anyone, her mother or otherwise. There was nothing to defend. She would meet with Peter and that would be the end of it.

"After all," she thought, *"it isn't likely, even if I were free to consider it, that Peter would be at all interested in having a relationship with me after all these years. Why, he is single by choice, so obviously he doesn't want the entanglements of a wife and marriage! Besides, first of all, you are not free to even consider another man"* she scolded herself, *"you have too many other things on your plate right now to let yourself go that direction, and taking care of Daniel is the biggest and most important of them all. You owe it to Daniel to maintain your loyalty to him, and love for him, now more than ever before."*

Smiling at Velma, Suzanne said, "Mama, let's do this; let's believe that Daniel is going to get better. My prayer is that he will be healed and our lives will go on together for a good long time. Please understand, I'm not thinking of getting involved with Peter, ever. It is just a friendship from a lifetime ago. I do feel that I should meet him for coffee, though. That is already set, and I don't feel that I can gracefully get out of it."

After a long, thoughtful look at Suzanne, Velma reached over, squeezed her hand and said, "Somehow, I feel this is not the end of it, but I know you are a woman of integrity and will honor your husband in all things."

"Now," Velma continued, "I thought you were going to help me gather those apples from the orchard. They sure aren't going to get themselves off the tree. If we don't get them in before we leave, there won't be enough to even make a pie with when we return in a few weeks. Those dad-gum blackbirds and raccoons will eat every last one in the blink of an eye!"

"Yes, we do need to get that done this morning," murmured Suzanne. "I also want to make sure all of your things are in order at the bank before we leave for Dallas on Monday. I can't believe they are trying to say you owe additional monies on the farm. Something just doesn't sound right there. When we paid the balance off just before Daniel became so ill, they were supposed to issue you the necessary papers and the title to the property within the month. Now here we are, a year and a half later still trying to bring closure to that. If I didn't know better, I would think old man Knowles at the bank was trying to take advantage of two lonely, little old ladies!"

"Well, he'd better watch out," replied Velma quite haughtily. "One of us is not so old, and one of us may be old and little, but she is also a tough, old bird!"

Jumping out of bed and pulling herself to her full height of five foot two inches, she proceeded to air box a few rounds. Suzanne laughed so hard she almost fell off the foot of the bed.

"Calm down, Mama, we will get this all figured out without fisticuffs!"

Still smiling, she stood and gathered up the tray with the dishes. As she headed for the door, Suzanne said, "Go on now, get dressed in your grubbies and let's go pick some apples. Then we can tackle Mr. Knowles and the property title issue."

After putting the dishes in the kitchen sink, Suzanne clattered back up the stairs from the kitchen to her room to grab her cell phone, which she had left lying on her dresser. While upstairs, she also brushed her teeth and checked to make sure she had her things straightened up.

Chances were they would have a busy day and she wanted to come back to a clean and comfortable room. Gathering a handful of towels and clothing, she decided to take them down to the laundry room and get a small load ready to wash. With Daniel being so ill, she never knew when she might have to pack in a hurry and head back home.

Hurrying, Velma jumped into her old gardening clothes and straightened her bed covers. Even though she wasn't sure how long she would be in Dallas with Suzanne and the kids, she really wanted to get the apples stored away. They would be here waiting for her when she came home and she looked forward to making fried apple pies for Thanksgiving.

"*Maybe,*" she thought, "*I will even have enough to dry a few and have them to nibble on during the cold winter evenings.*"

She remembered eating those with her own grandfather when just a child and the thought brought a smile to her face. Suddenly, she realized that she felt as if a huge burden had lifted off her shoulders. It was wonderful just to be alive and to have a sweet daughter like Suzanne.

Worry had been a part of her life for so long she hardly knew what to do when she let it go. But let it go she would. There was no point in wasting a perfectly lovely day on worry. And besides, hadn't George preached often enough that worry was a sin?

Heavens to Betsy, if he hadn't always given her a hard time about her habit of worrying. In fact, one year for Christmas, he had put a small worry stone in her stocking! She would never forget the look on his face as he watched her take it out and read the small note included with the stone. George loved a good joke better than most. She still had that stone and carried it in her pocket most days.

Velma scurried down the hallway from her bedroom to the kitchen. Just as she got to the kitchen door, she heard Suzanne's cell phone ring. Turning toward the stairwell, she waited at the bottom for her daughter to come down.

She hoped that Suzanne would not get caught up on a lengthy call and not be able to get on out to the orchard to help with the apples. Velma knew it would take them a good hour or possibly two to gather them and they had so much to do this day. She felt herself growing a bit impatient that Suzanne didn't just let the phone go into voice mail.

"Lord knows she's attached to that phone like it was her ball and chain," she fussed quietly.

Hearing only a few soft-spoken words here and there of Suzanne's dialogue, Velma couldn't get the gist of the conversation to tell if it would be a while until she was off. Flapping her hands in the air in a motion so much a part of her that she never even realized she was doing it, she went on into the kitchen. Clearing up the dishes from the morning, she set some meat on the counter to thaw for their evening meal.

Sensing more than hearing her, Velma realized that Suzanne was standing in the kitchen doorway. Glancing over at her, ready to urge her along, she bit the words off before they ever left her tongue.

"What is it, Suzie? What has you looking like you just saw a ghost?"

When Suzanne just stood there, all silent and white, Velma became more than a little concerned. Going to her daughter, she grabbed her by the arm and steered her toward a kitchen chair. Setting Suzanne down, she took her face in her hands. "What is it, Darling? What has happened? Is it Daniel? Is he worse?"

Drawing a deep, shuddering breath, Suzanne felt the flow of oxygen go through her lungs in a rush. Feeling more lightheaded than she cared to admit, she gripped her mother's hands and held on as if for dear life.

Looking at her mother with anguished eyes, she whispered raggedly, "Mama, Daniel tried to kill himself this morning."

As the awful words hung in the air between them, Velma tried to understand what her daughter was telling her.

"No! Not our Daniel! He would never do such a thing," Velma protested.

Grabbing her hands together and holding them against her chest, she sobbed, "Well, not when in his right mind, at least. Oh, Suzie, I am so sorry. We must get there as quickly as possible! Forget about the apples. I will get the neighbor boy to pick them for me. He could use the extra money anyway, with that new baby he and his young wife just had. Come now, let's see if we can get a flight out today. You want to be there as quickly as possible."

Hurriedly, Velma put the meat back in the freezer, and wiped down her counter tops with the damp dishtowel still in her hand. Clearly she was more upset than she dared to show.

For several long moments, Suzanne sat at the table still as a stone. Her mind refused to function, it was as if she had known all morning that something dreadful was going on with Daniel. How could she have known? But she had. She remembered the urgency to pray for him in her room earlier. Was it then that he had been so desperate that he felt the only answer was to take his own life?

Suzanne felt as if her heart might stop beating of its own accord. She felt hot and then cold. Just when she thought she might somehow understand this terrible thing, her mind went completely blank once again.

"Mother," she whispered, "Why? How could he even conceive of such a thing? He has been so confused for the past months, hardly knowing anyone or anything most of the time. This illness makes no sense. It makes me crazy! And I should have been there. What was I thinking to even consider coming here for a few days? I will never forgive myself."

Sobbing now, Suzanne threw herself into her mother's arms. Velma held her daughter tightly, knowing that words would have no meaning.

She rubbed Suzanne's shoulders and back as she made little crooning noises. She hoped somehow her child would know how deeply she shared her pain.

Finally, Suzanne got a grip on her emotions. Pulling away from her mother, although very unladylike, she wiped her nose on her shirt sleeve.

"Don't you have a tissue anywhere in this house, Mama? Really! I must have a tissue now."

Grabbing one from beside the breadbox, Velma handed it to her daughter. Suzanne blew her nose loudly and glanced up at her mother.

"I'm so sorry, Mama, you are right, I need to call the airlines. I hope that they can get us out of here quickly and we can do whatever needs to be done to help Daniel. What we can do, I have no way of knowing, but surely there is something that can be done to give him some peace."

Throwing the soaked tissue into the trashcan, Suzanne pulled her cell phone from her pocket and dialed the airline from the number programmed into her phone. There were, after all, some advantages to flying Delta regularly.

As if in a fog, she explained to the woman at reservations the details for why she needed to get their tickets changed to the next flight to Dallas. Giving the names of herself, Velma, and Autumn, Suzanne was relieved to learn that they could get seats on the 7:00 pm flight out. Hanging up the phone, she told her mother to get ready and they would go on into town and deal with the banking issues.

"We might as well make the most of this day and get as many things done as we possibly can. God only knows when we will be able to come back here. I am so sorry, Mama, I know that you wanted to gather your apples yourself, but I think it would be best to let that young man do it for us this time. By the time we get done at the bank, it will be time for me to meet with Peter for just a few minutes and then we will need to get home and get packed and headed to the airport."

Looking almost frantic, Suzanne continued, "I suppose I must meet him. After all, he is in a teacher's workshop so I'm sure his phone is off. It would be rather rude of me to cancel by way of a phone call to the school office. Besides, that would likely start more rumors than I am ready to deal with!"

Assuring her that it was fine, Velma told Suzanne that she was going to go ahead and clean up a little and pack her bag before they left for town. Suzanne trailed after her mother as she left the kitchen. Standing at the bottom of the stairwell, she felt as if in a daze as she tried to think of all that needed to be done before they could go to her husband.

She had already started the load of laundry, so that would need to be dried and folded. And she would have to awaken Autumn and help her get her bag packed. They would have to get Brenda home, and somehow explain to her why she could not go with them to Dallas this time. Oh, it was all just so hard to think about.

Feeling guilty that it would take even these few short hours to get back home to Dallas and to Daniel, she knew that some things were simply out of her control. Suddenly feeling weak in her knees, she slid helplessly down onto the worn treads of the stairwell. Burying her head in her hands, she wished she could cry the pain away. Perhaps if the tears would come again, she could break free of this horrible, icy grip which held her like a vice.

It came to her then that she would have to explain this terrible situation to her children. Moaning softly, she shuddered.

"How does one tell their children something of this nature? That their father is so desperate that he tried to end his own life. How can I help them understand that under normal circumstances their father would never do something like this? Oh God, please help me find the words to heal and not to wound. Please, Lord, help me. I am so afraid. This is not something I ever thought I would have to deal with."

CHAPTER 10

As her mother disappeared down the hallway, Suzanne sat on the old staircase for a moment longer. With her head in her hands, she quietly prayed that God would give her grace and strength for what lay ahead. After sitting there on the stairs for a short while, she rose slowly and went up to her room to shower and change.

As she was getting dressed, Suzanne told herself that she would go wake Autumn and tell her just as soon as she had a few moments to pull herself together. However, as she was putting the finishing touches to her hair, Autumn came bursting into her room.

"Mom," she cried, "Gram said that Dad is worse and we must go back to Dallas early. What happened, is he very ill? Are you still meeting with your friend, Mr. Clifton, today? When do we leave for home?"

Stopping the flow of questions with upraised hands, "Yes, Sweetheart," Suzanne replied. "Dr. Carey from the hospital in Dallas called and had some unsettling news regarding your dad. Please sit down and let me tell you what is going on. I was hoping to wait until later, but I feel you would want to know in order to be able to pray for Daddy."

Struggling with tears that were burning to be released, Suzanne proceeded to fill Autumn in on Daniel's attempt to take his life.

With agonized eyes filling her small face, Autumn, too, struggled to maintain her composure. "Mom," she whispered, "why is Daddy so unhappy? Why would he want to end his life?"

"Oh, Honey, if I knew the answer to that question I would be so glad to tell you. He really is not responsible for his actions right now. It is the illness, the medication and the stress. All of those combined are what has triggered this awful thing. Right now, what we have to concentrate on is tying up loose ends here and getting back home to be there for him. I've already called the airline; we will leave at seven o'clock this evening. I wish I had my car here and we would just take off now and drive home.

"However, I really do need to go to the bank with Mama and get that matter about her land title taken care of. And, I'm trying to decide what to do about Peter. Somehow, I feel that I need to go ahead and meet with him at least for a few minutes. I don't know why, but I just feel that he will care and will be praying for us all."

Looking closely at Autumn, she inquired, "Would that be upsetting to you, Honey?"

Reaching out and grabbing her mom tightly, Autumn choked out her answer. "Oh, Mom, of course, you should see him. He would think it terribly rude if you didn't fill him in on what's happened to Daddy. He seems like such a nice man and he obviously cares about what you and Dad are going through. I am just so worried about you, as well as about Daddy. I know that you are so tired. This must be very hard for you to deal with right now."

Leaning back and looking her mother in the eyes, Autumn continued, "In some ways, it makes me very angry that Daddy would do this to us. It's not just him that this hurts; it is actually more difficult for us to deal with than for him! Don't you think, though, that maybe he didn't quite know what he was doing?"

Before Suzanne could form a reply, Autumn continued, "Mom, have you told the boys yet? How will they deal with this? They, we all, are still hoping he will get better, you know."

"No, I haven't called them," Suzanne replied. "I would much rather be there with them when I tell them about this. I don't think it would be fair for them to hear it over the phone. Tonight, when we are all together, will be time enough. Dad is resting now and the staff are watching him closely, just in case he should try anything else. I will call Adam here shortly and tell him that we are coming home earlier than planned. That way he and Jamie will know we are heading home. I want them to meet us at the hospital as I have set up a late meeting with the doctor. My car is at the airport, so we don't have to worry about transportation back to the hospital once we are there."

"Now, if I am going to speak with Peter before we leave, we had best get moving. I need to finish my hair and makeup. Gram is going to take you and Brenda to the store with her for an hour or so while I meet with Peter. I had planned to have you girls go with me, but with this happening, I really just need a little quiet time to explain what is going on. I would rather that you not discuss the details of this with Brenda right now, do you understand? And, Honey, it is going to be best if Brenda stays home this time. I will explain to her that this just isn't a good time to make the trip to Dallas with us after all. I can only hope she and Karen will understand without having to have all the horrid details."

Drawing a deep breath, Suzanne continued, "If you should speak with either of your brothers, please don't let on that anything is wrong with your father. I truly do feel it's best if I give them the details in person. It will be hard enough for them even then."

"Sure, Mom, I understand, and I know that Brenda will too; even if she can't know all the stuff going on. She knows we are dealing with a lot right now," Autumn replied.

"And, for what it's worth, I'm really glad you have Mr. Clifton as a friend to turn to right now. Unlike Aunt Karen, I know how very much you love Dad and always will. Mr. Clifton seems like he would be a good friend. Brenda and I were talking earlier this morning, and we think you should just take it all one day at a time. God knows what is in the future and we know that He is still in control! Dad may eventually get well, and we will all be happy again. Mom, I've watched you care for Daddy over the past year, and even longer, even before we knew he was so terribly ill. It has not been at all easy for you. Just know that you have Gram and all of us kids with you, and we love you more than anything."

Putting her brush down and turning around slowly, Suzanne gently took Autumn by the shoulders and looked deeply into her caring, concerned brown eyes; eyes so much like her father's. Without saying anything, she pulled Autumn close and hugged her daughter to herself tightly for a long moment. Then, with a soft pat on the back, she pushed her gently away to look at her face to face.

"Autumn, Honey," Suzanne said, "know this, I will never do anything to bring shame to your Dad either in my heart or otherwise, neither while he is alive, nor if he should pass away. I love your father dearly; next to God, he and you children are my life."

Holding her daughter at arm's length, for a long thoughtful moment, Suzanne looked into Autumn's eyes; then she continued, "I am, however, grateful for a few moments in time to share with my old friend. I need to begin gathering myself together for what is ahead in the next weeks and months. I am not looking for more than friendship with Peter, if even that. Sometimes when things come about so unexpectedly, we must simply stop trying to figure it all out and trust the Lord. Knowing that He truly does know what is ahead. He always wants what is best for us. The Lord must know that I need a friend. If so, then I guess I will trust Him in that."

"Thank you for trying to understand where I am coming from in all of this. Now, go find Brenda and your grandmother and let's get to the bank. We will drop Brenda at her home later, so tell her to take her suitcase with her."

Autumn swung around to leave the room. Looking back over her shoulder mischievously, with a change of mood only a teenage girl could come up with, she said to her mother, "I love you, Mom. You are the best mama a girl could ever ask for!"

With a flip of her ponytail and a huge smile, Autumn bounced out of the room.

Slowly, Suzanne sank down to the edge of the bed. Absentmindedly smoothing the soft, quilted coverlet with her hand, she closed her eyes. "*Lord,*" she prayed quietly, "*help me to be strong for Daniel in the time that we have left. Let my family always see and be assured of my commitment to my husband; especially during this hard time. Whatever comes after that, Father, is in your hands. Amen.*"

After sitting for a moment more, Suzanne rose up from the bed, and smoothed her woolen sweater down over her jean-clad hips. Glancing in the wavy old mirror, she finished touching up her hair and applied a light coating of lipstick. Taking a deep breath, she left the security of her room, feeling she was prepared spiritually and emotionally for the meetings with Mr. Knowles, the banker, and then with Peter.

Arriving downstairs in the kitchen, she grabbed her purse and hurried outside to join Velma and the girls in the old station wagon Velma still insisted on driving. Suzanne remembered the day her daddy had bought the car for her mom. That had been a while ago.

It was the year before her dad had passed away unexpectedly from a heart attack. The car had been brand new and was exactly what Velma needed to take eggs and vegetables to the market where she sold them to the locals. It had served her well for many years, but it was a bit worse for the wear now. Suzanne was, in fact, a bit embarrassed to be seen driving or riding in it. She worried that some might think she was too tightfisted to help her mother get a newer, better car.

Suzanne had offered to buy her mother a new vehicle, but Velma was adamant that this one served her just fine. She could be as stubborn as a Missouri mule when the mood struck her. Eventually, Suzanne gave up, knowing that when the time came and her Mama needed a new car that she would be there to help. She supposed there was a good bit of sentimental value attached to the old clunker.

Climbing in on the driver's side, she told Velma that she would drop her and the girls off at the mini mall after they stopped by the bank. Then she would go on to meet Peter.

"That way, if I have the car, I can leave when I feel the need."

"Don't worry about us," Velma replied, "I've already arranged with my friend, Mattie, to give us a ride home when we are finished shopping. She is meeting us at the shoe store and after shopping for shoes, we will all go have a hamburger at the Dairy Bar before meeting you back at home. I'll have her run Brenda home on the way."

"Thanks, Mama," Suzanne said, reaching over to squeeze Velma's hand. "You are always one step ahead of me, aren't you?"

"Well," Velma replied, "that is questionable. You are always so organized and prepared, but I knew that you just might need a little extra time today. This way, you won't have to feel so rushed. Autumn and I will get all packed up and get the house closed up for the trip this evening. All we will have to do is grab our suitcases and head out when you get home. We will need to leave for the airport no later than four o'clock, so just keep an eye on the time."

After a quick stop at the bank, and a quick, but firm, discussion with the banker, Suzanne felt relieved. Mr. Knowles apologized profusely to them both about the mishap. He asked Velma to sign off on the necessary papers once again. He then stated that he would put in for a formal review of the loan payoff status, and would get back with Velma within a few days at most. Again, he assured them not to worry.

"It is all taken care of and was simply a clerical error," the portly little man insisted. "We will clear it all up on this end and send you a paid-in-full receipt and, of course, provide you with your land title via priority mail."

Suzanne was more than a little annoyed with his patronizing manner. In order to get things done, however, she was willing to put up with him this once. It seemed since dealing with the life and death issues surrounding Daniel's situation she had very little patience with the mundane things of this world.

"If people would just do their jobs right the first time there would be a lot less frustration in this world," Suzanne fumed silently as she picked up her purse to leave. Yet, she knew that this was not a perfect world and tried to let her annoyance roll off her like water from the proverbial duck's back.

Once done at the bank, Suzanne drove Velma and the girls to the shopping area. As her family hurried into the mall, Suzanne pulled away and drove on down the street to meet with Peter. She dreaded having to tell him of the latest happening in her life.

"How do you tell a near stranger that your husband, in a rare moment of clarity, tried to kill himself?" Suzanne wondered.

She realized that her palms were sweating and she felt ill all of a sudden.

"Why did I ever agree to meet with Peter? It's not like I owe him anything. Sometimes, I swear that I let people pull me here and there and everywhere. You would think that one day I would grow up and learn to say no! I mean, after all, I've gone over twenty-five years without even talking to the man, why is it so important to comply with what he wants now?"

Feeling more than a little vexed for putting herself in a situation of feeling she had to meet with Peter when she needed to be focused on getting back home to Daniel, Suzanne felt tears welling once again. Realizing that she was overly tired and stressed, and that this was just a little bump in the road, she stepped on the gas and drove the remaining distance to the coffee shop.

CHAPTER 11

P ULLING INTO THE parking lot of Miss Pitty Pat's Cafe, Suzanne saw that Peter's jeep was already parked there. Glancing in the rear view mirror to make sure her mascara wasn't smeared and that her hair was fairly neat, she took a couple of deep, cleansing breaths.

"Okay, girl, don't go making a fool of yourself now. This is simply a quick luncheon meeting with an old acquaintance. Keep it short and sweet, you have a plane to catch."

Swinging her slender legs out of the old station wagon and standing tall, she straightened her shoulders and walked up the steps to the door of the shop. Suzanne paused for a brief second to take a slow, calming breath. Exhaling, she gently pushed open the oval glassed door that was part of the original house built in 1840 and stepped inside.

She automatically glanced around to see if there was anyone she recognized sitting in the nearby booths. Surprisingly, the place was empty; well nearly. She spotted Peter at a back window table. He was quietly reading the local paper.

She walked gracefully toward him. It felt so natural to smile as he glanced up and then rose slowly to saunter over and meet her halfway across the room. She felt all her reservations and frustration melting away. Reaching out to grasp his extended hands, she again felt that sense of belonging and of being safe as his strong, work-calloused hands grasped hers.

A deep knowing welled up within her. This was a friendship that would stand the test of time. Strangely, even though they had never dated in high school, she felt a connection.

Peter stood there for a long moment, holding her soft hands in his strong ones; devouring her face with his murky green eyes, without saying a word. Finally, he simply gave her a crooked smile as he tucked her hand in his arm and walked her back to the table.

Again, she was catapulted back to the night of homecoming when she had walked across center court with her hand lightly resting in the crook of his arm. Glancing up at his strong profile, she thought he looked as handsome as he had back then. Perhaps even more so with the maturity of the years. She noticed a slight sprinkling of gray around his temples.

"At least," she thought, *"I'm not growing older alone!"*

With Daniel being so much older than she was, she had never really thought that much about getting older. No matter how many years she accumulated, Daniel was always the perfectly dignified, older gentleman; the husband who treasured her and made her feel young and beautiful. At least until things had gotten so bad. Lately, she felt as if she had aged a hundred years in a few months. She knew he had.

Seating her at the table as if she were made of porcelain, Peter returned to his chair and folded the paper to put it aside as the waitress came over to take their order. Suzanne remained very quiet as she ordered her usual fare; mineral water with lime and a tossed salad. Peter ordered a large cheeseburger with fries and coffee.

As the waitress left the table, Peter teased Suzanne gently about watching her girlish figure. Smiling back, although with unexplained shadows in her eyes, Suzanne assured him that that was exactly what she was doing.

A moment of quiet reflection came over both Peter and Suzanne. Her elbows on the table, chin on the heel of her hand, she searched out each feature of his face; the tiny little scar just below his left eyebrow, the way his hair glistened with gold highlights as the sun struck it just so. Suddenly, she struggled against an insane urge to run a fingertip down his firm jaw line and explore the strong muscles of his throat and neck. In her heart of hearts, Suzanne knew that it was a good thing she lived hundreds of miles from this man. Temptation might be a terribly strong thing, otherwise.

Peter sat quietly and watched her looking at him, as if memorizing each and every feature. After a long, deliberate pause, he reached across the table and took her hand from under her chin. He sat holding it, quietly looking at the perfect oval shape of her softly colored nails. Gently, he outlined a rosy fingertip.

Then, cupping her hand in his, he glanced up at her and said, "Tell me about it. What is breaking your heart this afternoon and making those gorgeous blue eyes of yours so melancholy and sad? And, by the way, where are those girls of yours. Don't tell me that you gave them the slip! I thought for sure you said we needed a chaperone."

The smile in his eyes said she could trust him.

With a deep, quiet strength, Suzanne lifted her chin and looked steadily back at him. "Peter," she replied, "I really don't know you at all after all these years, yet, somehow I feel I've known you forever. Even more, I feel that I can trust you."

He knew by the look on her face that this was not the time for light banter; something was seriously wrong. Releasing her hand and settling back in his seat, he drew a deep breath. It was harder than he had dreamed it would be, not to want to fix the problem, whatever it was. Not to be able to make her world safe and right somehow felt wrong. And yet, she was not his, and her problems were not his to fix.

Gripping her hands together firmly, almost as if to take back how his touch felt, she lowered her eyes to the table. After a long, silent pause, Suzanne looked back up at Peter. She pressed her fingertips together tightly. Trying to gain control of her emotions, for a long moment she concentrated on simply breathing. After a moment, she started talking very quietly and carefully.

"This is all just so very hard. As you probably already know, I met and married my husband, Daniel, a little over twenty-five years ago. At the time, there were many ugly rumors, which I found out about much later, of my having to get married. Rumors of dark, ugly things happening, or I surely would not have married him so abruptly. All of those things were lies. In all honesty, I was simply very young and naive and Daniel literally swept me off my feet. He was so mature, stable, and everything a girl could dream of, and he was very charming."

Pausing, she drew a circle in the vinyl tablecloth with her fingernail. Finally, with a deep sigh she continued, "I fell deeply in love with him within a few short weeks. Or, perhaps it was love at first sight. Regardless, when he suggested a hurried marriage after only a few months of courtship, I didn't hesitate. He had been married before, and had a young son who needed a mother. I didn't want to wait any longer to become a wife and mother. Simply put, I guess that I needed to be needed. I also felt loved and cherished from the very first moment I met him. He has always been a wonderful husband."

Pausing, she stared steadily at Peter. "Are you sure you want to be bored with all of this?" she inquired with a tiny quirk of a smile.

Peter sat there quietly thinking, *"Little does she know how many questions she just answered for me in this short time, after all these years!"*

Choosing his words carefully, he responded, "Suzanne, I only want to know whatever you are willing to tell me. If it hurts you to talk about this, know that you can keep still. It will not change the way I feel about you. However, I do have a question. Why was it so impossible for you to see how I felt about you back then? Did you not realize that you were all I thought about? All I dreamed about?"

"Peter," she half laughed, half sobbed, "of course I didn't. Don't you realize how things were? With Daddy being so very strict about who we could date, and with never having the money to go to the parties and movies, I simply never gave dating a thought! That last year of school, when I became a little more involved in afterschool events, was my first glimpse of what being part of the in-crowd could be like."

"Perhaps that had something to do with my reaction to Daniel's proposal. I saw an opportunity to be my own person, set my own course, for the first time in my life. For years, I had wondered why no one ever asked me for dates. I used to wonder if I was ugly, or had bad hygiene habits, or what? Then I found out that everyone was afraid of my Dad's rules and regulations. Don't get me wrong, Daddy was really a big old teddy bear and we all have great memories of him, but he could come across as being plain old scary to those few guys who ever got up enough nerve to get close to one of his precious daughters! Also, the fact that he was the loudest Baptist preacher in town didn't help any."

Daring to laugh at herself helped Suzanne to find her balance again.

Peter sighed deeply, "So, what you are saying is that I just wasn't persistent enough, right?"

"What do you mean by persistent enough? I don't understand," Suzanne replied.

"Well," Peter said hesitantly, "I did call once, to ask you to the Junior prom, but your Dad answered the phone. While he didn't actually tell me I couldn't talk to you, by the time he got done asking all his questions, I was a nervous wreck. I wound up babbling something unintelligible and apologizing for calling. Then I quickly hung up. I've often wondered if he ever told you that I had called."

"No!" Suzanne exclaimed.

"You actually called to ask me to the prom? I would have walked over hot coals to be asked to go with you! However, thinking back on it, I do remember Dad mentioning one evening that some guy had called that day. However, he couldn't remember who it was, or which one of us girls he was asking about. I never imagined it would be for me, I certainly would never have thought to name you as a possibility!"

"But why not?" exclaimed Peter. "That is what I meant. Didn't you even have a clue that I was crazy about you?"

"Not even a clue," Suzanne responded calmly. "You see, Peter, you were in a different league from me. It would have been like reaching for the stars to have even hoped to have you care about me. Besides, we were both so very young, you know?"

Sadly, Peter shook his head. "Do you realize how many years I've spent wondering about all of this? Rarely a day has gone by that I've not thought of you and wondered where it all went wrong?"

"Peter," Suzanne urged, "perhaps it just wasn't meant to be. That doesn't mean we can't be friends now, does it?"

Just then, the waitress brought their food. As she sat it at their places, Peter stroked Suzanne's face with his eyes. As soon as the girl left to return to the kitchen, Peter responded. "If friendship is all I can have with you, then I will grab for it with both hands. However, I will never stop regretting all the joys and pleasures that have been lost with the years."

"Peter, please don't do this. I really would like to be friends if that is possible. But, I can't even think about the what if's, or the lost pleasures as you put it. If so, I would be doing a great injustice to Daniel and our relationship, and that I will never do."

Chagrined, Peter dropped his eyes to his plate for a long moment. Finally looking up at Suzanne, he murmured, "I'm sorry, Suzanne, I didn't mean to come across as if I was hitting on you. That is not my intent. I let the years of thinking get the better of me, forgive me if you can."

"I believe you, Peter. If I didn't, I would be walking out of that door right now. May I suggest we call a truce?"

Smiling tentatively at Suzanne, Peter said, "Yes! Now, let's eat our food and then I want to take you to my pasture and show you my new foal."

"You have horses?" Suzanne exclaimed, glad of a change of subject. "Do you know how much I love horses, especially newborns?"

They visited back and forth, as they ate their meal. It felt so natural to sit there together, almost as if they had always been friends.

Peter finished his last bite of the gigantic burger, wiped his mouth with his napkin, and said, "Well, are you ready to go see my horses?"

With a shadow falling over her face, Suzanne replied. "Peter, I didn't want to spoil our lunch, however, seeing the horses will have to wait. We had some bad news about Daniel this morning. Mama and Autumn and I are leaving this evening for Dallas. I have a lot to do before we leave, otherwise you couldn't stop me from checking out your new colt."

"What is wrong? Is Daniel worse?" Peter looked genuinely concerned. "I could see in your eyes that something was wrong. You really are terrible at hiding your feelings, you know."

Suzanne debated over whether to tell him the truth, or simply leave it that Daniel was doing poorly. Knowing deep in her heart that Peter would understand, she whispered the words, "Daniel tried to commit suicide early this morning, Peter."

Drawing those crazy invisible circles on the tablecloth with her fingernail again, she glanced up at him and suggested that they go somewhere more private to talk. The restaurant had suddenly filled with people and the noise level had increased until it was difficult to talk in a normal tone of voice.

"I'm really not comfortable sharing all of this where someone might overhear, and I don't have a lot of time. We were able to get the earliest flight out; leaving this evening to go back home. I know there is nothing we can actually do, but I need to be there with my husband and my boys."

Lifting anguished eyes to look at Peter, she was relieved to see no condemnation on his face. Instead, his eyes were filled with nothing but compassion and concern.

Tossing his napkin on the table, Peter shoved his chair . "C'mon, I have something I want to show you. It won't take long, but I think it might be very special to you right now."

Paying the bill, he ushered Suzanne out of the cafe and helped her into his jeep. Getting in the vehicle on the driver's side, he started the engine.

Reaching deep into his heart, he said a silent prayer for wisdom and patience.

"*Lord, you sure do know how to keep a man on his toes,*" he laughed to himself.

CHAPTER 12

DRIVING DOWN THE street without saying a word, Peter took a sharp left and wound his way through the back streets of the little town until he finally came out at the highway. Taking another left, he drove quickly down the hill and around the bend to an ancient iron bridge hanging precariously over the lazy Buffalo river.

Turning into the incline to go around and down under the bridge, they came to an old city park that had seen better years. Pulling up under a stand of tall pines, Peter turned the engine off.

Staring straight ahead, hands crossed over the steering wheel, he said, "Suzanne, before we continue our earlier conversation, I think that there is something I should tell you."

Without giving her a chance to respond, Peter rushed quickly ahead with his thoughts.

"As you have probably heard, I went through a pretty tough period a few years back. After being single all of my life, I finally decided to begin seriously looking for a wife and a life mate. I'm not proud to admit it, but I met a young woman at a couple's bar, and we started dating. I found out that she had been married before and had a small son, but that didn't matter to me. She was beautiful, witty and charming, and she captured my heart, to say nothing of my desire. She presented herself as very sincere and acted as if she wanted a family and a home. In reality, though, she was looking for someone to provide her a place to live and a father for her son, while she continued her promiscuous lifestyle."

Smiling ironically, he continued, "Initially, I couldn't see beyond the smiles and sweet words, and was basically taken in hook, line and sinker. We were soon engaged to be married. I put her on a pedestal and did every-thing I could to make her love me. Inevitably, I moved her and her son in with me. I started paying her bills and we began talking wedding dates."

"Throughout the process of moving toward the wedding, however, I finally realized that she did not love me. It seems she didn't even love her own child. In fact, I don't believe she knew how to love anyone other than herself and her sinful desires. She actually told me at one point that she was only in the relationship for the convenience. This was very difficult for me to accept because I thought I had fallen in love with her. If I'm hon-est with myself, I was more in love with the idea of being a family man and a father. It's what I've always wanted. I did realize at some point that I didn't love her, but I was committed to keep my word."

Pausing briefly, hands holding tightly to the steering wheel, Peter glanced over at Suzanne to garner her response to his tale. Seeing her huge blue eyes looking quietly, trustingly at him, he inhaled sharply.

Continuing, he confessed, "I wanted to call off the wedding. I knew in my heart that it was a disaster waiting to happen. She insisted that she still wanted to be married. I am still not sure why she felt she needed to follow through with a marriage that she clearly didn't want. So, against my better judgment, I stuck with it out of a sense of responsibility, and, because I thought somehow I could change her. The day of the wedding came and I went to the church at the appointed time, fully intending to follow through with the marriage. After waiting for over an hour, with no bride in sight, my mother spoke with me. She finally convinced me that my erstwhile fiancé was not going to show up."

Peter allowed himself a small laugh of derision. "It turned out she had left me for the next man in her life; one of many, I soon learned. It was very hard for me to accept, and to let go; especially of her little boy. He and I had bonded and were the best of friends."

"I really wanted a family and all that it represented. I was so tired of the lonely nights and lonelier holidays with only my folks who have grown older. I needed and wanted the companionship of a wife and children! I honestly had convinced myself that if I tried hard enough I could make it work. In retrospect, I realize that I actually got off easy. I'm sure we would have been divorced by now and that would have been one more thing to deal with that I certainly didn't need. But pride is a funny thing, and it stung for quite a while. Sadly, it was only a year later that she was killed in a car crash, leaving her little boy to live with his grandparents."

"Do you still see him?" Suzanne asked.

"Only occasionally. They live in another state and it is difficult with the distance and all, but we do stay in touch, especially on his birthday and at Christmas."

Suzanne murmured her sorrow on his behalf. Touching his arm briefly, she let him know that she was listening and cared.

Sitting quietly for a moment longer, Peter tapped his thumbs against the steering wheel before continuing.

"Through my pain in all of that, I began to seek a higher source. I realized that there had to be something, or someone, to fill the void in my life. I was pretty sure it was not another relationship. At least not right away. Maybe I was afraid of getting hurt again. Nevertheless, I began to read my Bible and to seek divine answers for the first time in my life. As I did so, Christ began to become very real to me. Eventually, I found my way to a little church a few miles from here. I stopped by one day for a visit with the pastor. Even though I was very leery of talking to anyone about all of my confusion and mixed up thoughts, I felt compelled to speak with this man."

Clearing his throat, Peter tried hard not to become emotional.

"As soon as I met Pastor Sands, there was an immediate connection in the Spirit. We talked for over four hours. He led me to know Jesus Christ as my personal Lord and Savior that day. That was the beginning of a new way of life. No, it was literally a *new life* for me! Since that time I've been attending church there and love being a part of a group of Bible believing Christians."

Realizing that he had been running on and on, and feeling more than a little embarrassed, Peter said, "Wow! I've talked nonstop. We are supposed to be discussing your situation. I am truly sorry."

Sitting quietly, looking out her car window with her head turned away from him, Suzanne battled the tears that threatened to overflow.

"Lord," she thought, *"what are you trying to tell me through all of this?"*

Slowly turning her head back toward Peter, she gazed at him through the glow of luminescent tears. Reaching out a gentle hand, she grasped hold of his strong, tanned fingers.

Squeezing softly, she whispered, "Oh, Peter, you don't know how happy it makes me to hear this. I've wondered in years past if you would somehow find your way to Him. To know that you are walking with the Lord makes telling you what I must tell you so much easier."

Carefully and slowly, Suzanne began to tell Peter about the phone call she had received a few hours earlier. How the hospital staff had found Daniel in the shower, fully clothed, but with his wrists cut open in an attempt to end his own life. With tears flowing freely now, Suzanne attempted to keep her voice calm.

"Peter," she said, "I've known the Lord all my life, but over the past few months I've come to the point of truly questioning His keeping grace for the first time ever!"

With a shuddering breath, she hurried on, "Watching Daniel go through the terrible and difficult process with this disease has shaken my faith to the very core. I have struggled with trying to understand how and why God could let something like this happen to someone who loves Him as much as Daniel always has. Then there are my children! It breaks my heart to see them struggle to deal with all of this. But, in spite of everything, I must trust and believe that they will be stronger people for it all.

Hearing about your situation and how it brought you to Christ gives me hope to keep on keeping on."

Feeling completely emotionally drained, Suzanne slumped against the cushion of the jeep and sat with her head bowed. Peter, not knowing how to respond, sat quietly praying for wisdom and for the right words to say.

Squeezing Suzanne's fingers, he finally said, "Come on, I want to show you something."

Opening his car door, he strode around to help Suzanne out of the jeep. Taking her by the elbow, he helped her across a pile of large boulders. Slowly, they continued to work their way through the opening of a natural rock formation. The huge rocks created the perfect spot to sit and rest. One could look out over the river cascading along in its hurry to get to the ocean far away. The mist from the river sprayed gently over them as Peter carefully seated Suzanne on the natural bench that years of wind and rain had formed in the stone.

Sitting beside her, wrapping his arm around her to provide her his warmth in the cool breeze, he gently urged her to look out over the tossing waters. Just over the river was a low hanging branch of a gnarly old dogwood tree. Pointing, he showed her what to look for. At the end of the branch, nestled carefully in the crook of the limb, was a bird's nest.

Peter murmured in her ear, "All last spring I would come here to spend time with the Lord in prayer. At that time, in the nest, was a mother Cardinal sitting on her eggs, carefully protecting them from the spray off the river. As the breeze came and went, the nest swayed back and forth even as it does now, with a gentle rhythm. The Lord seemed to be showing me that the mother bird had built her nest right out over the tumbling waters in an attempt to keep her little ones safe from predators. Then, when they began to hatch out and even got ready to fly, she found that she had to have even more trust in the Lord; trust that He would keep them from falling into the rough waters below. I realized then that if she could trust Him with something so precious as her babies, I could trust

Him with my life. Can't we trust Him with Daniel's life, as well as your own? Even if Daniel only has a few months or weeks to live, God can keep him, and you, through it all. None of us have a promise of tomorrow. Will you trust Him with me, for your Daniel?"

Squeezing Suzanne's shoulder, Peter grew silent, waiting for her to absorb the thought. Sighing deeply, Suzanne leaned her head back against Peter's solid shoulder. Looking high up into the tall old pine tree above them, she sat there for a while not saying anything. After some time she turned toward him. Shifting her position to look up at him, she leaned earnestly forward.

"Peter," she asked, "why do you suppose God has allowed us to connect in this way at just this time? I mean, it's not like we can be real friends or anything. I live so far away, and we both have our lives to live. My husband could go on the way he is for a long time, and I am committed completely to being there for him. I love Daniel and will for the rest of my life. I don't understand why now, after all these years, we have been brought together."

Smiling crookedly, Peter took his time answering and then drawled, "Well, maybe the Lord just wanted you to know that you don't have to go through this alone."

"Or," lifting his hand to stop her quick input, "maybe He wants to grow me and test me in my Christ walk."

Shrugging, Peter hurried on before she could interrupt, "Who knows, maybe there are more lessons to be learned than we even realize at this time."

Cocking her head inquisitively, Suzanne asked, "How can God be growing you through my painful situation?"

Looking down at his worn old cowboy boots, Peter was silent for a moment.

"Lord," he whispered in his heart, *"should I open my heart to her and tell her I still love her, or should I wait?"*

Listening to the voice of the Holy Spirit deep inside his heart, he knew that he should hold off with these thoughts for the time being.

Raising his serious, troubled eyes to meet Suzanne's inquiring gaze, Peter replied, "When a friend is hurting, those around them hurt as well. Perhaps God wants me to share your pain as you walk through this valley with Daniel. If I can be there as a friend and make things easier for you, I would count that a privilege."

"*Lord*," he prayed silently again, "*you will have to help me with this one. How can I be close to her, loving her as I do, without letting her know?*"

The reply came back clearly in his heart, "*My Grace is sufficient, says the Lord.*"

Suzanne, unaware of all that was happening in Peter's heart and soul, glanced down at her watch and exclaimed, "Peter, we have been here over an hour! I really must go back and get prepared to leave for Dallas. I am going to be running like a crazy woman as it is!"

Pausing again, she looked at Peter with a deep, penetrating look. Leaning in toward him, she said, "Peter Clifton, I am so grateful to God for sending you my way. Had you not been here, I'm not sure how I could have found the strength to go back to Dallas to face what awaits me there. If you are willing to be my friend and go through this time with me, I accept your offer. I just hope that you don't wind up despising me for being the weak and weary individual that I am!"

Before Peter could protest, Suzanne grabbed his hand and jumped to her feet. Swinging around to have one last look at the simple little nest clinging to the swaying limb of the dogwood tree, she softly said, "May my strength of purpose and trust in the Lord be as great as that of the little mother bird as she watched her young ones take the leap of faith out over that tumbling water!"

Pulling Peter with her, she headed back toward his jeep. Once there, she escorted him to the driver's side and opened the door for him. Then, grinning like a kid, she climbed in and bounced across the padded seat to her side.

"Come on, slow poke," she exclaimed. "I've got places to go and people to see!"

"Suzanne Brummell Parker, you are a witch!" Peter exclaimed.

She laughed a deep throaty laugh as she clicked on her seat belt.

Smiling, he thought, *"One minute you have my heart wrapped around your little finger in sympathy and the next you are teasing me beyond endurance. All the while you hardly realize the effect you have on my poor old heart."*

Jumping quickly into the jeep, he started the engine and maneuvered around to return to the road. "Do you have time for coffee?" he asked, looking over at the incredibly lovely woman beside him.

"Oh no!" Suzanne replied. "I really do need to get back. Mama and Autumn will think I have fallen off the face of the earth! Peter, thank you again for lunch and for everything."

Glancing up at him, she laughed softly. "You know," she said, "I feel like I have found something that was long lost. I am glad that we are truly going to be friends."

At that moment, they arrived back at Miss Pitty Pat's and Peter pulled in beside Velma's old beat up station wagon. Shutting off his engine, he leaned back against the seat.

"Well," he said, "time sure flies when you're having fun!"

Glancing over at her, he asked Suzanne, "Do you think it would be considered out of line if an old friend called you up from time to time? And, do you happen to have email?"

Then, answering himself, he mumbled with a red face, "But, of course, you would with all that you do in your work. How dumb of me to even ask."

"Yes," replied Suzanne, "I have a private email address and no, I don't think it would be out of line if we talk occasionally! That's what friends are for, isn't it? Let me get my purse out of Mama's car and I will give you one of my business cards with all of my information on it."

Getting out of the jeep, Suzanne unlocked the door to her mother's car, reached in and grabbed her bag from where she had left it earlier.

Taking out a card, she handed it over to Peter as he slid from the driver's seat to stand beside her.

"Peter," she said, "if you don't mind, I plan to tell my boys about our friendship. That way, if you call and one of them answers the phone, they won't be taken off guard. Or, if big mouth, Miss Autumn, speaks up, they won't think I'm hiding anything. My boys tend to be a little over protective at times. Especially now that their father is so ill."

"Of course," Peter replied. "I hope to get to know your sons in the future and I know that Autumn and I are going to be the best of friends. She is a great kid."

"Thanks," replied Suzanne. "Now," she said briskly, "I really must go."

Peter held her with his look. "*I wish I had held you a while longer down at the river while I had the chance,*" he thought.

Mentally shaking his head to clear his mind from those thoughts, he said instead, "Well, my friend, you will be in my thoughts and prayers. I wish you a safe journey."

Opening the door to the car for her, Peter watched silently as Suzanne slid into the driver's seat and closed the door. Quickly she rolled down the window. Reaching out, she clasped Peter's hand one last time.

"Thank you again," she smiled. "I really treasure the time spent with you today."

He stood silent, lost on what to say, as words simply seemed to have left his vocabulary strangled. Instead, looking at her with piercing eyes that seemed to see straight through her, he stood tall, with the sun at his back, saying nothing.

Slowly, Suzanne withdrew her hand. Starting the engine, she smiled somewhat uncertainly up at Peter again, and then shifted into gear and drove out of the parking lot.

As she drove away, she prayed, "*Lord, this is so strange, I feel like I am leaving something precious behind. Help me not to have inappropriate feelings* toward Peter. You know my heart belongs to Daniel, and to You. Keep me strong through this time ahead."

As she left the driveway of Miss Pitty Pat's, Suzanne realized that she really needed to stop by and see her sister, Karen. They had parted on such bad terms the night before, and she hated to leave things so undone. In spite of their differences and outlook on life, she truly did love Karen and didn't want to return home with hard feelings between them.

Deciding not to call ahead, she drove the few miles to Karen's home. After she and Bill had divorced, Karen had gotten a very good job with an attorney and had been able to purchase the home she and Bill had been buying.

It was a lovely French Country home with lots of native rock, and windows everywhere. And yet, even with the beautiful home, an incredible daughter and son, and a good job, Karen was not happy. She had allowed the difficult things of this world to make her bitter. It was so sad and such a waste of a beautiful life.

Pulling into Karen's drive, Suzanne saw that her sister was in the side yard trimming her roses. Grateful that she would not have to go inside and prolong the visit, Suzanne took a deep breath and said a quick prayer for wisdom.

Stepping out of the vehicle, she watched as Karen lifted her hand to shade her eyes, looking to see who had pulled into her drive. After a moment, she dropped her hand and turned her back to her advancing visitor.

Standing uncertainly just a few steps from her sister, wishing things were different, Suzanne spoke softly, "Karen, I know that you saw me arrive, will you not turn and speak with me for a moment?"

Karen stood perfectly still for a long moment. Finally she turned slowly, looking at Suzanne with anger written across her features. "What do you want? Isn't it enough that you made a fool of me last night?"

Although Suzanne had expected to find her sister angry, the venom in her voice took her off guard momentarily. Quick tears filled her eyes. "Karen, do you really despise me so much? Do you think I would do anything to hurt Daniel, or you for that matter?"

"Well, what else would you expect me to think, Suzanne? Especially when you top off last night's episode by going God knows where with Peter Clifton for well over an hour today. Suzanne, you don't have to live in this community with their small mindset, enduring the pity and scorn as I do. I've lived with it most of my life, living down the rumors of Bill Ivey and his other women, his drinking, his carousing. I have no intention of having to apologize for my very own sister every time I show my face in public."

Immediately, Suzanne knew that someone had already reported her visit with Peter to her sister. A momentary image of an older woman at Miss Pitty Pat's flashed across her thoughts. She knew the name would come to her eventually, but right now she was too hurt and angry to even try and remember.

"Karen, I don't know who has called you to tattle on me, but it is ridiculous. Peter and I met for a few short minutes at Miss Pitty Pat's. He then invited me down to the river to show me something that he thought might help in this time of dealing with Daniel's situation. I do not need, nor intend, to defend my situation in this. If you choose to think the worst of me then so be it. I love you, and I stopped by here today to see if we might be able to work out whatever issues might be between us. I can see now, however, that you are in no frame of mind to be reasonable."

By way of an answer, Karen once again turned her back to Suzanne and silently continued pruning the rose bush in front of her. Suzanne stood for another long moment, wishing with all her heart that her sister would not be so stubborn.

Finally, realizing that she was wasting precious time, she turned and made her way back to the car. Sitting with bowed head for a moment, Suzanne allowed the tears to escape down her cheeks.

"Perhaps I was wrong to go with Peter, Lord. I suppose I should have simply declined and gone on my way rather than meeting with him at all today," she murmured.

Angry at herself, Suzanne continued talking to her heavenly Father. *"It certainly has not helped this situation any. And while I believe that Peter and I could be friends in the coming months, I don't know where it could lead other than that. After all, if Daniel lives or dies, I am his wife and that is the way I want it to be. If I become a widow, it will not be any time soon that I will be welcoming another man into my life."*

With a stubborn expression on her face, turning the engine on and putting the car into gear, Suzanne backed her mother's station wagon out of the driveway. Throwing her sister one last sorrowful look, she prayed a silent prayer that the Lord would somehow do a healing in Karen's heart and help her to one day break free of the bitterness that held her in its grip.

Getting back to her mother's house and getting to the airport was the most important thing on her mind at the moment. Karen would have to wait for another day.

"I tried," Suzanne spoke to no one but herself. *"I tried."*

One last, lonely tear crept out of the corner of her eye and tracked its way down her cheek. Swiping it away impatiently, Suzanne grabbed a tissue from the box in the console and blew her nose.

"Enough. No more crying today. I have to get home to Daniel and I must be strong a while longer for my children. There will be time enough for crying when Daniel is gone."

CHAPTER 13

As Suzanne drove away from Miss Pitty Pat's Cafe, Peter turned and noticed a rather heavy-set woman sitting at a table near the window. She saw him looking at her and immediately grabbed her purse and came rushing out of the coffee shop. The woman hurried as fast as her short little legs would carry her, toward a small grey car. Opening the door, she looked accusingly back at him as she stuffed herself into the vehicle.

She reminded him somewhat of a plump sausage and he had to stifle a chuckle. It really wasn't charitable to have these kinds of thoughts about the poor old lady. He had known her his entire life and knew she was actually quite sweet. She and her tall skinny husband ran the local grocery store and knew everyone in the surrounding county. They always reminded him of the childhood nursery rhyme of Jack Spratt and his wife.

Briefly, Peter wondered why she had glared at him in such a way, before dismissing it as unimportant. Climbing into his old jeep, he threw it into gear and headed toward his farm. Perhaps seeing to his horses would take his mind off Suzanne.

Smiling wryly to himself he acknowledged, "Not much chance of that, old man!"

It wasn't until later in the day when going into town to pick up his mail he had forgotten to get earlier, that he again ran into the strange little lady. As he was entering the post office, she was coming out. She stopped and held onto the door, keeping him from going inside.

"Aren't you the man I saw with Suzanne Parker this morning?" she barked.

Standing in a relaxed pose, Peter attempted to figure out why she would ask him such a strange question. "Well, yes, I was with her having a bite of lunch at Miss Pitty Pat's around noon today. I feel sure you are aware of that since you watched us from the café window. Why? Is that a concern for you?"

Looking at him through squinted eyes, the woman replied, "I happen to be Karen Ivey's best friend. Karen Ivey is Suzanne's sister, and she told me what a disgraceful thing you and Suzanne pulled off last night. I am ashamed to know you, young man. And, I do know you, to be sure. Your mama and daddy have been coming to my grocery store for more years than I can count."

"Then why are you speaking to me, my Dear Lady, of something that is clearly no concern of yours? If what I have done were so despicable, I would think you would want nothing to do with me. And besides, I have always understood that one is innocent until proven guilty. Is it possible, do you think, that Karen could have been a little mistaken in her assessment of the entire situation?"

"Karen is not a liar!" the woman fairly screeched.

Peter sighed deeply. "Please, Mrs. Quigley, I have known you all my life. Now do you really think that Velma's daughter, or I for that matter, would do anything morally wrong? Particularly right out in front of God and everybody! Think about it for a moment. Karen simply came upon a situation that she didn't understand. Suzanne had been telling me about a situation with a family member who is ill and I was offering her a little comfort and concern. Why, I feel sure that I would have done the same had it been you in those circumstances!"

Pausing and looking up at him with a questioning look on her face, Mrs. Quigley suddenly chuckled and replied, "Yes, Peter, I do believe you would. You are one of those rare men who is truly a gentleman in every situation. And, I imagine if I was upset you would take me in those strong arms of yours and give me a hug. In fact, come to think of it, I would be deeply hurt if you did not!"

"Let me talk to my friend and see if I can calm her down. Karen means well, but this whole thing with her brother-in-law has just about torn her heart out. Oh yes, I do know all about it. But never you mind, I will see what damage control I can do starting immediately. Thank you for clearing this matter up in my mind, Dear. Now, I must run along and talk with Karen before she tells the whole county that you and that sweet Suzanne are fixing to have something more than a bite of lunch!"

Smiling sweetly, she stood on tiptoe as she reached up to kiss his cheek. Bending to meet her halfway, Peter drew her close in a warm hug and whispered in her ear. "You are a dear, even if you do try to hide it behind a blustery exterior."

Giggling like a schoolgirl, Mrs. Quigley smacked him on the arm with her pocketbook.

"Get on with you now, Peter! We will have none of that."

Sashaying off, she was as proud as any grandmother might have been. To have the handsome Peter Clifton say something so very nice to her, and to give her an embrace, right out in clear sight of God and everybody, just made her day. She was smiling from ear to ear. The funny little lady climbed into her vehicle and drove away.

Peter sighed deeply. Sometimes the joys of living in small town America were overshadowed by the lack of privacy and simple consideration of others. Hurrying on inside, he gathered the mail from his box and quickly made his way back to his truck. He wanted to make a quick stop by his parent's home at some point during the late afternoon or evening. He'd not been there in a few days. With his dad recovering from his heart attack, Peter knew it was important for him to stay in touch with both his mother and his father.

But for now, he needed to take care of his animals. There was something therapeutic about being around his horses and cows. Some days, like today, he could hardly wait to be on his little ranch, listening to the sounds of nature all around him. Once they were fed and cared for, he could go spend a little time with his mom and dad without worrying about the animals.

Knowing that Suzanne would be hurt if the rumors continued, however, he was glad that he'd stopped long enough to have the conversation with Mrs. Quigley. She was one of those individuals who were either for you or against you. To have her understanding the situation and helping to squelch the rumors could only help.

Thinking about Suzanne made him smile his slow easy smile. He'd put the situation of where their relationship might go in the future totally in the hands of the Lord. However, he felt no catch in his spirit, nor did he feel that it was in any way wrong, to be a part of her life at this time. In fact, he valued that she had made her position quite clear regarding her love for her husband and her desire to do nothing to cause him shame or harm. A woman like that was worth her weight in gold.

Over the coming weeks, he determined, he would call her every few days to check on Daniel and to see how they were holding up. For sure, a part of him wanted to get on a plane and fly out there to be with her. But, the sensible part of his brain told him that it would be too much too soon at this time in their relationship.

Strangely, he grieved for the man that he had never known. And being the man that he was, Peter hoped and prayed that, in spite of everything, Daniel would get better. Even though that prayer meant that he would never stand a chance of having a life with Suzanne, he prayed it anyway.

He knew the next few months would fly swiftly by as he taught at the high school in the mornings and worked his farm in the late afternoons and evenings. He had several head of cattle now and, of course, his horses. His pride and joy was the new foal that had been sired by a famous stud. The little fellow was already showing promise of living up to his father's name.

Who knew, one of these days they might be at the Kentucky Derby. Peter had long dreamed of having a horse that could compete in the national races. That dream might be coming true sooner than he had thought possible.

"*If Suzanne could be a part of that,*" he thought, "*I would be a happy man.*"

No sooner had that thought entered his mind, than he recognized that he had no right to be thinking this way. Immediately, Peter bowed his head, right there beside the haystack and prayed. He asked God to forgive him for thinking of this woman in a way that was not permissible at this time in their lives.

"*Father, help me to keep pure thoughts as I pray for Suzanne and her family over the coming weeks. Lord, I do love her and I accept that. I also accept the fact that I have no right to think of her as mine. I thank you that I have the privilege of being her friend, and if I can ever be of help to her, I trust you to lead, guide, and direct me. For now, I give Suzanne to you. Please, Lord, take care of her and her family. If it is your will that Daniel be healed I pray for that now. I give you all praise and honor, Lord. In Jesus' name, amen.*"

With a feeling of peace in his heart, Peter completed his outdoor chores before going into his lonely home to fix a bite of supper and grade some papers. He knew deep in his heart that he was on the right track and that nothing the enemy could do would cause him to fail.

Climbing into his truck and driving to his folks' place a while later, Peter remembered that he had promised to fix a loose shutter on their lovely, old two-story home. He hoped he had enough daylight left, but it sure felt good to have his own chores finished and those dang papers graded. The paperwork was the one thing he really disliked about teaching. It could make a fella crazy if you let it. But, as in all of life, there were some things a person enjoyed, and others they just endured.

Pulling into his parent's driveway, he drew a deep breath. He wanted to tell his mother about the afternoon with Suzanne, and yet, he was afraid to. There were so many emotions raging against each other in his heart that he wasn't sure he could even articulate what he was feeling. Going inside, he found his mother happily making a batch of muscadine jelly. Grabbing her from behind, Peter gave her a warm hug.

Smiling up at him from her tiny height of five feet nothing, Nadine Clifton lifted a spoon of jelly she had been blowing on to cool.

"Here, you silly boy, tell me what you think of my jelly. I'm thinking I might just enter a few jars in the fair, if it sets up good."

Lifting his head and sniffing the air, Peter inquired, "Is that warm buttermilk biscuits I'm smelling?"

"It sure is! I thought warm biscuits with butter and some of this fresh jelly would add a nice touch to our supper. Your daddy has been feeling a little under the weather this evening and I felt this might be just the thing to help him feel better. That, and you stopping by for a visit, of course. I do hope you will have a plate with us."

Moving toward the stove, she listened as her son continued talking. She loved this boy child of hers more than words could describe. He was one of the most dependable and responsible young men she had ever known.

"Well, I can't stay long, Mom. I just remembered a while ago that I had promised to fix the shutter on that upstairs window. It's supposed to storm later tonight and I wanted to get that done so it won't come blowing off if the wind gets up. Besides, I already ate my supper. However, I sure won't turn down a biscuit with fresh muscadine jelly."

"Oh, well, that is so nice of you, Son. Your daddy has been worrying himself half-silly about that shutter. In fact, we got in a bit of a tiff this morning because he was bound and determined to get the ladder out and climb up and fix it himself. I let him know, in no uncertain terms, that he was not going to do that. In fact, I threatened to tie him to the bed in his pajamas if he even thought about it a minute longer! I swear, you would think the man just wants to have another heart attack!"

Laughing, Nadine pulled a tray of golden brown biscuits from the oven.

"You might as well sample these biscuits while they are warm, then you can get on with the window shutter. Call your father to come in and eat with us, if you will. I have a feeling he is more depressed than feeling sick. A good visit with you will cheer him right up."

"Sure, Mom, but first let me ask you something. Do you remember Suzanne Brummell, from school?"

"Well, of course, I do, Peter! I may be getting up in years, but I am by far not senile yet. Why, what is it you want to know?"

"It isn't so much what I want to know, Mother, as to ask you to be in prayer for her. It is all quite hush, hush, for now. You see, her husband is quite ill and may not be around much longer. I would just feel better knowing that you are lifting her and her family up in prayer."

Nadine stood by the stove, holding her hot pad in her hand. Looking long and hard at her son, she finally responded, "Peter, of course, I will be praying. I am assuming that you have been in communication with Suzanne. Yes, I heard that she was in town for a short visit. You know nothing happens around here that does not cause a stir of some sort. I also got a call from Mrs. Quigley this afternoon, telling me what a wonderful and thoughtful son I have."

Stirring her pot slowly, she continued, "I wondered how long it would take you to get around to telling me about your luncheon with Suzanne. And, of course, where you and she took off to after lunch. According to Mrs. Quigley, you were gone for the better part of an hour before you brought her back to pick up her mother's car. Really, Peter, don't you know by now that there is nothing that does not get noticed by the busy bodies of this town?"

Groaning and holding his head in his hands, Peter sank into the chair at the kitchen table.

"For real, Mother? She called to tell you how long we were gone? That right there is exactly why sometimes I just want to leave here and never return. Does a person not have a right to any privacy? I mean, it's not like we were having a clandestine meeting or anything. If that were the case, Suzanne certainly would not have parked her car right out in the most conspicuous place in town! It was a spur of the moment thing. She was telling me about Daniel's illness and was getting emotional. Rather than have her break down in tears in front of the waitress and anyone else who might be watching, I invited her to ride down to the river with me. I took her to that spot where the mother Cardinal had her nest this spring. Remember? I told you about it several months ago."

"Yes, Dear, I do remember, and I am absolutely positive that your time together was quite innocent. I trust you completely, my son, and strangely enough, I also trust that young lady. That is not the issue, though. You seem to want me to be aware of your interest in her; an interest that has spanned many years. And as long as you are aware that she is tied to deep commitments, I will not scold you, nor tell you how to run your life."

Sighing deeply, Nadine continued. "Yes, I will pray for Suzanne and her family. If what you say is true, she will need all the prayers she can get. It is a terrible thing to watch someone you love dying right before your very eyes. Alzheimer's disease is one of the most horrible. It steals the identity of the person, yet leaves their soul and body intact to endure until the end. And before you scold me for knowing what Daniel's illness is, it has been common knowledge with the gossips for a good month or more. They are all just too kind to let on to Velma that they know."

With a sniff, Nadine reached for her apron and wiped a tear from the corner of her eye.

"The Lord knows I feel for Suzanne. Your father is a breath away from crossing over Jordan at any given moment if he should have another heart attack. If I leave the room and come back, I never know whether he will be lying in that chair dead, or be sitting up fussing at me for not bringing him a cup of tea. Such is life, we must live each day as a blessing from the Lord, and try not to think too much about what tomorrow might bring."

Leaning over to kiss her son on the top of his curly head, she urged him to go in and get his father for supper.

"The good Lord knows I don't know what I would do without you. You are my strength. It is no wonder Suzanne was drawn to spending time with you. You are one of those men who seem to put the world back on its axis with no effort. Now, please go get your father before this food dries out too much to enjoy. And then you'd best get that shutter fixed before it gets too dark to see what you are doing."

With one last sniff and a swipe of a wayward tear, Nadine bustled around setting plates on the table. She treasured every moment spent in her son's presence, and hated that she had let herself get all emotional over things that neither she, nor he, could change.

Peter went to the door leading into the family room, to see his father already getting up out of his recliner.

"Is that buttermilk biscuits I smell, son?" he said with a twinkle in his deep brown eyes. "I may not be able to do much around here, but I'll declare that I can eat as many of those as you can!"

Peter enjoyed the next hour or so with his parents. It grieved him to see them both growing older so quickly. It almost seemed they had aged overnight following his father's heart attack.

Taking time to sit and eat with them was a simple thing, and yet he knew it would give them joy for the rest of the week. Peter knew that he was more engaged with his parents than many others were, and yet he wished there were more hours in the day to allow him to help with things they needed done.

He then wondered how they would have managed if he had married someone and moved away. This was something he'd rarely given a thought to since he had chosen to live and work close by all his life.

"*I suppose it would work out,*" he thought. And yet, he knew it would be difficult to ever leave his parents alone for long.

Brushing off the worrisome thought, he teased with his mother for a bit as they readied up the kitchen. She would never think of stopping for the night as long as there was a thing out of place. It didn't take long, and Peter cherished the time with the two of them.

Once done with that he hurried out to the garage and found the hammer and nails. It didn't take him more than a few minutes to reattach the shutter. Glad that he could do even this simple thing, he hummed as he put the tools away once again and returned to the kitchen to tell his folks goodbye.

As he was preparing to leave, his father told him to have a good night. He then ambled back to the living room to catch the early news broadcast, leaving Peter and his mother alone. Looking over at her son, Nadine smiled, then picked up the conversation where they had left off earlier.

"Son, I know you don't want to hear me nagging at you, and I hope that's not how you will take what I have to say. However, being your mother, I know a lot more about you than you might sometimes realize. I know that for many years you have held Suzanne Brummell up as the standard for every relationship you have been in; at least the remembrances you have of Suzanne. I've sometimes worried that you may have held her to too high of a standard, putting her on a pedestal so to speak."

Pausing to draw in a deep breath, Nadine continued, as Peter sat on the tall stool at the kitchen counter, patiently waiting for the rest of what his mother had to say.

"More than anything, I don't want to see you be hurt through all of this. Suzanne has lived a very different life from what you have. Oh, I have no doubt that she has grown and matured into a lovely woman, wife and mother. But she is not the same girl that you cherished and adored. She may never be the woman you need. I hope you are prepared for the rejection that could come if she simply chooses not to want or need you in her life once things with Daniel are done."

"Darling, boy. It breaks my heart to think that all these years could be for naught, and that your heart could be broken once again. Please, Son, guard your heart just a little, for your own sake, if you will."

Peter sat for several long moments digesting what his mother was trying to convey. He knew without a doubt that she had only his best interests at heart. However, he wanted, no needed, her to understand that he was truly trusting the Lord with his life as never before.

"Mother, dearest," Peter began, "thank you for voicing your concerns, and for caring so much for my wellbeing. I understand why you feel you need to caution me, but please know that I am not going to rush into anything. Besides, this thing with Suzanne may never come to be, as much as I would desire it. Even if we are just to be friends for the rest of our lives, I will have had that. She clearly loves her husband, and I would do nothing to diminish that part of who she is. In fact, the very fact that she is true to him, even in his sickness, is just another confirmation of the kind of woman I believe her to be. And, if someday, somehow, God ordains that we be together, then I will feel that I am the luckiest man in the world. Tell me that if this ever happens that you will love her for my sake, if nothing else."

Nadine hurried to assure her son that she would indeed love the woman he loved.

"I will be praying that the Lord will guide each of you along this way. I just wanted to caution you a bit. You are lonely and ready for a new phase of life. But it may be months, or even years, before Suzanne has processed through her grief and loss. Even when she does, you and she may find that your paths will go separate ways. If it turns out that she falls in love with you, and wants to be in your life, your father and I will welcome her and her children with open arms."

"Now," the little mother scolded, "let's not fret on this anymore tonight. I know without a doubt that you will do what is best and right. If it is meant to be it will all work out in the end!"

Standing, Peter smiled at his mother as he prepared to leave.

"You are amazing, Nadine Clifton. Somehow you manage to make me feel like the most incredible man in the world, while also feeling like a boy in need of a good scolding once again! It must be a mother's gift. Well, I must be off, I have enjoyed our meal and our little visit tonight. I can't imagine a world without you in it. That shutter should be just fine. If it gets to banging again be sure and let me know."

Giving his mother a warm hug and waving a hand at his father in farewell, Peter let himself out of the house. He drove down the drive in the dusk as his parents settled in to watch the evening news. With a deep sigh, he looked up at the sky, wondering how the flight was going for Suzanne and her family.

"Lord, please keep them safe in your hands, and help them to make the best decisions possible for Daniel and for the needs of their family."

Knowing that this was one more thing that he had no power to control, Peter gave the worries back to his Lord and Savior. Remembering the days when he had felt so lost and afraid, he was grateful for the knowledge that his heavenly Father truly did have everything under control.

As soon as they had landed and had a moment to collect themselves, he fully intended to call Suzanne and check on how things were going. Peter knew that he had to be careful or he would wind up being a pest. That was the last thing he wanted. However, he felt such a burden for her, and a desire to be engaged in her life as much as possible during this difficult time.

Heading toward home, he smiled as he realized how close he had come to not attending the Fall Festival the evening before. Crowds were one thing he avoided at all costs.

"It's funny," he puzzled to himself, *"how just one quick decision may affect the rest of one's life. I'm sure glad I decided to attend the festival. Really glad."*

CHAPTER 14

LITTLE DID SUZANNE know that back at Karen's house, Karen turned and watched her drive away. The sorrow etched across Karen's face was enough to break a lesser woman.

Waiting until Suzanne had made the turn, Karen dropped her pruning shears where she stood and hurried to her screened in back porch. Opening the door, she fairly flew into the shadowy room. Falling into one of the brightly cushioned wicker chairs, she began to cry as she had not cried in years.

"Oh God, why do I have to be such a hateful person? Why do I push everyone in my life away? I don't want to be like that, but something just comes over me and I feel such anger, such hatred. Oh, dear God, if you really can hear me, please forgive me for my ugly heart, and please, help me to find my way back to you, and back to peace."

After her fit of crying had worn itself out, Karen sat in the quiet peace of the afternoon. To her wounded spirit, it was magical to simply sit; listening to the sounds of birds calling, and the wind whispering in the leaves of her tulip tree. Shifting slightly, she curled her legs up under her and leaned back in the comforting embrace of the cushions.

Feeling better than she had in years, she suddenly realized that God truly had heard her cry. He did care that she wanted forgiveness. Her heart felt whole and clean like it had not since before she had married Bill. She felt completely loved by her heavenly Father. Wonderingly she simply sat for well over an hour.

After a while, she heard Brenda in the kitchen calling her name. She had not even realized that someone had clearly dropped her daughter off at home. Getting up and stretching her cramped legs, she let herself in through the back door.

"I'm here, Darling. What did you need?"

"Oh, Mother! I was about to wonder what had happened to you. I'd looked all over upstairs and down and you were nowhere to be found. It frightened me more than a little. Are you alright?"

"Oh, Brenda, I am so sorry. I am sorry that you would even have to feel frightened for your mother. I am sorry that I have let life become so difficult for you these past few years. Can you ever forgive me?"

Brenda stood with open mouth, watching her mother. "Who are you, and what did you do with my mother?" she finally blurted out.

Karen laughed shakily. "Well, I am your mother, just a new and better mother, I hope. I realized this afternoon that I have been one of the most bitter, selfish and inconsiderate people ever. I prayed, Brenda, and I asked God to forgive me for my sins. I know that He did, because I feel clean and new for the first time in many years. But I may need your help a little longer. I intend to get off all the prescription pills I'm on and to stop drinking. It will not be easy, but I am determined to do it."

It took a few minutes for Brenda to reply. She wanted so desperately to believe her mother, but she had seen Karen go through too many phases to take her newly found salvation at face value. And yet, she didn't want to discourage her mother either. Anything would be better than having to deal with the craziness of life when her mom got zoned out on pills and booze.

"Mom, if there is anything I can do, please tell me. You know I will do anything to help you find your way."

"Well, for starters, Sweetheart, I am going to gather up every bottle of pills and alcohol I can find, and I want you to help me flush them down the toilet."

Unbelievingly, Brenda tentatively replied, "Are you sure, Mom? 'Cause once they are gone you won't be able to go back. Not without a great deal of trouble and expense."

The wise girl knew that her mother had connived for years to get her various doctors to give her pills that the others knew nothing about. If this truly was a life changing experience, however, she surely didn't want to be a stumbling block; keeping her mother from the freedom she desperately needed.

"Brenda, I know better than anyone how hard this will be. I expect that I will go through withdrawals for the next several days. I beg you now, whatever I threaten, whatever I say or do, do not let me leave this house. And just keep feeding me black coffee, chicken soup and crackers until it is done. It's not going to be easy or pretty."

Somberly, Brenda nodded. She hoped she was up to the task ahead of her, and was very glad her younger brother was at their father's for the next week. Together she and Karen went through every room in the house, starting with Karen's bathroom. They gathered an astounding supply of prescription and liquor bottles.

As she followed her mother from room to room, Brenda could not believe some of the places where Karen had hidden her stash. There were bottles behind books in the bookcases, between cushions in the furniture, and even in the laundry hamper.

At last, Karen stood at the kitchen sink and began opening bottles of alcohol. Shakily, she began pouring bottle after bottle down the drain. Brenda stood disbelievingly by, amazed at the determination shown clearly on her mother's face.

Once the alcohol was all gone, Karen took the many bottles of pills, instructing Brenda to take the caps off and hand her the bottles, together they began disposing of the drugs down the toilet. Flushing every little bit to clear the drain, they continued until every last bottle was gone.

Brenda had watched carefully to see that her mother didn't slip a few pills here and there in her pockets, but to her surprise, Karen never wavered. Finally, as the last few pills made their way to the sewers below, Karen stood back and laughed unsteadily.

"Well, there. Now that is done. I am a bit drained, Dear. What say we have a nice cup of tea and then I think I will lie down for a bit."

Karen had been through a rehab program several years before, and she knew quite well what was coming. However, she didn't see the need to frighten her daughter overly much. After all, it was get through it or die trying at this point.

The next few days went painfully by as Karen battled her demons. Brenda took off school on Thursday and Friday, giving her mother the much needed help in getting through the roughest part. By Sunday, Karen was still weak and shaky, her eyes sunken and skin pale. But she knew she would make it now. Looking at Brenda over a strong cup of black coffee on Monday morning she realized that it was teacher's conference week. That meant Brenda would be home all week; she smiled.

"I'm glad you have this week off school, Brenda. If I can just make it a few more days I think we will be on the home stretch. I want you to know how much I appreciate you and love you. This was the hardest part and, together, we made it. I am so sorry that you had to see your mother in these conditions, but I promise you, this will be the last time I ever put you through something of this sort. I am never going back to that way of life again. I am going to get well, and I am going to make you proud of me."

The next weeks took on new meaning for Brenda as she saw her mother grow in the Lord, join a women's Bible study and become a new person in Christ. They did things together as mother and daughter that they had never done before. Things like joining a gym and taking art classes together.

At first she was skeptical as she waited to see if the old Karen would come creeping back in. However, week after week passed and Karen only became stronger and better. Finally Brenda and others had to realize and accept that God had completely healed her heart and her mind.

Brenda begged her mother to call her sister and tell Suzanne what was happening in her life, but Karen waited.

"I just want to make sure that I can do this before I tell her," was her standard response when questioned. "And besides, she has way too much on her plate to be bothering her right now. There will be a time that is right, and when it is, I will talk with her."

And so, Brenda relished the fact that she had the mother she had always dreamed of having. As a family, they were happier than she could ever remember being.

She debated calling Autumn, but she knew that they were going through problems of their own. "Besides," she thought with a little spurt of rebellion, "there will be time enough for telling the world about Mom's recovery when I know it's going to last."

She wished with all her heart that her mother would have talked to her Aunt Suzanne when she came by the house a few weeks earlier, but that was out of her control. She could not imagine shoving a sister aside for anything. It had long been her heart's desire that she had a sister to share her burdens with. Autumn was as close to a sister as she would ever have, and while she treasured their friendship, it still wasn't the same.

Praying was all she knew to do. Surely if God could heal Karen from the addictions she had been in bondage to, he could also heal her heart toward her sister.

CHAPTER 15

As Suzanne prepared her bags for the trip back to Dallas, she felt suddenly as if the whole world was on her shoulders. Pausing to look out the upstairs window toward the apple orchard, she breathed deeply. The trees were waving in the breeze. Here and there a golden leaf would fall and drift silently to the ground.

"Lord," she prayed silently, "*please, give me strength for the days and weeks ahead. You know that I have loved Daniel, even in the most difficult times of our marriage, but, Lord, I am so tired and feel so unprepared for what is ahead. Provide me with your strength. Sometimes this responsibility of caring for Daniel seems so big, and I feel so helpless to carry it alone. I need you to carry it for me, Father. And please, give my children strength to hold up as well, and give them understanding that only comes from you.*"

Wiping a lone tear from her cheek, Suzanne moved slowly across the room. Taking one last look around the precious refuge, she picked up her bags and straightened her shoulders. Inhaling deeply, she grasped the doorknob in her trembling hand and stepped out of the room. Reluctantly, she pulled the door closed behind her, as she left the one place that had always represented safety and peace to her.

As the door latched with a hollow click, Autumn came bounding out of the room down the hall.

"Mom," she cried, "we'd better get going or we're going to miss our flight! Gram is already at the car."

Grabbing Suzanne's carry bag from her, she clattered down the old staircase ahead of her mother.

Suzanne followed more slowly. Sliding her hand lovingly down the worn banister, she felt the peace of her heavenly Father surround her. Strangely enough, it seemed as if she sensed the presence of her dad as well.

Whispering softly, she said, "Goodbye, Daddy, I have a feeling it may be a while until we return. I love you, forever and always."

As she reached the back door, it seemed the entire backyard was in a frenzy. Old Barney was barking and jumping. Velma's best friend, Mattie, was laughing and talking as she assured Velma that she would keep an eye on everything. All the while, she was waving her arms and hurrying them all into the automobile.

"Yes, yes, I will get the boy to come pick your dad-blasted apples. If you will stop worrying for one little moment, and simply trust that we have enough sense around here to do a few things, that would be good!"

Suzanne smiled quietly, only her mother's dearest friend could get away with scolding her so soundly and not get her own ears boxed.

Making sure the door was locked and the screen door was firmly in place, Suzanne gave Mattie a last hug and climbed in the car with her family. They all waved goodbye until they could no longer see Mattie standing under the massive oak tree.

"Well," Velma said with a twinkle in her eye as she gripped the steering wheel, "if I drive like your daddy used to, we should make it to the airport in just under an hour!"

"Lord, help us!" Suzanne smiled back. "I would rather get there in one piece."

Checking her watch, she told Velma, "Seriously, Mama, we have plenty of time. Just get in the fast lane and hold it steady and we should be right on time. If you don't mind, I think I will just lie back and close my eyes for a bit. I feel quite weary after the day we have had."

"Sure, Suzie, lie back and rest. I know where I am going. Of course, if this is just a ploy to keep from telling me about your visit with Peter, then I am going to be pretty mad at you!"

"Mother, it is not a ploy! I am tired to the bone and there is really nothing to tell. I visited with an old friend for an hour or so and told him about the situation with my husband. That is pretty much the gist of it. Now, may I please rest?"

When Velma didn't respond, Suzanne reached over and patted her on the arm.

"I love you, Mama. I didn't mean to sound short with you, but I am very overwhelmed right now."

"I know, love," Velma replied, "and I should not badger you with my silly teasing. Please do rest while you can, the evening ahead is going to have stress enough for us all."

Suzanne let her head fall back against the headrest, closed her eyes and left everything in her mother's capable hands. To have nothing to do, and to not be in charge for even a few moments felt heavenly.

As she drove on toward the airport, Velma prayed quietly for God's peace on the family and His traveling mercies over them all. She also prayed for the boys and the heartache that seemed inevitable over the next few days.

Glad that she could give her burdens to her heavenly Father, she smiled and began softly humming *Amazing Grace*. The sweet presence of the Holy Spirit surrounded her and it seemed she could smell a sweet perfume in the air.

Autumn was reading a book in the back seat, content for the time being to escape into the world of fiction. Although she had been disappointed when it was decided that Brenda should stay at home, she seemed to be taking it in stride.

"Because young people are incredibly flexible," thought Velma. *"Somehow they seem to roll with the punches better than us older folk."*

It was turning out to be a beautiful fall day and the sun was shining. It seemed odd that there was such sadness waiting for them on the other end of the trip.

"*Strange*," thought Velma, "*the sun should not be shining so beautifully on such a sad day. But,*" she admitted to herself, "*I sure am glad it is.*"

Suddenly, in the stillness of the quiet car, Suzanne's cell phone shrilled out. Jerking awake, she fumbled around in her bag until she found it and flipped it open to answer the call.

"Hello? Yes, Jamie, we are on the way to the airport."

Looking at Velma, she said, "Mama, where are we now?"

Velma replied that they were over two-thirds of the way there and should be checked in and on the plane within half an hour. Suzanne relayed this on to Jamie. She then asked that he get in touch with Adam and arrange to meet them at her house around eight-thirty; explaining that they would all go from there to the hospital to see their dad.

"Mom," Jamie insisted on the other end, "what exactly is going on? You guys weren't supposed to be back for several days. What happened to change that? Is Dad worse? I tried calling Dr. Carey, but he said I had to speak with you and that Dad is holding his own. What does that mean?"

"Oh, Jamie, I really didn't want to discuss this over the phone. Can't you just wait until I get there, please?"

"Mom," he replied, "Adam and I are no longer children and you really should trust us enough to tell us anything we need to know. We want to be there for you and Dad, but we can't if you keep things from us."

"Jamie, I don't mean to make it seem that I'm keeping things from you, but this is just so hard. I wanted to tell you both together. Your Dad has been very depressed, especially so since his last episode and they changed his medicine."

Drawing a deep breath, Suzanne spoke gently, "Jamie, Dr. Carey said that your father tried to take his own life this morning."

A long moment of silence followed as Jamie absorbed this news. Finally, he responded in a raspy tone, clearly trying not to let his emotions get the better of him.

"How? What did they say that he did? Are you sure it wasn't just a medicine that reacted with him? You know that has happened before."

"Jamie, he took the metal edge off the shower unit and tried to slice his wrists. He clearly knew, momentarily at least, what he was doing and he intended to end his suffering."

Suzanne sighed, "Luckily, Son, the aide found him before any serious damage occurred. Nevertheless, they are very concerned, as he does not seem to be snapping out of the depression. The meds are not working well at all. I spoke with Dr. Carey earlier this afternoon, before we left Mama's house, and he said your father is now refusing to eat or drink. The doctor indicated that we will probably have to decide very quickly what to do next as it appears your father is determined to see an end to this."

"What are our options, Mom? Can't we just put him on a feeding tube?" Jamie asked in a deeply worried voice.

"I'm not sure, but I don't think so," Suzanne replied. "Your father had a living trust made up about a year and a half ago stating that if he ever became seriously ill that he would not want to be put on any kind of life support. You know your father; he did very thorough research about this illness and tried to be prepared for any event related to it."

"What about this suicide attempt? That doesn't sound like Dad at all."

"Well," Suzanne responded, "Dr. Carey said that we can't hold him responsible because it is a combination of the illness and the medication each taking their toll on him."

"If he just refuses to eat, what will happen then, Mom? Will he just give up and die?"

"I'm not sure, Sweetheart. These are all questions we will have to discuss with the doctor. That is why I want all of us to be there this evening. That way, all of our questions can be presented at one time. Then we will all know as much about what we are facing as is possible."

Shifting in her seat she saw the traffic was getting crazy, "I'm sorry, Jamie, I've got to go now, traffic is getting quite heavy and I need to help

Gram watch for the exit to the airport. Take care, and I will see you boys in a few hours. If you want to meet with Adam and fill him in, that is fine with me. Please let him know why I held off on sharing this with you both over the phone. Actually, tell him that I did try calling him this morning after Dr. Carey called, but he was teaching a class. I was so upset I didn't even leave a message. other than to say that the doctor had called and that we were coming back home."

"Sure, Mom, I'll go by their house right now. He is there working on grading finals, but I will bring him up to date. Mom, we love you and we will all get through this together."

"Thank you, Son. I love you children more than words can ever express. I am so glad I have each of you to walk through this dark time with me. Bye now; be careful as you are out and about and I will see you after while."

Slowly hanging the phone up, Suzanne glanced in the backseat at Autumn. She was sound asleep, with headphones on and her book lying in her lap.

Giving her mom a brief update on what Jamie had said, Suzanne fought to keep tears from falling again.

"I must stop this crying, there will be plenty of time for that when this is all done."

"Oh, Suzie, tears are good for you. They bring healing to the soul. But, I do understand, you must be strong for a while longer. Look!" she chirped. "We made it right on time!"

Pulling into long-term parking, they woke Autumn and grabbed their bags. Getting through check-in was always a tedious process, but they finally reached their gate just as the boarding began. Suzanne had splurged and used some of their frequent flier miles to upgrade the three of them to first class. She figured that it was well deserved.

The flight went well. Velma fell asleep almost as soon as her head hit the back of her seat. Autumn reverted to listening to her headphones again. Suzanne had opted for the window seat and sat looking out at the fluffy white clouds and bits of blue sky.

Her mind wandered back to the early years with Daniel. She remembered that, at times, she had been deeply lonely in a way that was difficult to describe. He loved her; she never doubted that. In fact, it was almost an obsessive love that was sometimes overwhelming in its intensity. She supposed that may have come from the loss of his first wife. And yet, in many ways, he lived his life pretty much on his own, leaving her to deal with the raising of the children and managing the home.

He was constantly on the road traveling to speaking events, workshops and ministry retreats. Or, he was in his study, at the church or at home, working on the next sermon series or the next book. The years that he was in school for his doctoral degree seemed to drag on forever, and were even lonelier. There were times when she'd sometimes felt like a single mom; well, other than the fact that she never had to worry about how to pay the bills.

Daniel had always been a good provider. But she was the one who attended the children's school events, handled the household items, paid their bills, managed the household problems; and most difficult of all, dealt with the disciplinary issues with the children.

Sometimes it seemed Daniel was only home often enough to disrupt their normal routine. When he was home, he felt he should step in and make up for all the time that he was gone. He had never understood her frustration over the inconsistency of his disciplinary methods, nor the fact that the children had resented him stepping in when they were used to their mother handling things. Somehow, though, they seemed to muddle through.

Suzanne loved being a mom, but the world of being a mother and handling the decisions and choices for her children by herself more often than not was, at times, overwhelming. Add to that the responsibility of being a full time pastor's wife, serving on ministry boards, doing fundraisers, and helping with a growing congregation; it was oftentimes exhausting beyond words.

Occasionally, she had wondered why she continued trying to make sense out of something that there was no sense to. The world of ministry was perhaps the loneliest world she could ever imagine. While it fulfilled her in the sense that she had more than ample opportunity to minister to others and be an instrument of God, she had learned early on that she could trust very few. Being the lead pastor's wife was like walking a tight-rope. Sometimes she nearly fell off the rope, and at others, she simply held on for dear life.

And yet, thinking back on the past twenty-five years, she knew that she would do it all over again with Daniel if the opportunity arose. After all, there were her children, her few very close friends, and of course, her husband. Through the Alzheimer's she had come to realize that she loved Daniel more than she'd ever dreamed possible. Theirs had been a charmed life in many ways. She had seen and experienced places and people that many would never dream of seeing or knowing.

Smiling to herself, she remembered the time that they had gone on a trip to Peru. The two weeks there had been like a dream vacation, even though Daniel was speaking and doing research the entire time. She had wandered through the bazaars and walked on sandy beaches in a part of the world that only a few Americans even knew existed.

And then there were the trips to his beloved Scotland. Daniel had taken great pleasure in taking her and the children to his homeland. They, in turn, had fallen in love with the country, the people and the customs.

"*No,*" she thought, "*I wouldn't necessarily want to do all of it over, but I wouldn't trade the experiences I've had either.*"

Closing her eyes, she drifted into a restful doze, waking only when the tires of the jetliner touched down on the tarmac.

CHAPTER 16

U PON ARRIVING IN Dallas and getting off their flight, they were pleasantly surprised to find both Adam and Jamie waiting for them as they disembarked. It wasn't until Suzanne saw her sons that she realized how good it was to have their warm smiles and bear hugs to welcome her home. It was a boost to her spirits for what was ahead of them.

Adam explained that his wife, Deborah, was unable to come with them, as their little girl, Sandi, was not feeling well. As he was giving everyone gigantic bear hugs, he told his mother that Sandi was running a slight fever and had kept them up half the night.

"Deborah thinks she is just teething, but, it sure made for a long night."

"But why did you feel you had to meet us here?" inquired Suzanne. "Don't get me wrong, I'm thrilled you did, but it really wasn't necessary. I had planned to meet up with you all at home and then drive over to the hospital together."

"Well, Mom," Jamie drawled, "we figured if we met you here then you'd be obligated to take us all to supper before we head to the hospital. That hospital food could kill a person!"

With muted laughter, sensitive to the seriousness of their purpose for gathering, everyone agreed that a bite of supper would be a good idea. It seemed to dawn on them that they were being silly and frivolous when their father, and husband, was lying in a hospital bed after literally trying to kill himself. Sobering instantly, each of them became quiet and solemn.

Suzanne, looking around at her children, recognized that the seriousness of Daniel's situation was weighing heavy on them. She realized it was imperative that she explain more of the situation surrounding their dad.

Adam especially seemed distant and cool. She realized that he was a bit hurt that she had not contacted him immediately with the details surrounding his father. She reached for him, their eldest, and pulled him to her side.

"Sweetheart, I know that Jamie spoke with you about your dad. I'm sorry that I wasn't here to give you the details myself. I just couldn't find a way to tell either of you what was happening. When Jamie persisted in knowing, I felt he could better tell you than hearing it from me on the telephone."

Adam wrapped his long arm around her. Leaning down, he pressed a kiss on the top of her head.

"It's alright, Mother. I know it's so hard, but we will get through this together. I actually ran over to the hospital and sat with Dad for a while this afternoon. As I held his hand, tears slipped out of his eyes, even though his lids remained closed. I think he knows that we care, and he knows that he is not alone. That's what's important right now, that we each realize we are none of us alone in this thing."

With tears in her own eyes, Suzanne smiled up at her tall eldest son. Reaching up, she touched his cheek. "I'm so glad you were able to go, Adam. That means more to me than you can ever know."

Looking at the others, she said, "Well, let's get going. We need to get to the hospital and see the doctor before he leaves for the night. He told me just to give him a call when we arrive. He graciously agreed to meet us after his evening rounds. I don't think it will hurt anything if we stop and get a bite to eat first. I know Mama and Autumn must be starving, and I am a little hungry, too. We've hardly had a moment to stop and eat all day."

As they gathered their luggage and headed toward the parking area, Suzanne reminded Adam and Jamie that she had her car parked in the long term parking area.

"Not anymore," Jamie crowed. "We know you always leave your parking receipt under the dash, and of course, Adam has a spare key, so we went on over and picked the car up. Both Adam's minivan and your Jaguar are just across the walkway in hourly parking."

"Oh my," Suzanne smiled, "you guys are just too much! We are so weary with the drive from Mama's house and then the flight. It is nice to be so well taken care of. I might even let you and Adam chauffeur, then I can just sit back and enjoy the ride for a change."

"Great!" Adam yelped. "I wanted to drive your car but Jamie won the honor of bringing it around when we got here."

"And how might he have done that?" Velma chuckled. "By being smarter, or just by being so good looking?"

"Grams," Adam laughed, "the only thing in Jamie's favor is that he would be younger than me! I challenge you that he is not smarter nor better looking!"

Velma just laughed and hugged her dear grandson close. She loved all of Suzanne's children more than life itself.

"So how did he win?" Autumn laughed. She adored both of her big brothers and thought them each near perfect.

"I'll let Jamie explain that," Adam chuckled.

Looking just a bit chagrined, Jamie pulled on his left ear lobe. A trait so like his father that it caused Suzanne's throat to constrict.

"Well," he drawled in his best south Texas manner, "I bet old Adam here that I could talk my way out of the speeding ticket that was just about to be mine, seeing as how we'd just been pulled over for going ninety-five in a seventy mile zone!"

"Jamie!" Suzanne, Velma, and Autumn all gasped in unison.

"Aw, Mom," Adam purred, "didn't you know Jamie always drives like that?"

Jamie immediately defended himself and hit Adam on the shoulder with his large fist.

"Listen, big brother," he said, "you better clam up before I start telling a few tales of my own."

As everyone responded with laughter, Velma inquired, "So, Jamie, how did you talk your way out of the ticket?"

With a bright smile and a glint of mischievousness in his sparkling blue eyes, Jamie replied, "Well, Grams, sometimes you do what you have to do. I simply told the officer that I was on my way to pick up three of the prettiest women in the state of Texas. I said that I was so excited I totally failed to realize how fast the old van was going! That officer just grunted and told me I'd better slow it down in the future or he'd give me double trouble next time!"

As everyone laughed, Adam and Autumn finished loading the van with all the bags.

"Okay," said Jamie, "who's going to ride with me and all of Sandi's cookie crumbs?"

Autumn replied that she would, "But only if you promise to teach me how to drive just like you!"

"Deal!" responded Jamie, and then looking at Suzanne, he shrugged and grinned as he apologized sheepishly. Then he asked, "Shall we stop by the Rib Ranch before we head on to the hospital?"

"Oh yes," Velma exclaimed, "they have great food. Let's go."

And so it was decided.

After helping his mother and grandmother into the car, Adam slid into the driver's seat.

"Mom, are you sure that you trust me with this thing?" he asked as he ran his hand lovingly over the steering wheel.

"Sure," replied Suzanne, "I know you'll be careful. Besides, if you dent it you'll be paying far longer than you would care to think about!"

At that, Adam laughed and said, "You are probably right there!"

Slowly, he pulled out into traffic to follow Jamie toward the restaurant. From time to time, Suzanne would peek at him from the corner of her eye just to check on how he was doing. Once he glanced over, caught her looking at him, and just grinned from ear to ear.

It shook Suzanne to the core to realize just how much she loved this man-boy of hers. He was such a combination of Daniel and his deceased mother, and yet he was completely his own man. Needless to say, he'd picked up several of Suzanne's mannerisms over the years as well. Strangely enough, he was the only one of her children who ever called her Mother, and that mostly when he was being very sentimental. He was a wonderful son and she loved him with all her heart.

Sometimes when she looked at her children, she marveled at the miracle each of them represented, and at how uniquely God had created each of them to be. She supposed Adam was a little extra special since he came to her as part of a package deal. She had loved him on sight. They shared a special bond that somehow surpassed the fact that she was not his biological mother. She would forever be grateful for the opportunity to have been able to finish raising this very amazing young man. He was her rock in times of trouble these past few years.

CHAPTER 17

ONCE AT THE restaurant, it took only a few moments to be settled and to place their order. While they were waiting for their food, a somber silence fell over the normally happy group.

"Mom," Jamie asked, "would you like to give us the details as you know them concerning Dad?"

Slowly raising her lovely blue eyes to look at her children, Suzanne experienced a stab of pain and sadness that was beyond words. After looking directly at each of them, she responded to Jamie.

"Son," she said, "you understand that I do not have all the details. However, as I've told you, from what I could understand from Dr. Carey, your father tried to take his own life this morning. We believe this was a result of the illness and medication, but, of course, we can't be totally sure. Your father has been very depressed. In his more lucid moments, he has actually talked about wanting to have all to do with this illness over and done with. Who can ever really know what is in the mind of someone suffering this way. Perhaps we will learn more when we get to our meeting with the doctor this evening."

Taking a sip of water, she continued, "I am so sorry about this, I know you all love your father so much. If there were any way to keep this pain from you, I would do that. Our biggest challenge at this time is to be there for him without letting him know of our fear and concern for him. And most importantly, to let him know we love him in every way. As of this afternoon late, the doctor informed me that your father is now

131

refusing to eat or drink. We may have a very tough decision ahead of us in the next few days; whether to agree to life support or not. Your father has it established in his living trust that he does not want to go on life support, regardless of the situation. However, the lawyer may figure a way around that and we may be faced with a very hard decision on his behalf. It is not a thing to be taken lightly, putting someone on life support."

Looking at Adam directly, she said, "Adam, Honey, you have been very quiet, is there anything you want to say or ask?"

Turning the stem of his water glass round and round in his long fingers, Adam swallowed hard. Looking up at his mother, he said, "Mother, I want you to know that you have my one-hundred-percent support in any decisions that must be made. I know, without a doubt, that you love my father; have loved him for nearly a lifetime, and through many hardships. Whatever I can do to help you, I am here."

Looking at Jamie, Suzanne saw that he wanted to speak and motioned for him to go ahead.

"Mom," Jamie said, "you know that they have given Dad no hope of recovery, other than a literal miracle, at this late stage in the disease. What do you think our choice should be?"

Bowing her head and closing her eyes briefly, Suzanne drew in a deep, slow breath and then exhaled slowly as she raised her head to look at her children.

"As difficult as this is for me to say," Suzanne responded, "and believe me, I have prayed and prayed over this, even before the situation this morning. I feel strongly that I know what your father would want. He would not want to be on life support, but to let time take its course. I will support him in this final decision; I know that he would want to end his life with dignity and in God's timing. He would not want to be on life support to simply lie there for weeks or months on end. I feel the attempt this morning to take his life was in a moment of desperation, and likely due largely to the medications."

Pausing to clear her throat that was suddenly clogged with tears, Suzanne swallowed a drink of water before continuing.

"I trust that you children will support and love me as I do what I know he would want done. It will not be easy and may, in fact, not be over soon, but it is clearly what your father wants. I will do everything in my power to abide by his wishes and allow him that final choice of living, or dying, as he deserves. Of course, I would never condone his taking his own life, nor any sort of plan that would consist of helping him to die! But on the other hand, if he is ready to go on to glory, and it is the time for the Lord to take him on naturally, I will not come between the Lord and Daniel's desire. If the Lord chooses to take Daniel, then we must all be prepared for that end."

They all sat in a somber silence for several long moments. Adam cleared his throat and spoke up at last, "Mother, as hard as this is for all of us, I'm glad that you are helping us all to prepare for what is ahead. I admire and love you more than you can know. Dad is ready to go, I've known this for a while now. If God isn't going to heal him, then I'm ready to see him take Dad on."

"Thank you, Adam. I believe we all feel the same. This last year, especially these last months have been terrible for all of us, your father most of all. God in his infinite wisdom will do what is best."

"Now," Suzanne continued as her face clouded with emotion, "there is something I must share with you boys at this time. I've already talked with Autumn about it and don't want to have any surprises come up. While at Mama's this past week, yesterday in fact, I encountered an old friend from high school whom I've not spoken to, nor really even thought about, in many years."

"We talked for a brief time last evening, and this afternoon we met for an hour or so over lunch and had a short visit. He has come to know the Lord over the past few years and has asked if he might stand by me as a friend and prayer warrior over the next days and weeks. I have agreed to this, and have agreed that he may call or email me from time to time as well."

Drawing a deep breath, Suzanne continued, "Boys, I did not want you to hear about this by accident, or perhaps even screen a call for me and not be aware of who he is. I trust that you know that I will always be faithful to your father in every way. I think that goes without saying. Daniel is my husband and the father of you children. As long as there is a chance of hope, I will continue to pray for a miracle of healing and that we can live out a long and happy life together. Nothing will ever change my love for your father."

Taking another sip of her water, Suzanne breathed deeply as the boys sat silently watching her, clearly wanting to hear the rest of what she had to say.

Clearing her throat, she continued, "However, in spite of the way it may look to some, I feel that God has brought Peter into my life again for a purpose. It somehow seems right to know that my friend is there; praying for us and encouraging me as we go along this journey. I want to ask if any of you have a problem with this. I totally trust your input and wisdom. If there is any concern, or if you feel this is inappropriate, I will cut the friendship off immediately."

Slowly, Adam and Jamie looked across the table at each other. After a moment, Jamie gave Adam a small nod. As if completely detached, Suzanne realized that they had just communicated in a very real way with each other; as she had often seen them do in the past. She marveled at the closeness in these two brothers who had different mothers and were a decade apart in years. Yet, their bond was so tight that they could communicate with no words needed. With bated breath, everyone at the table waited for Adam to speak.

Even though Adam could be quite funny at times, there was a serious side of him that everyone respected. Reaching across the table, Adam threw aside the raveled paper napkin she had torn to shreds. Gently, he cradled her smaller hand in his large, strong hands; hands so like his father's.

With a look in his eyes that was far beyond his years, Adam softly said, "Mother, we have watched you struggle for this past year, and even beyond. If there is anything, or anyone who could bring you a small measure of comfort, both now or later, then we are all for it. No one could ever doubt your love, respect and commitment to Dad; not if they knew you at all. Anyone else simply doesn't matter. I don't know who this friend of yours is, but I know he must be a pretty terrific guy if he recognizes your worth!"

"Here, here!" Jamie cheered.

Adam glanced at him again and Jamie instantly quieted down.

Adam continued holding Suzanne's hand as he spoke. "Mother," he said, "and to me, you are truly my mother, even though you certainly aren't old enough, and you didn't give birth to me. You have loved and nurtured me as if I was your very own child. I'll never forget the way you opened your arms and your heart to me when I was a lonely little boy of nine years. You brought laughter and joy back into our lives after losing my mother. Dad and I had been so lost and alone and you were like a bright ray of sunshine in our lives. I have at times been frustrated with Dad over the past few years when on occasion I would see him act out in anger, especially these last couple of years when he was acting out more and more. Then, when we found out about his illness, I understood that the Alzheimer's must have been the reason for much of his behavior. You have stood firm through all of the storm, your love for Dad has never been in question. You are a woman of deep integrity and strength. We will stand by you in every way during this time."

Suzanne sat there with silent tears streaming down her face as she realized how utterly blessed she was to have these three wonderful children. About that time, Autumn, who had been quiet for perhaps the longest time in her whole life, blurted out, "Well, I've had the privilege of meeting Mom's friend, Mr. Peter Clifton, and he is a great guy and considers

Mom to be his friend. I, for one, am glad she has him praying for her and Daddy, and for all of us!"

Everyone responded positively as Suzanne mopped her streaming tears.

"Now," Suzanne exclaimed, "we really must wrap up here and be on our way. After all, the doctor agreed to meet us after hours. I certainly don't want to keep him waiting too much longer on us. I felt it would be best to see him before I rushed to see your father. I also knew Mother and Autumn would be starving by the time we landed, and I wanted time to explain your father's situation to you both in person. Therefore, I intentionally asked if Dr. Carey could meet us later than he normally would have. After assuring me that an extra hour would not make a difference, we agreed to approximately a ten o'clock appointment time. He was very kind and understanding of the situation."

Just then, Suzanne's cell phone rang and as she answered, a gentle smile came swirling across her face. Everyone was silent as she said, "Yes, Peter... yes, we are here all safe and sound... yes, I've told the boys that you are praying for us as we go to meet with the doctor... yes, they are fine with you praying and checking on things... okay... yes... goodbye. Oh, and Peter, thank you for calling."

Suzanne hung up with a bemused look. Slowly placing the cell phone back in her purse, she looked up to find everyone watching her, varying looks of interest on their faces.

Turning slightly pink, she exclaimed, "Well, I told you he might be calling!"

As everyone tried to hide their smiles, Velma murmured, "Well let's see, we've been on the ground all of an hour; this should be quite interesting! I am glad you know that you have a lot of people holding you accountable right now... not that you need it, of course. I'm just saying."

Scolding her mother for being silly, Suzanne stood up and urged her children to get their things. "We really must get to the hospital. The doctor will be waiting for us, and I really want to speak with him. I also need to see Daniel. I plan to stay with him for the night. So boys, I will trust you to get Grams and Autumn home safely. I couldn't bear to leave your father alone another night."

Arriving at the hospital, they were ushered into Dr. Carey's pristine office. Suzanne wished she could turn the clock back a few years to a time when there was no need for these doctor visits; to a time when Alzheimer's was just something she had read about in a magazine.

The doctor came in with his usual brisk manner. Filling them in quickly regarding Daniel's situation, he presented the facts to them in clear and precise terms.

"We don't know how this disease works exactly. However, as you can see, in some patients there are times of lucidity. It is then the patient is more often than not desperate, acutely aware of the hopelessness of their situation. The best we can do is to encourage them, be there for them and protect them from themselves. As Daniel has made it quite clear that he does not want to be put on life support, there is really very little we can do except be by his side as much as possible. Of course, we will provide him with every comfort available."

When asked, he assured them that Daniel was in good hands, but that if he was ready to let go of this life there was really nothing they could do but give him the dignity he deserved.

Leaving the doctor's office, they went up the elevator and down the long winding hallways to where Daniel was resting in his room. Each one spent a few moments talking softly to him, but he lay as quiet and still as if already gone. Even when Autumn knelt beside her beloved daddy and whispered she loved him, he never stirred.

Brokenheartedly, they all left; except Suzanne. She settled in beside her husband in the big reclining chair and sat holding his hand until the wee hours of the night. Finally, exhausted, she slept.

The next days and weeks flew by swiftly as the family was called upon to make several tough decisions regarding Daniel's care. He steadily declined, and Suzanne was forced to make the decision not to put him on life support.

She knew that this decision alone was one of the most difficult she would ever make in her life. Yet, she knew that Daniel truly wanted to be finished with the hell on earth that he was living through. Even in his confused state of mind, he wanted to be free. She could not find it in herself to deny him that final dignity.

As the weeks passed, Peter called on a regular basis, but they only talked for brief moments. He sent several lovely floral arrangements to Daniel's room; and always, there would be a card addressed to the family, reminding them of his prayers on all their behalf.

There was never a hint of anything beyond the most proper and respectful consideration in his contacts. He spoke with whichever of the family happened to answer the phone, and always expressed his concern and care for them all. Adam in particular came to respect the kind man and to look forward to meeting and thanking him someday for his prayers and concern.

Suzanne spent every possible moment at the nursing facility with Daniel once he was moved back there. She lost weight as the days went by, yet refused to leave the husband of her youth. She sat beside him and read to Daniel every day.

At times, she simply sat and held his hand in a silence that said more than words could have expressed. Constantly on her mind was the fact that any moment could be their last. One day, as she sat quietly singing an old hymn to him, she could have sworn that his mouth twitched into a smile. Of course, it was difficult to tell, but she chose to believe it was true.

In the wee hours of one long night when the saga first began, he had been particularly lucid and they had talked at length. He had begged her to find someone to live out her life with.

"You are too young, my Darling, to live alone for the long years ahead of you. I want you to be happy, happier than I have been able to make you."

Suzanne had assured Daniel that she had never been anything but happy with him, and that she couldn't bear to think of her life without him. At his insistence that she find someone to love, she finally compromised and told him then that she would let the Lord direct her path.

That night, as he seemed so aware and so kind, she had shed tears of grief for the love she and Daniel were soon to lose. She cried with a sad, yet heartfelt joy that Daniel had been able to share with her, and she with him one last time. Suzanne assured him again of her love and reminded him of how proud she had always been of him.

Suzanne knew that she would never forget that moment when he had squeezed her fingers tightly, as a single tear made its way from the corner of his eye onto the stack of starched white pillows beneath his head.

In a whisper, barely audible above the whir of machines, Daniel had murmured, "'Tis good, Sweetheart, 'tis so good, I am ready to go now. It has been a long battle and I am tired. Be happy, my pet; please, be happy. I am sorry you must go through this. I am sorry that you must grieve when I am gone."

He whispered a few more words to Suzanne, saying he loved her and wanted her to follow her heart when the time was right. "I don't want to think of you being alone, my love. I know what that is like. I've been there, you know; after Joanna died."

Daniel asked her to take care of their children, especially Autumn, his baby girl.

"I wanted so badly to walk her down the aisle on her wedding day. It was simply not meant to be," Daniel whispered sadly.

They talked quietly for a few more moments, the last few moments they had together, before he was totally gone to her.

Suzanne knew she would forever cherish these last few softly spoken words of conversation with Daniel. They were over too soon, but at least they gave her something to hold on to in the days ahead.

Even as she watched, Daniel slowly faded back into the land of the lost. He lay quietly resting, glancing around the room from time to time as if looking for someone he knew and finding no one. His eyes were empty now of any emotion or awareness of who she was. The heartache was almost more than she could bear; and still she sat on beside him.

Not many days later, on a bright fall day in Dallas, Daniel Parker went to be with the Lord. His family stood beside his hospital bed praying that the Lord would be merciful and kind to him in his passing. The children surrounded Suzanne and Daniel, waiting quietly with their beloved parents for that final parting after a lifetime of love.

Up until the very last moment, Daniel had lain as still as could be, eyes closed, barely breathing, with just the hint of a tiny smile hovering over his lips. Suzanne knew deep in her heart that she would forever remember that smile. It was almost as if Daniel realized that they all were there, and wanted to assure them that everything was going to be alright. He was ready to storm the gates of heaven and begin his new life in glory.

After a while, he breathed in a deep sigh and slowly released his breath. In the hush of the quiet hospital room, Daniel winged his way to glory.

Suzanne Parker held her husband's hand tightly as he took his final breath. She knew without a doubt that Daniel had indeed stormed the gates of heaven as he reached that long awaited destination. He had often preached that to be absent from this body was to be present with the heavenly Father. He was there now, she had no doubt.

CHAPTER 18

ADAM PARKER SAT in the empty hospital room, holding on to his father's cold, lifeless hand. He'd urged Jamie and Autumn to take their mother home. Their dad was gone, and their mother was an exhausted, broken shell of herself.

Assuring Suzanne that he would sit there with her husband until the funeral home came to pick him up, he begged his mother not to stay to see the body removed.

"It will be too hard on you, Mother. Please, let me sit here with Dad for the little while until they come. You guys go on home and try and rest a little. Deb, you go with them, too, and make sure that Sandi is all right. I know she is missing her mama. I'll find out from the Director what would be a good time tomorrow for us to come by the office and get the arrangements all finalized. It won't be long now until it will all be finished and over."

Wiping tears from her cheeks, Suzanne bowed to her eldest son's wisdom. "I think you are right, Adam. I don't think I could bear to see them roll Daniel out of this room. My heart aches too much now, that would be the final straw. Besides, I know that you want a few last minutes with him, and that's the way it should be. Come on, Jamie, walk with me; and you too Autumn, honey. I just need to feel you close to me right now."

Leaning over the side of the bed, with eyes swollen from her tears, Suzanne gazed upon her beloved husband's face one last time. Reaching out involuntarily, she touched his quickly cooling cheek, realizing that he had just the hint of a stubble from his shave the day before. Lovingly, she stroked his cheek, as if memorizing every detail one last time. With a broken sob, she turned to Adam, and fell into his open arms.

"Oh," she gasped, "it's just too hard. Yes, yes, I will go now. Thank you, Adam, for sparing me this one last thing. I can't bear any more. I just can't bear any more."

And so he sat alone, waiting. The shadowy room seemed filled with images of the past. Leaning his head back against the green plastic chair, he allowed his heart to remember. The memories took him back to a time when it was just him and his dad.

His mother had died in a horrid car crash the day before his first birthday. She had been out running errands, gathering all the things needed to give him the most wonderful birthday party of all times. According to the police report, a distracted driver ran through a red light, killing her on impact.

While Adam realized that he didn't have any actual memories of his mother, as he was much too young when it happened, he had grown up feeling as if he'd known her. His father had talked of her often, especially when it was just the two of them. Daniel had loved Joanna deeply. They had met in college and had dated for nearly two years before moving into marriage.

Joanna had been a very deliberate, detailed person, and she'd insisted that they go by the rules in planning the wedding and their life. She had been ecstatic when she found out the year after she graduated from college that she was pregnant. In usual Joanna style, she staged telling Daniel about the baby, and immediately began preparation for the nursery and the new baby soon to come.

There was rarely a day in his growing up that Adam had not grieved for and wished he'd gotten to know and love the beautiful, vibrant woman depicted in the pictures in their home. Before Suzanne and his father married it had been worse. He'd lain awake many a night imagining his mother coming into his room to tell him bedtime stories, or to tickle and tease with him. He'd listened to other kids talk about the warm, oven-baked cookies after school and their wonderful birthday parties and felt cheated in every way.

Adam remembered when he was about eight or nine, his father taking him to baseball games and soccer. His mind swirled with emotion as he thought back to the two of them sitting in front of the television on cold winter nights with a huge bowl of popcorn as they watched re-runs of The Courtship of Eddie's Father. He had felt a kinship with Eddie and was glad he had a father who played with him and took him places. But, oh, how he'd wished for a mother, too.

His dad had told him, "When the time is right, the right one will come along, Son." And so she had.

Realizing that he still held his father's now cold hand, Adam slowly, almost reverently released it and carefully placed it back on the bed. Sitting forward with his head in his hands, he wept as he realized that in many regards he was now an adult orphan. Sure, he had Suzanne, and he adored her; but, the reality was, both his birth parents were gone.

To be only in his early thirties and to have lost both parents was a hard thing. He dwelt for a time on some of the conversations he'd had with his father in the last year. Knowing that he was dying, Daniel had tried to convey to his children every memory he could dredge up. He'd reminded Adam of his heritage, on both sides; and Daniel had begged Adam to always remember both him and his mother with love.

"I'm going to be with Joanna soon, Son. In many ways I can hardly wait. I loved your mom with everything in me during that time of my life. There has not been a day gone by that I haven't missed her like an ache in my bones. However, I also love Suzanne, and I worry about her. She doesn't deserve to be left alone at such a young age. A woman in her early forties is hardly old enough to be called a widow, much less be alone for long. If she finds someone to love and marry, please, don't you and the other children hold her back from that. She deserves all the happiness she can find."

Adam had let his dad talk it through, nodding and agreeing as was appropriate. At that point, he was careful, as everyone was, to do nothing to upset or aggravate Daniel. As much as it broke his heart to have these conversations, he'd let them ebb and flow, simply letting the river of emotions take their course.

And now it was done; all the talking, all the remembering and sharing, it was over. He was now the head of this family, with a little girl of his own to lead and guide. The tired, heartbroken young man hardly felt up to the task.

Hearing the sound of sharp laughter, quickly muffled, Adam stood and stretched his back. It seemed he'd been sitting there forever. Glancing at his watch he realized it had been nearly an hour. Wondering where the attendants were who would come to move his father's remains, he started toward the door, a bit of impatience in his step. Just then, the door swung wide, admitting an intern that looked young enough to still be in high school.

"Well, there you are! This must be Mr. Daniel Parker's room. We are here to take the body to the morgue," the bold young man blurted out entirely too cheerily. Reaching toward the bed, he yanked the sheet off Daniel's still form, revealing the shrunken body of the man who had once been strong and sturdy.

Immediately, Adam reacted. Grabbing the sheet, he quickly covered his father again. Through gritted teeth, he spoke, "You, young man, will treat my father with respect. If you can't find it in yourself to do so, then I will be speaking with your superior immediately."

Realizing that he'd upset the son of the man who had just passed away, the intern apologized sheepishly. "Hey, man, I didn't mean anything by it. We are just given instruction to take him downstairs to be transported. We will be careful, I promise you. I will personally see to it. Oh, and by the way, did you want me to remove his wedding band? Most people like to take those kinds of things home with them."

Adam realized then that they had all been so distracted and distraught that no one had given a thought to Daniel still having on his wedding band.

"Of course, if you don't mind, I will do it. I know my mother would want to keep that. Can you give me just a minute longer, please?"

The younger man, realizing that he owed at least that to the son, stepped quietly out into the hallway again, letting the door close softly behind himself.

Gently, Adam lifted his father's left hand. It took no effort at all to remove the carved, gold wedding band. His father's body had shrunk so much in the last few months it was a miracle he'd not lost the ring. Checking the nightstand, he found his father's watch and several other small items. Gathering them up, he tucked them in his jeans pocket.

Realizing, with a catch in this throat, that this was the moment, the last time before the funeral that he would ever see his father, he leaned over the bed one more time. Gazing at the face he knew he would never forget, Adam felt tears sliding down his throat as he fought them back.

"Goodbye, Dad," he whispered with a raspy voice.

It was all he could do to maintain his composure.

Clearing his throat, he stepped to the door and invited the young intern back into the room. Watching them begin to move the rolling hospital bed out of the room with his father simply lying there was the hardest thing Adam had ever had to do.

The lost little boy inside of him wanted to run down the long hallway after them, yelling for them to stop. The grownup man that he was watched silently, hands in his pockets, as they turned the corner and wheeled the bed onto the waiting elevator. Fighting the urge to give in to his overwhelming grief, Adam turned and walked slowly in the other direction.

The next couple of days passed in a whirlwind as they met with the funeral director, wrote out the obituary, created a slide show of Daniel's life, and chose flowers with loving care. The visitation came and went in a blur of people and emotion. Thousands of people stood in line for hours on end, determined to give homage to the man who had been their pastor and friend.

Suzanne and her children were gracious to each person, shaking hands, and listening to remembrances that spanned the years of Daniel's life. The sanctuary where Daniel had preached thousands of sermons was filled with the love of those he had ministered to so often.

It was more than a little overwhelming, and yet there was a sense of preciousness to it all that made every moment worthwhile.

At home later that night, Suzanne held the small golden circle that Adam had given to her in the palm of her hand. In her mind, she relived the exact moment when Daniel had taken his final breath. As strange as it would be to try to explain to anyone, she had felt almost as if a thread holding them together had snapped at his leaving; as if, by his death they truly were no longer bound.

"Until death do us part," she whispered.

The ring felt cool in her palm. It had been hand carved, designed by a friend of Daniel's in Scotland and was worth a small fortune. Dazed from exhaustion and grief, the shattered woman wondered what she was to do with it.

Glancing at her left hand, she realized that the lovely wedding and engagement ring Daniel had given her so long ago were now a symbol of all that was lost to her. Without him there to wear his, hers too had lost their meaning.

Biting her lower lip, Suzanne stared down at the rings a few moments longer. Somehow, she was not yet ready to remove them. That was so final. Even the thought of taking off the rings Daniel had given her was more than she could bear.

Finally, she slipped his ring in her desk drawer, telling herself that she would worry about that another day.

"I'm simply too exhausted to decide on something that important tonight."

At the funeral the next day, Suzanne was not at all surprised, upon turning at a slight movement behind her, to find Peter reaching for her elbow. Nothing in the world could have felt more natural to Suzanne than Peter being at her side as she laid her husband to rest.

Knowing that the future was in God's hands, she trusted Him completely to guide and direct her steps. If that future was to include Peter, she knew it was only because God was giving her a second chance to have joy, even in the midst of her mourning. He would show her when the time was right to even consider such a thing.

CHAPTER 19

PETER HAD FLOWN in for the afternoon of the funeral and planned to stay one night before going back. When Suzanne realized that he was not planning to stay in town any longer than that, she was strangely relieved. It somehow felt right to know that Peter would be there to say farewell to Daniel, but she knew also that she needed time alone to grieve and adjust to life without her husband.

Later that night, after Suzanne had spent time with her family and friends, the house grew very quiet, as one by one everyone went home. Soon, Autumn and Velma were in their beds fast asleep, exhausted from the events of the weeks behind them. Suzanne found herself wandering through the strangely empty house like a wraith. It was so odd how it seemed as if suddenly Daniel's presence was no more a part of their home; especially strange, considering the fact that he had been in the nursing facility and hospital for months now. There was a feeling of emptiness in the rooms, which she had never felt before.

A little after ten o'clock, Suzanne was surprised and more than a little perturbed, when her cell phone rang and she saw from the caller ID that it was Peter. He apologized for calling so late, and explained that he was calling to ask if it was all right for him to come back over to her home for a short time.

"I realize it is very late, but I need to see you and I think there are some things we need to talk about. Since I am leaving early in the morning, this is my only opportunity to share with you what is on my heart."

After several long moments of silence, Suzanne replied, "Yes, Peter, you may come over. It has been a long day, as you can imagine, and I am very tired; but I will see you tonight. I was sitting here just now thinking about Daniel, and asking the Lord to guide and direct my thoughts, when the phone rang. Please, give me just a few moments to make myself presentable, and then come on over."

Offering Peter some coffee a little while later, Suzanne wondered briefly if she should have had him come. She didn't want to ever do anything to dishonor Daniel's memory. Her mother and Autumn were both asleep upstairs, and the boys were in their own homes. Somehow, it bothered her that Peter had insisted on coming over. While she knew her children liked him, and trusted her, she would never want them to think she was capable of seeing another man in a romantic way on the evening of their father's funeral.

After a few moments of chit chat, Suzanne asked Peter if he would like to walk out on the back patio with her.

"We can talk comfortably there without fear of disturbing Mama and Autumn. We will have complete privacy to talk, as the neighbors' homes are quite a distance away."

"Sure," he replied. "Suzanne, I don't mean to distress you. Perhaps it was selfish, but, I just wanted to be with you tonight for a little while, and to let you know that I am here for you if you need anything in the coming weeks."

Walking to the patio door without responding, Suzanne switched on the small lights placed here and there around the beautiful garden area. The underwater pool lights caused the water to shimmer with a beautiful glow as a small waterfall cascaded at the far end.

Motioning for Peter to precede her, she closed the French doors softly behind them. Moving into the moonlit night, she breathed deeply of the flowers that seemed to grow year round in the gentle climate.

As they began to talk softly, Peter asked Suzanne, "Are you holding up alright? I can't begin to tell you how much I admire your strength. The care you have shown Daniel and your family over the past weeks and days has astounded everyone. You are an amazing woman."

She murmured that she was as good as could be under the circumstances. They walked in silence for a few long moments. Finally, Peter could not stand the distance he felt growing between them. Searching for something to say to ease the tension, he blurted out, "Suzanne, may I now ask you to tell me what that question was that you never got to ask all those months ago at the fall festival?"

"Well," she replied carefully, "it is a little difficult to put into words. I'm not even sure this is the best time."

Giving a deep sigh, she continued, "Especially now, with all the emotions of the day and this terribly long week resting on my heart. Somehow, it seems so trivial in retrospect, but yes, I will tell you. Please don't think I am silly, but I was wondering that night, if you had ever thought about the night of our homecoming court. I wondered if you remembered it being as wonderful and magical as I remember it being. And, do you know if the fellows on the team picked me as queen out of respect, or was it simply a joke that I never caught on to? I've wondered about that from time to time," she murmured softly.

Standing there under the stars with moonlight in her hair, Peter thought he had never seen anyone so beautiful, and yet so vulnerable. It dawned on him in that moment that the sweet, strong woman who was Suzanne Parker could be wounded deeply by him if he were not careful. No one around her seemed to be aware of just how tender and raw her feelings were. However, he did. He knew that the words he spoke now might forever seal the fate of their future. In fact, the very fact that he had dared to come to see her on this night, of all nights, might very well seal their fate.

Reaching out to cup her chin in his hand, he looked directly into her eyes for a long moment. "Suzanne," he said, "there has not been a day gone by in the past twenty-five years that I have not thought of that night and wished it had never ended. My only regret then, and now, was that you were not my very own, my special girl. The kiss that I gave you that night to appease the guys on the team would later come back to haunt me over the years. Many times, I regretted not rushing out of that gym with you immediately following the game, and making you realize how much I cared for you. As to the guys, I know for a fact that they, each and every one, felt that you were the girl who best represented our school for that time. Every fella on the team admired and cared about you in some little way."

Peter paused quietly for a few moments and then continued, "I've wished so often throughout the years that I had convinced you that I wanted you in my life forever. Even now, I wonder what it would have been like to have shared the past twenty-five years with you; raising our children together. I also wonder, is it too late for us to perhaps have a hope and a future together?"

Sensing a further withdrawal on Suzanne's part, Peter realized that he had said too much, too soon. Catching his breath, Peter pulled her close as he whispered, "Oh, Suzanne, forgive me. I am a fool for pressing you too soon. I know it is much too early to speak of love and marriage. You have just today laid your husband to rest. It may not be the right time now; but as soon as you have mourned the loss of Daniel and are ready to live life again, I will claim your heart as mine."

Suzanne stood quietly within his grasp.

After a moment, she pulled away and glanced up at him as she replied, "Peter, I am too sad, and too exhausted to have this discussion. If there is to be something between us, I pray the Lord will show us both at the right time. Now, however, I just need time to heal and to rest. My heart is broken with the loss of my Daniel. I don't think I fully realized just how much I loved him and relied on his steadfastness until he was laid to rest today. Please, don't expect anything of me just yet. I have nothing left to give. I am given out."

A tiny sob escaped her lips before she could swallow it down.

Appalled at his own selfish behavior, and feeling helpless beyond words, Peter held her for a moment longer in the moonlight, unable to let her go. He wished with all his heart he could make things right for this woman he adored.

Suzanne endured his embrace, but gave nothing in return.

Realizing that there was nothing he could do for the time being, he silently bowed his heart and his will to the Father above. Assuring Suzanne that he understood, and apologizing for pressing her too soon, Peter released her from his grasp. They continued their walk in the moonlight, both of them lost in their own private world of loneliness and sorrow.

They talked for a little while longer of mundane things; and then Peter took leave of the woman he loved. He told her that he would call her the next morning before his flight left. He yearned to ask her if he could kiss her goodbye, but something stopped him. It was too soon.

Looking up at him with tears shining in her eyes, Suzanne simply stood there, waiting for him to leave. Lost and alone in her grief.

"Goodbye," he murmured as he turned to leave.

"Thank you for understanding, Peter. Truly, thank you." Suzanne whispered, as he walked across the damp grass to his car.

CHAPTER 20

T HE NEXT WEEKS and months passed in a blur for Suzanne as she began
to learn to live her life without Daniel being the center of everything
she thought or did. She found that life moved on in spite of the pain of
loss. Slowly, she sought to find new joy in the midst of the overwhelming
sorrow.

There were huge decisions to be made, such as whether to put her
home on the market, whether to continue living in Dallas close to her
sons or to move back to her little hometown with her mother. Eventually,
she decided to keep the house. It was paid for, and was such a part of
their children's history that she simply could not bear to part with it.
Reasoning it out she decided that if nothing else, if she did ever marry
again, she could let one of her children live in it and raise their family in
the grand old mansion.

The rooms echoed with so many memories of the good times they had
all experienced as the children grew that she just could not bring herself
to move away, not yet anyway. And Autumn had experienced enough
change in her life for the time being. She was just entering high school and
with her father dying, she needed the stability of her own home and her
room with all of her things around her.

The next months were spent picking up the pieces of her life and
determining what she wanted and needed for her future. April came, and
with it the presentation of the award for Daniel's book. Adam did a spec-
tacular job of representing his father, with a huge, larger than life portrait

of Daniel on an easel beside him. It was more of a tribute to the absent author than an award ceremony.

Suzanne sat with tears running down her face, wiping her eyes with a damp handkerchief from time to time. It was amazing to her how many people had shown up to honor Daniel, and how many people loved his work. She wondered again if he had ever truly understood how admired and loved he had been.

At the end, Adam received a standing ovation for his touching remarks and remembrances of his father. In the following months, the book sales far exceeded the expectations of their publisher. While this was wonderful in the added financial security it provided the family, it once again underscored depths of sadness for Suzanne. She wondered what Daniel would have felt had he been able to see how loved his works were.

Adam and his wife made sure that Suzanne and Autumn never wanted for anything. He also spent time with Jamie and helped him process through his grief. Suzanne could not have been more proud of her eldest son had he been the firstborn of her own body. He was an unfailing support in his care for his younger brother and sister, and his love for them all touched a chord in Suzanne's heart that nothing else could have done.

Perhaps, it was his early years of being without a mother that gave him such insight and compassion into what his younger siblings were experiencing. It seemed he anticipated each stage of grief they were experiencing before it was even recognized by either of them.

Velma had gone back home a few days after the funeral. She knew that Suzanne needed time to heal and mourn. She remembered well those early days after George had passed on that she had simply wanted, needed, to be alone. Theirs had been such a busy life with their small church activities and the farm work. She had rather taken for granted the small pleasures which made up the whole of their life.

It wasn't until George was gone that she came to realize how much she had truly enjoyed being the wife of a country pastor, ad hock farmer.

With many of their activities revolving around the seasons, she had perhaps taken for granted that it would always be so.

However, nothing was forever. As hard as life was at times, the good always outweighed the bad.

She knew that Suzanne would come to rights in her own self, and with the Lord's help, find a balance in her life. However, it might take a little time. Time did seem to heal all wounds; it just took some a little longer than others.

Yet, Velma worried for her daughter. As they talked on the phone every evening, she could hear the deepening of the loss in her voice. Little did she know that Suzanne had almost stopped eating, and was up all hours of the day and night, going through Daniel's things, trying to deal with so many details of the incredible man's life.

She had lost so much weight that Autumn was almost beside herself with worry about her mother. Adam and Jamie had both tried taking her to lunch and talking with her, but nothing seemed to help.

Suzanne knew that she was allowing her grief to consume her. She could feel the vacuum that she was in, but there seemed little she could do to break free of it. The weekly phone calls from Peter did little to clear the fog she was in; in fact, they sometimes made her despair even more. Had she not had the responsibility of caring for Autumn and seeing that she did well in school, Suzanne wondered if she could even manage to keep from breaking down completely.

She tried with everything within her to understand and determine why she felt such an unending sorrow. She had known for months that Daniel was dying, she had thought she was prepared for that loss. And yet, she felt that if only they had gotten a little more time she might have been better prepared.

There were days on end that she stayed in her dressing gown, wandering through the huge home, alone and lonely. Autumn was off at school, and the boys were busy, as was to be expected. Suzanne tried reading, sewing and gardening in an attempt to fill the void, but nothing worked. She awoke in the middle of the night more often than not, reaching for Daniel, only to find his side of the bed empty and cold. The sorrow would sweep over her afresh and anew, threatening to break her soul into pieces so tiny a puff of wind would blow them away.

As the months passed following Daniel's death, Deborah and Adam began to worry about Suzanne. They saw her pulling away from family and friends more and more, and it was evident that she was not eating. The weight seemed to have fallen off her frame in short order. When questioned, Autumn shared that Suzanne just pretended to eat and would then throw plate after plate of food in the trash.

While getting ready for bed one night, Adam urged Deborah to spend time with his mother.

"After all, if anyone in this family can understand her grief, besides Gram that is, it would be you, Deb. Having lost your first husband you would be able to help my mother find her way through this grieving better than any of the rest of us."

"Yes, but I didn't lose my husband to death, Adam. You know that as well as I do. Harry left me, and that's quite a lot different than having a spouse die."

"Not really, Sweetheart. I've heard it said that divorce is sometimes worse than a death. At least when a loved one dies you can find closure and come to terms with the loss eventually. Especially when you know you will see them again in glory. I'll always believe that those of you who can overcome a divorce are the strongest of us all. You have to live with the loss many times over. Each time your old anniversary rolls around, every time you see a particular kind of vehicle, every time you see a person that looks like that person looked. Yes, you must live with it every day of your life. And so, I think if you could talk to mother, let her talk to you, it might help."

Deborah agreed and called her mother-in-law the next morning on the pretext of having Suzanne come spend some time with her granddaughter.

Suzanne responded that she would love to come to Deborah's home that afternoon to play with the baby and visit for a little while. She was a little surprised upon arriving to learn that the baby was fast asleep and likely would be for several hours.

Ushering her into the tiny kitchen, Deborah offered Suzanne a glass of sparkling lemonade and seated her at the kitchen table. "Here you go, I thought a bite of lunch might be just the thing," the younger woman smiled.

They visited for a short while as Suzanne barely nibbled at the golden croissant filled with chicken salad. Deborah had fixed it knowing this was one of her mother-in-law's favorite luncheon meals. The bouquet of bright daises in the fruit jar sitting in the middle of the table did little to alleviate Suzanne's feelings of sorrow and sadness.

Shoving the barely touched sandwich plate aside, Suzanne sat staring out the kitchen window for a long while. Deborah was quiet, letting her collect her thoughts, knowing she would talk when she was ready.

After a while, turning toward the young woman whom she had come to love as a daughter, Suzanne cleared her throat and tried to speak. Instead, to her own surprise and embarrassment, harsh sobs roiled up out of her inner being, nearly suffocating her. Bowing her head, shoulders shaking, she cried as she had not cried since the night Daniel had died. It was as if once released the dam was determined to turn into a flood.

For a long while Deborah simply knelt beside her husband's mother with her arm around her, letting Suzanne work through the grief in the only way possible. After a while, handing her another tissue to replace the sopping wet ones in her hand, Deborah began to talk.

"You know, Suzanne, after Harry left me, I thought the whole world had ended. I even, for one tiny moment, thought about ending it all. Life was so hard, and at times it felt like there was nothing left worth living for. He embarrassed me in front of my entire family and community by having the affair with my best friend. The hurt that I felt from the two of them was like a double edged sword cutting me from every direction. There were days that I wanted to lash out, to hurt them as they'd hurt me, or even more. But, I knew that if I ever sank to their level it would all be over. All I knew to do was call on the Lord and let Him guide me through my grief, hurt and anger. Oh, I know it's not the same to lose someone to divorce as it is to death, but the grief is still very real in either situation. You will get past this. Life has so much left to give and you will find new joy and happiness. I did, and you will too."

Sitting back on her heels she simply waited.

Finally, after what seemed an eternity, Suzanne whispered hoarsely, "I am just so angry at Daniel for leaving me. There, I said it aloud. I am angry, and I know that is so very foolish. I know that if he'd had his way he would have grown old with me, enjoying our children and grandchildren to a ripe old age. Why am I being so foolish?"

"Ah, dear Mother o' mine," Deborah whispered back, "that is so much a normal part of the grieving process. Anger is what burns the sorrow from our souls. But, to get stuck in the anger is so not what you want to do. It will consume you. Instead, let the Lord take your anger, your hurt, and your sorrow and let Him replace it with peace, with love, and with joy."

"Oh my," Deborah laughed softly, "here I am preaching to the choir! If anyone knows these things it is you. I was thinking, however, maybe a visit to Pastor David might be good. You could go visit him, you know, and maybe he could help process things from a different perspective."

Wiping her tears once again, Suzanne smiled down at the beautiful young woman kneeling beside her, "What did I ever do to deserve you? God surely blessed me when he brought you into our lives."

"Thank you, sweet daughter, I needed this visit and this talk. I admire you so greatly for the strength that has grown in you these past few years. Sometimes, I remember the broken, wounded girl that Adam brought home that first time, and I marvel. Never will I forget seeing the shadow of hurt in your eyes and wondering if you could love my son the way he deserved to be loved. And here we are these five years later, and you have proven once again what a huge heart you have. I love you, Deborah. You are a treasure to me. Yes, I may just do that. Go talk with Pastor David. He is a wise young man. And he understood Daniel so well."

They talked for another hour. Suzanne shared with Deborah her fears of trying to bring another man into their lives.

"Peter is so persistent, you know. He tries so hard to give me room to grieve. I know he does. But he has waited a lifetime to be with me, and he grows impatient at times. We actually got into quite an argument the other night when I told him I needed more time. If he had his way we would be married already. And while I think I might be falling in love with him, I just don't know that I am ready to take that big of a step just yet. Deep down inside, I think perhaps I feel like I'm betraying Daniel by even considering something like falling in love again."

"Suzanne, Daniel knew what it was like to be left alone after his first wife died. You know that he grieved for Adam's mother. He loved her deeply. And yet, when you came into his life he was the first to recognize that God had favored him greatly with a second chance for love. He would be the last person on this earth to discourage you from living the rest of your life with a man who adores and loves you. Daniel wanted you to find happiness again. I know because he talked to Adam about it once, shortly after he was diagnosed with his illness. He urged Adam to encourage you to grasp and hold onto a new love when that time came."

Surprise covered Suzanne's face. "I didn't know he'd talked to Adam. He did talk to me on a couple of occasions, urging me to carry on with my life. Even toward the end, he urged me to love again if that love was offered. And yet, I have held on to my sorrow like a mantle, a protective covering. I know it will take time, but somewhere deep inside of me I do desire to be loved again. To be wanted as a woman. It has been so long. Longer than you can possibly imagine. Daniel was gone from me, from us all, long before his final months of illness. I tried so hard to never let him down, to love him in the midst of all the changes. But sometimes, Deborah, it was so very difficult. For so long, especially these past couple of years, he was not the Daniel I'd known and loved. It was such a surprise when he seemed to make full circle and became the sweet, wonderful man I'd always loved just before the end. It almost gave me hope that he would get well and recover in spite of what the doctors said."

"Of course, he didn't," Suzanne ended quietly.

Sitting silently for a while, the two women enjoyed the comfort of simply being together. Suzanne realized with a start how much she had come to love and admire her daughter-in-law.

"*Adam is truly blessed,*" she thought.

Gathering up the plates, Suzanne helped Deborah clean the already spotless kitchen. As they finished, Sandi awoke and began calling for her mother. Her voice came sweetly over the baby intercom system.

Deborah smiled and whispered to Suzanne, "Why don't you go in and get her out of her crib? She will be thrilled to see her Grammy."

Glad for a reprieve from the ever present sorrow, Suzanne hurried to the nursery to retrieve her beloved granddaughter. Lifting the sweet smelling little girl in her arms, she waltzed her around the pretty room, humming a light hearted song. Little Sandi giggled and grabbed for her Grammy's earrings. "Me wear." She wanted so badly to wear the dangly baubles that Suzanne had hanging from her earlobes.

"I promise you, my darling, when you are old enough Grammy will get you the prettiest pair of earrings possible! You shall have your glamour for sure."

Returning to the kitchen, Suzanne stayed for another hour or so playing with the baby and talking and laughing with Deborah. Adam came home just as she was getting ready to leave. Giving his mother a bear hug, he exclaimed how glad he was to see her.

"We have missed hearing your laughter, Mother. You must come around more often and stay as long as you would like; in fact, why don't you stay for dinner tonight?"

"Oh, my darling, I would love to, but Autumn will be home by now and I really need to be home to have dinner with her. That big old house is so lonely when one is there all by themselves. But we will both come by one evening very soon and have dinner with you all. I really need to get on home now. Deborah, it's been wonderful visiting with you and Sandi. Thank you from the bottom of my heart for the invitation to come by this afternoon. I love you all and will see you soon."

As Suzanne drove away, Adam wrapped his long arm around Deborah's waist and pulled her close. Nuzzling her hair, he whispered, "Thanks, Sweetheart, it was so good to hear my mother laughing again. You clearly helped her break through the barrier of her grief, even if only for a little while."

"I think she will begin to mend now," Deborah murmured. "It was a quite a breakthrough afternoon, a much needed one I do think. You do know how much I love your mother, Adam. I have worried about her as much as you have. She shared several things today that she has carried bottled up inside for too long. Now, perhaps she can move forward. I also encouraged her to go see the pastor and talk to him if that would help her. It must be so confusing to have loved someone so deeply, as she did your father, and then to find another who loves her just as much. I think it's all been a bit overwhelming to her."

"Do you think she is questioning her feelings for Peter?" Adam inquired sharply.

"Oh, I don't think it's that so much as the feelings of guilt for perhaps feeling too much too soon. Peter is a very persuasive man, and he has not held back in letting Suzanne know how much he desires to be with her. She, on the other hand, has to find a way to let go of the love she has had for your father for so many years."

Seeing the look of obstinacy crossing her husband's face, Deborah rephrased her comment, "Not let go of the love, Adam, so much as learning to let that love have its own special place in her heart while still finding her way to loving Peter. It's a bit complicated."

With a mock scowl, Adam replied, "Well, all I can say is that she has the best cheerleader and coach around in you. If anyone can help her find her way, I am sure you can."

Turning as one, they made their way back toward the kitchen, Sandi toddling along behind them. Adam knew without a doubt that his mother would be fine. She was made of sterner stuff than anyone he knew. He just hoped that Peter was a good enough man to fill his father's shoes. Somehow, deep down, he felt he might just be.

DAYS TURNED INTO weeks following Suzanne's visit with Deborah. Her clothing still hung from her frame, and she knew she looked like a proverbial scarecrow. It seemed the longer Daniel was gone, the more she missed her husband. She wondered if she would ever get beyond her grief.

Finally, going to her pastor's office early one morning, she hesitatingly asked the young secretary if she might speak with him. Ushering her immediately into the pastor's private suite, the girl hurried to get the exhausted looking woman a glass of cold water.

She had known Suzanne all of her life, had been baptized by Daniel when he was the pastor. Never had she seen the lovely older woman looking so tired and haggard. Something was surely dreadfully wrong. She hoped Suzanne was not ill with some terrible disease. It had been almost a year since her husband's death. Surely she was not grieving herself to death.

Catching the pastor in the hallway, the young woman hurriedly expressed to him that Mrs. Parker was in his office waiting for him. She also explained that she was quite worried at how Suzanne appeared.

"She is not at all herself!" the younger woman exclaimed. "I would say that Mrs. Parker has not been eating right, she has lost a lot of weight! And you know that she was never very heavy to begin with!"

The pastor hurried to meet with Suzanne, concern written on his countenance. Upon arriving in the office, he crossed the carpeted room to grasp Suzanne by the hands. She turned from the broad window where she stood looking out at the scene, one she had looked at many times over the years.

This had once been Daniel's office, and she had come here on a regular basis to meet him for lunch, or to spend a few moments with him before a service or going to a meeting together. A feeling of rightness came over her as she looked into the face of the rather plump young man who waited so earnestly to serve her.

"Dear Pastor, please do not look so very concerned! I know that I am a frightful mess right now, but I am trying to find my way. I thought perhaps it might help if I spoke with you."

Drawing her toward the settee, the pastor seated her gently and then took the chair across from her. Leaning in toward her, he smiled a genuine smile of appreciation for the woman who had mentored him for so many years.

"How may I help you, Mrs. Parker?"

Suzanne gazed at her fingertips, realizing that she needed a manicure in the worst way. She had stopped caring for her own personal needs and just tried to get through each day as it came. Days that dragged on endlessly, it seemed.

Finally, she whispered into the quiet stillness of the room, "It is just so very hard to understand what God expects of me now that my husband is gone. I feel like a ship without a rudder. I truly don't know how to carry on."

Glancing up at the minister, Suzanne felt her eyes welling up with the seemingly never-ending tears. "Oh, David, I never dreamed it would be so hard losing Daniel. We had grown to be such a part of one another, and my entire life has been built around whatever he had going on, and with caring for our children, our home and our church family. I honestly don't know how to start over, how to become a whole person again. I feel as if I am only half of what I was for so long."

They spent the better part of an hour talking and praying together. Suzanne told her pastor about the friendship, and possible love that could be had between her and Peter.

"I just don't know if I am ready to move into another marriage relationship at any time in the near future," she exclaimed. "And yet, I can't imagine living for years and years alone, especially once Autumn is grown and off on her own."

In utter misery she sat, waiting for the pastor, or God himself, to send her a sign; to show her the way.

Finally, the pastor, who was younger than her by a good fifteen years, leaned back in his chair. Speaking gently, but firmly, he replied, "Suzanne, I have known you literally all my life. I have watched you raise your sons, and you have done a terrific job with that. You have a daughter that any mother would be glad to call her own. Daniel and you served this congregation well, and for longer than any pastor before or since has done. You do not have to feel guilty for anything, or about anything. If God is directing you to a new phase of life, a new life partner, then you are free to accept that for the gift that it is. Clearly, your husband wanted only what was good and best for you. My suggestion to you is that you let go of what is behind you, and look ahead to what is before you. Lift up your eyes, let God bless you, and rejoice in the goodness that He wants to bestow upon you."

Pausing for a breath, he continued, "It sounds to me as if this man, Peter, is a good Christian man. Furthermore, he loves you; there is no doubt of that. Now, it is up to you to decide if you can love him in return. There is, therefore, no condemnation in Christ Jesus. Go forward and live your life to the fullest, as long as it is pleasing to Him. Complete your grieving, for sure, but don't become trapped in the grief. That will do no one any good. God wants to bless you, and you need to reach out with both hands and receive those blessings. Daniel has been gone nearly a year now. It may be time to begin letting go."

With a feeling of relief such as she had not known for many months, Suzanne sat almost as if dazed. Finally, glancing up and smiling a tentative smile, she reached a slender hand toward the minister.

"Thank you, David," she whispered, as tears welled in her eyes, threatening to escape. "I accept your counsel, and I will do my best to honor God in all that I decide to do."

Wiping her eyes with her sodden handkerchief, she made her farewells and went home to reflect on the conversation further.

Suzanne had no more than gotten home and changed into comfortable old sweat pants than the doorbell rang. Realizing that Autumn wasn't home from school yet, she ran lightly down the stairs. She felt the weight of her sorrow beginning to lighten for the first time in nearly two years.

She'd realized in talking with Pastor David earlier that she had begun grieving for Daniel nearly a year before he'd passed away. The loss of their ministry position, watching her husband steadily become worse, and hanging on to her sanity by a thread, had taken its toll on her. Just knowing that she was going to be all right, and her family would survive, even without Daniel at the helm gave her hope.

Swinging the door wide, she smiled at the young delivery woman standing patiently at the stoop. Recognizing her as a member of the church she had served for so many years, Suzanne greeted her warmly.

"What do you have for me today, dear?"

"Hello, Mrs. Parker, I have a package for you that requires a signature, if you don't mind."

"Well, what a surprise," Suzanne murmured. "Who is it from? I am not expecting anything that I know of at this time."

Holding the package out to where Suzanne could read the return address, the girl pointed to it. It was from the nursing facility where Daniel had spent his last few months.

"It looks like it might be a few of your husband's belongings," she smiled.

Suzanne signed the electronic pad offered and took the package with a bemused look on her face. Shaking the package like a child, she wondered what could be in it. She had been sure they had gotten everything from his bedside table and in his room. Glancing back up at the delivery girl as she turned to leave, Suzanne smiled and turned to go inside. She reached for the door to close it as she turned to say goodbye.

With a jaunty farewell, the younger woman jogged back to her delivery truck, her brown rubber-soled shoes making a swishing sound on the pavement as she hurried to stay on schedule.

Suzanne closed the door softly, suddenly glad to be home alone for once. Padding in her sock feet toward the kitchen, she set the package down on the butcher-block center island.

Turning away from the brown paper square, she set a large green mug under the coffee maker spout. Feeling the need for a cup of warm tea, she reached for the tea caddy. Waiting for the tea to steep, she studied the package from across the distance between the island and the kitchen sink. Somehow, she wished she could force it to reveal its contents simply by staring at it. For some unknown reason the very presence of the box stole her peace of mind. It made her want to run fast and far.

Shaking off the feeling, and chiding herself for being silly, she added a dab of honey to the Lady Gray Tea. Lifting her mug, she settled silently into the tall chair nestled next to the island. For several long moments she simply sat holding the mug between her hands. She was cold for some reason. Certainly it was not at all cold in the house. It had to be a case of nerves. She sipped her tea, relishing the warmth that flooded through her, assuring her that all would be well.

Finally, knowing that Autumn would be home from school in an hour or so, Suzanne slowly set her mug down and reached for the package, pulling it toward herself. She closed her eyes for a long moment, her hand resting lightly on the top, as she prayed that the Lord would give her strength to handle whatever was inside the brown wrapper.

Pulling on the tape that held the bundle together, she gently unwrapped it, layer by layer. As the final wrapper fell open, she saw a bundle of letters all tied together with a dark brown shoestring. Clearly, it was one of Daniel's from the pair of brown oxfords he so loved to wear.

Wondering how on earth he had kept one, as everything of any form of danger had been removed from his room following his attempted suicide, she held it lightly between the fingers of her left hand. Lifting the thin brown cord, she touched it briefly to her lips, the faint, sharp fragrance causing tears to spring unbidden to her eyes.

"Will I ever stop crying at unexpected remembrances of Daniel?" Suzanne breathed softly.

Brushing the tears from her lashes, Suzanne forced herself to not cry. Even as she brushed aside the overwhelming grief, she lifted a stark white, folded note that was lying on the very top of the stack. Opening it cautiously, Suzanne saw the crisp handwriting of the head nurse of the facility. Reading it swiftly, she learned that the staff had found the letters stuffed under and between the mattresses of Daniel's bed.

An apology followed for the time that had elapsed in sending the documents. The nursing assistant responsible for finding them had stuffed them in a drawer and forgotten them for the months since Daniel's demise. The head nurse assured Suzanne that the letters were intact, just as they had found them, and she hoped that the lapse in time would not create a hardship in any way concerning what might be contained within.

A momentary spurt of anger welled up within Suzanne at the incompetence, even as she immediately realized that everything happened in God's perfect time, and for His glory. Laying the note aside, she made a mental notation to herself to call and thank the staff for following through with sending the package.

Lifting the bundle of letters, she held them loosely, glancing through them to see her name on the front of all but a few. In addition to the ones addressed to her, there was one for each of her children. It dawned on her that the letters were dated in the upper right hand corner.

The ones to her were in sequential order from the time that Daniel was admitted to the nursing facility many months before. Granted, there were long gaps between the dates on the letters, and some of the writing was smudged and uneven, a bare resemblance of Daniel's precise handwriting.

Setting the three letters addressed to the children to one side, she sorted through the ones for herself, making sure that they were in date order. Reaching for a knife from the holder sitting in the middle of the island, she carefully sliced open the edge of the first envelope. Pulling the sheets of vellum from their hiding place and opening their folds, she silently began reading Daniel's farewell to her.

The first letter was quite coherent as he described his day. It was filled with the feelings he experienced as he strove to adjust to the differences in being displaced from his usual surroundings. He begged her to forgive him for allowing this illness to overwhelm their life. In usual Daniel style, he scattered scriptures throughout the pages, reminding Suzanne that this life we live is temporal, and that there is a greater life ahead for us all if we only press on and run the race with diligence. He closed by telling her how much he loved her and their children and asking her to take care of their Autumn, especially in the days to come.

Letter after letter, Suzanne sat and read, each one breaking her heart into even smaller pieces, as she gave up the struggle to maintain her composure. In some, Daniel was quite aware of his circumstances. He urged her to remember certain things that they had talked about, particularly regarding the financial aspects of her care and that of the children.

Had she not known how desperately ill he was, Suzanne would almost have questioned the illness that had taken her husband. His thoughts were well laid out and so much like the man he had been. Then again, he would ramble on for page after page, making little to no sense. The pain of his confusion crashing at her from the messy, scrambled words. Often, he referred to his mother and father who had both been gone for more years than she could remember. Yet, to him, they were as real at that moment as though he were a young child once again.

With her heart breaking, she read on and on, once again grateful for the solitude that was hers. Knowing without a doubt that God in His infinite wisdom truly does know exactly what we need and is there to provide it if only we will trust Him.

Finally, finishing all but the last one, she sat holding that one for a long while. She wondered if she had the strength to complete this chore. Already, she felt as if someone had forced her into an air tunnel and pulled her inside out.

Realizing that she did not have to read this one until she was ready, she gently tied all the others together, and set them aside. Lifting the final letter, she tucked it into her jacket pocket and patted it with one soft little pat, before taking the others and stashing them in the safe in the library. Deciding that she would have the boys over for dinner the next evening, and of course Adam's wife and little girl, she would then give them and Autumn the letters from their father. It would be a time of emotional healing for them all.

With a sigh of relief, she wandered up to their room, her room. It still felt so very strange to remember at the oddest of times that this was no longer a shared room, but was indeed hers alone. She had been thinking about having the room completely redone. Somehow she felt she needed that; not to do away with Daniel, but more so to make it her own. It had been nearly two full years since he had last spent time with her in this room, and she felt a change was needed.

Placing the final letter from Daniel in the little side drawer of her desk, she sank into the soft wing-back chair next to the window to watch for Autumn, who would be eager to tell her about her day. Suzanne felt numb beyond belief.

The letters had brought back so many emotions, so many memories of moments shared with her husband; moments that would never be theirs again. There was the way he laughed at the little things that upset her; the way his eyes crinkled at the corners just before he leaned in to her to give her a kiss, even as he teased her about being the only girl in the world for him. And then, there was the way he could make her so mad in one instance, and so thrilled in the next.

No one had ever been able to evoke the emotions in her that Daniel could. His gallant, old-world ways had charmed her from the very moment they had met. She never grew tired of his Scottish burr as he purred her name in the dark of the night.

Suddenly, she could stand the suspense no more. She had to know what his final letter said. Nearly leaping from the chair, she yanked the drawer open; the very one she had so gently closed just moments before.

Angrily, she ripped the envelope open, completely beside herself with the emotions raging through her being. Wondering, needing desperately to know, if it was more of the rambling on and on, or if Daniel had some final word for her, something that might help her find her way in the months and years ahead.

Sinking slowly to the soft carpet beneath her feet, she unfolded the sheets before her. She opened them carefully, as if they were as fragile as fairy dust. Gasping to pull air into her tortured lungs, trying desperately not to let the tears fall again, she saw the clear, precise handwriting that she knew so well.

Taking in the words as if in a daze, Suzanne read of his love for her, of his own grief as he accepted that there was no hope for him to get better and live the life he so loved. She could literally hear the lilt of his accent as she read the first few words. Daniel had written her a letter so filled with himself and his need to let her know how much she meant to him that she was completely overwhelmed. The final few words were her undoing.

"My Darling Suzanne, it is with wonder that I look forward to seeing my Savior face to face. I know that Heaven is meant to be spent glorifying Him and I am so ready for that marvelous experience. At the same time, my heart is ripped in two, as

my heaven on earth was my time with you. Never in my wildest dreams did I ever imagine having someone as beautiful, as lovely, and as precious as you with whom to spend these past years. I consider myself the most blessed man ever to have walked the face of this earth. It is with such deep sorrow that I prepare to leave you.

However, know this, Dear One, there will come a day when we will be reunited again. Oh, not as man and wife, certainly. The Word tells us that there will be no giving or taking in marriage in glory. We shall, however, be friends for eternity, my dear. We will never have to part again. We will rejoice and praise our Savior together forever.

Until then, my Darling, I want; no, I need to know that you are happy. If you should find love again, then I tell you with everything within me that I give my blessing for this union. I do remember that we discussed this in times past. Somehow I feel that you might need to hear again, in tangible form, that I truly want you to find love. I need to know that you are not alone but are happy.

Your happiness is the one thing that has always given me the greatest joy. When I found you, after Joanna had died, I knew that God had given me a double portion on this earth. I wish that for you, my Darling; a double portion of His love and joy. Never feel guilty for loving again. It is the way of life on this earth. It is His way of making our sorrow a little easier to bear.

If you will allow yourself to love again, to have hope and happiness for the days left to you, I pray that you will find a joy that will carry you from this life into the next. I will be waiting for you there, with arms opened wide. Until then, my Darling, until then.

With All My Love ~ Forever and Beyond. Daniel."

As tears flowed in an unstoppable flood, Suzanne gave thanks for the man she had loved for so many years. She realized that she had perhaps never truly appreciated the deep and pure love that Daniel had for her. Suzanne wished with everything within her that she could tell him again just how much she admired and loved him. The very fact that he would want her happiness above all else was proof enough that his love was of a higher plane than any she had ever known, or likely ever would know.

Hearing the sound of the downstairs door closing softly, and Autumn's footsteps on the stairs, she rose unsteadily. Stuffing the precious letter into the now crumpled envelope, she moved on silent feet to place it in the drawer again. Suzanne knew without a doubt that this was a letter she would read again and again throughout the coming years.

As Autumn's voice sang out her usual cheery greeting, Suzanne responded, albeit somewhat muffled, as she blew her nose as quietly as she could. Hurrying into the lovely bathroom that she and Daniel had designed for their personal enjoyment, she rinsed her face with cold water. She patted her face with a soft terrycloth towel and peered into the mirror. Surprised that her eyes and nose were no more red than they were, she flicked some powder over her face and straightened her jacket. Her children had seen enough tears from their mother to last a lifetime, it was time that they saw the joy of the Lord in her face.

Turning just as Autumn flew into her room, Suzanne reached for her daughter and wrapped the startled girl in a tight hug. After several long seconds, she leaned back and smiled into the warm brown eyes of her daughter. The fact that those same eyes were so very much like the ones of the man she had loved and lost gave her a sense of completeness.

"What say we go get some pizza? I imagine that you are starved. You can tell me all about your day at school and the band practice afterward. Does that sound fun?"

Nodding her head, all the while watching her mother with wide puzzled eyes, Autumn had to ask, "Is everything all right, Mom? You aren't sick or anything are you? You look almost as if you have been crying. Is everything all right with you and Peter? You haven't had a lover's quarrel have you?"

Laughing delightedly, Suzanne responded, "Oh, my darling girl! Of course, Peter and I are fine. How could we have a lover's quarrel when we are not yet lovers? Seriously, where do you come up with these ideas? I am quite simply glad, to the very bones of my body that you are my beautiful, wonderful daughter. I am especially grateful that you are here with me right now."

Feeling slightly lightheaded, Suzanne ushered her daughter out of her room, and down the stairs. Afraid that if they stayed in the room a moment longer she would begin blubbering like a baby, Suzanne wanted so desperately to tell her daughter about the letters from her father. She was determined, however, to tell the three children at the same time.

Knowing Autumn as she did, if she even hinted of the letters, there would be no peace until her curiosity had been satisfied. Besides, she needed time to process the last letter from Daniel before sharing it with anyone, even her precious daughter.

Together they climbed into Suzanne's svelte Jaguar and drove to the Pizza Palace. Ordering their usual, they enjoyed the time together. Autumn was full of funny stories of her afternoon classes and the band students who could not quite get their parts right. Laughing with her daughter, Suzanne realized once again how very blessed she was.

She ate two huge pieces of pizza, realizing with a start that this was the first time in a long while that food tasted good to her.

Suzanne shared with Autumn that she was going to invite her brothers for dinner the next evening. They planned a meal fit for a king, choosing a few favorite items for each brother. Autumn reminded her mother that little Sandi loved pigs in a blanket, so they added that delicacy to the menu.

Suzanne pulled her phone from her purse and called each of the boys, giving them the details for dinner and assuring that they could indeed be there. As she did so, she realized just how long it had been since they had enjoyed a real family dinner. Even though Daniel would be missing, a part of him would always be with them. Especially tomorrow night when she shared the letters he had written to his loved ones.

A deep peace took hold of her as she walked in her garden later that evening. A knowing that all would be well flooded over her. For a moment, it seemed as if she sensed Daniel standing beside her as she breathed in the fragrance of his favorite rose.

"Thank you, my Darling, for giving me the permission I so clearly needed to continue living my life. I will always love you, my Daniel. But I must heal, and I realize that I must keep on living, for my own sake, and for that of our children."

With a smile on her face, Suzanne stood in the cool, quiet breeze as she felt her heart begin to unfurl in the healing presence of the Holy Spirit.

The following evening they all gathered in the family room following a meal to be remembered for months to come. Suzanne had gotten the letters from Daniel out of their hiding place a little earlier. She had them laying on her desk, waiting for the time to share them with the family.

Asking everyone for their attention, she waited for a moment. Lifting her hand with the letters in it, she explained briefly how she had come by the letters. She told them that she had already read her letters from her husband. Then she handed one remaining letter to each of the three children.

Quietly, each person sat, holding the envelopes in their fingers for several long silent moments. Even little Sandi was quiet as she watched her daddy with huge eyes. Finally, Jamie reached across and lifted a letter opener from the desk. Slicing the envelope, he silently passed the opener on to Autumn. She in turn passed it on to Adam. In unison, they all three opened their letters and read them silently. Tears flowed as each one felt the special touch their father gave them as his words ministered to each one individually.

Suzanne knew that she would forever be grateful to Daniel for this final act of kindness. His boys in particular needed this closure. They all needed the hope of a future with their father.

CHAPTER 22

A FTER SITTING IN silence with only a sniffle heard here and there as they
finished reading their letters, Adam finally broke the prolonged stillness. Reaching out and capturing his wife's hand, he in turn took hold of
Autumn's hand on the other side.

"I think it would be good if we all spent some time in prayer, Dad has
given us a beautiful gift in his final letters. It would be appropriate to let
our heavenly Father know that we are grateful."

Each person in the room took hold of the hand of the person beside
them, forming a tight knit circle of love and compassion. Adam again took
the lead. Praying aloud, he thanked the Lord for each person in his family
and for giving them a last glimpse into their father's heart.

A quiet gentleness swept over the room as the Holy Spirit ministered
to each individual. Finally, Suzanne broke the silence, thanking Adam for
the prayer and all of them for coming over. She then informed her children that she had made fresh strawberry shortcake and iced tea for dessert
before they all headed out.

"Deborah, if you will assist me, we can carry the dessert in and have it
here by the fireplace. Adam, would you mind putting another log on the
fire, Son? I realize that it isn't really cold enough for a fire, but I needed
the warmth of the flames tonight."

Adam rose from his dad's comfy chair and removed the fireplace
screen, tossing another large log on the coals. It was quite a luxury to have
a real wood burning fireplace in Dallas, one that Daniel had insisted on

having installed when building the house. He knew how much Suzanne loved the smell and feel of a real fire. His desire had always been to make her the happiest woman alive.

Jamie suggested to Adam that they bring in a few more logs for their mother.

"You know she will sit up long after we are gone, and the stack is getting pretty low."

Together they made quick work of carrying in a good supply of firewood, more than she would need that night. It felt good to do even that little thing to help.

Hurrying to help Suzanne, Deborah followed her mother-in-law into the kitchen. As Suzanne bustled about getting the premade desserts in their lovely crystal dishes out of the fridge, Deborah filled glasses with ice. She then poured the tea slowly into each one. Up to now she had been very quiet. Finally, she set the tea pitcher down and looked over at Suzanne.

"Mom," she inquired, she had only begun calling her mother-in-law 'mom' in the last few weeks. Before, she had stammered and hum-hawed her way around using a name.

"Why do you suppose Dad didn't write me a letter? I am the only one, well besides Sandi, of course, that he didn't include in his final missives."

Suzanne stood with her back to Deborah for a long moment, not moving a muscle. She realized it was a deep hurt she heard in the younger woman's voice. Turning slowly, she looked at Deborah, taking a deep breath before replying.

"I am so sorry, Honey, that this has clearly hurt you. You must realize that to Daniel you were still just a friend of the family, for the most part. He likely did not even cognitively understand that you and Adam were married, the illness has been going on much longer than you can imagine. Even though he performed your ceremony three years ago, that was one of the last real acts of ministry that he did. His mind was already going, well before then. By the time Sandi was born he had little ability to understand that she was his granddaughter. To him she was just another little child. That is why when you took her to visit he rarely spoke to her or wanted to play with her. He had no real sense of connection. If it helps, he did mention in his letter to me that he hoped you and Adam would one day marry. He felt you were the perfect girl for our son. He clearly confused the past with the present in many instances."

With a small sniffle, Deborah nodded her head in silent understanding. She stood like a lost, forlorn child as she absorbed the words Suzanne spoke. Feeling her sorrow, Suzanne stepped around the kitchen island and wrapped her in a warm hug.

"Oh, Deborah, I love you so much. You know that of all the girls in the world there is not another that could be right for our Adam. You are truly my dear daughter and I don't ever want you to feel left out of this family for any reason. Do you understand me?"

Nodding, Deborah reached and grabbed a tissue from the ever available box to wipe her nose and eyes.

"Suzanne. . . Mom, I love this family so much. I needed to hear that from you just now. You know that my own father and mother rarely show emotion. They are so emotionally detached it is awful. I have only heard them, either one, say the words 'I love you' maybe two or three times in my entire life. The warmth and love in this home is what drew me to your family, and to Adam, in the first place. Thank you for answering my question. I was trying so hard not to let my hurt feelings get the best of me, but at the same time I was truly feeling a little left field and left out."

Giggling a little, she continued, "I would have likely kept Adam up half the night going over the whys and wherefores, and the Lord knows the poor guy needs his sleep!"

"Are you alright now, Dear?" Suzanne quizzed her gently.

"Yes. Yes, I really am. I guess I just needed to say the words and hear your response. It makes perfect sense, and I know that Dad knew how much I loved him. I just am so happy he let the family know how deeply he cared for all of us. It really does help, doesn't it?"

"It does. It surely does." Suzanne murmured.

"Now, let's get these in to the others before the ice all melts and the whipped topping is beyond repair!"

Meanwhile, back in the family room, Adam, Jamie and Autumn were having a heartfelt talk as well. Each one shared tidbits from their letter with the others. It was a time of healing, and renewing of their bond as siblings as they realized the finality of their father being well and truly gone.

Jamie spoke up, saying, "Well, Adam, old man, I guess the burden of being the head of this clan of misfits falls on your shoulders now. If anyone can handle that load, I am quite sure you can. I am grateful that Dad left us each with a sense of purpose and responsibility for Mom. She has been strong for so long but it is time she had a break. Perhaps we should work out some kind of a schedule of when we will do certain things for her, and when each of us will take a little extra time to spend with her. I know for myself that when I get busy with school and work I forget for days at a time to even call her. Autumn, if you notice that happening, please give me a text or a call and nudge me a bit to follow through."

Adam smiled at his younger brother, "That is excellent wisdom, Jamie. Thank you for thinking of this. I get so busy with a wife and child, along with work and school that I sometimes realize that days have gone by and I've barely connected with Mother or Autumn. We must do a better job in the future of keeping them close."

Autumn giggled and told them both, "Well, you must promise not to growl at me when I do remind you, because it will likely come up sooner than you think. And while we are talking, how serious do you think Mom is about Mr. Clifton? He calls her nearly every evening now, and even a couple of times a day on the weekends. Do you think it is proper for him to do so? I mean, he seems really nice, but Dad has only been gone such a short while. . ."

As her voice trailed off, Adam picked up the thread of the conversation. "Well, Autumn, that is a real concern, but I think we must let time take its course with this one. If either of you have a problem or a real concern with Peter, please let me know. The last thing I want is our mother making the mistake of a lifetime as she processes through her grief."

Clearing his throat, Adam continued, "I believe he is in love with her, and likely has been for a lot longer than we even realize. However, I don't think Mother is the kind of woman who will make rash decisions concerning him or anyone else. In fact, I don't know if she has even had the time or the desire to think of him in that way. Mr. Peter Clifton may well have his work cut out for himself in convincing Suzanne Brummell Parker to be his bride."

Just then Suzanne and Deborah entered with the dessert. The mood lightened as little Sandi danced around excitedly on her little toddler legs, urging them to enjoy the wonderful treat. A sense of love and peace settled over the home where they had all grown up. Even little Sandi seemed to know that there was joy to be found in her Grammy's house again.

CHAPTER 23

J AMIE CALLED HIS mom on his way home from work the next evening after they had all gotten together and read Daniel's letters. As soon as she heard his voice, Suzanne knew something was wrong.

"Mom, can we get together and talk? I'm having a really hard time right now after reading Dad's letter. I guess it's hit me that he really isn't coming back. He's not just over in the hospital like he was for so long. . . you know?"

"Of course, Sweetheart! Can you come on by now? Autumn is at a friend's house for the evening. We could have a bite to eat and just visit a while. If you'd like you could even relax and take a dip in the pool. You know there are several pairs of your swimming trunks here."

"Thanks, Mom, I'll be by soon. I just need to stop by the bank and then run in the store for some dog food. Rambo is about out and he gets cranky when I don't feed him."

Laughing together they hung up and Suzanne busied herself with preparing a light supper of salad and a grilled chicken breast. Jamie was the easiest of her kids to feed.

"That boy will eat rocks if there is nothing else around." Suzanne smiled to herself.

It dawned on her of a sudden that Jamie was no longer a boy. Sitting down on one of her kitchen chairs, she sat for several moments with hands in her lap absorbing this fact. Where had time gone? When had her children grown up so quickly?

Realizing the date, Suzanne had a sudden panic attack. It had just dawned on her that Autumn's birthday had come and gone the month before.

"My goodness, Autumn is sixteen. Oh no, I missed her birthday. How on earth did I miss my daughter's birthday? How come no one reminded me?"

Jumping up and looking frantically at her calendar, she realized that she had indeed missed her daughter's sixteenth birthday. Heartbroken, she realized that she had been so tied up in her own grief and pain that she had let one of the most important days in a teenage girl's life slip past.

"We must fix this immediately!" Suzanne said out loud. "Oh my gosh, I am so ashamed of myself. And apparently the boys forgot as well. And Autumn, being Autumn of course, never mentioned a word about it."

Just then Jamie pulled into the driveway. Suzanne heard his car and hurried into the living room. She watched as the tall, slender young man crawled out of his little sports car and leaned down to retrieve a huge bouquet of mixed flowers. Smiling a little at his sweetness, she stepped back behind the curtain so that he would not see her spying on him. It warmed her heart to see him straighten his jacket as he glanced toward the door. Clearly, he wanted his mama to be proud of him.

Using his key to let himself in, as Suzanne slipped back to the kitchen, Jamie shouted, "Mother o' mine! Wherefore art thou?"

This was always his favorite greeting when he'd been gone for a while. He'd been doing this for years, since he could talk really. It was something he'd come up with when very small and it had stuck. Suzanne loved to hear his voice ring out with the joy and love he shared everywhere he went.

Acting surprised, she turned and met him halfway into the kitchen. Grabbing each other in a tight hug, mother and son embraced. It was as if they'd not seen each other in weeks, certainly not the night before.

Pulling the flowers from behind his back, Jamie presented them as a gift to a queen. Grinning from ear to ear, he said with a flourish, "See,

Peter is not the only fella who has good taste in flowers! For my own, very special mother, flowers for the fairest flower in the garden of life."

Laughing, Suzanne accepted the bouquet with a tiny curtsey. Jamie, always her most dramatic of children, was clearly a Scotsman through and through. He was so like his father that at times it startled her. She knew that one day some young woman would be a lucky lady to catch her son's eye. She almost dreaded that day as she knew she would lose a part of him that could never be recovered. And yet, she would never hold him back from the kind of love his father and she had known. She prayed daily that he and Autumn would both find Christian life mates and would live long, happy lives with them.

Suzanne grabbed a lovely Lennox vase from the china cabinet and filled it with cool water. She carefully arranged the colorful flowers to show them off to their best advantage.

"Thank you for the flowers, Jamie. They are beautiful, and I will enjoy them as long as they last."

Settling into their late afternoon luncheon, Suzanne brought up about Autumn's birthday. Jamie was as mortified as she had been to realize that they had all let his little sister down in such a way.

"We must do something about that immediately! I am totally surprised that Adam or Deborah didn't remember! They are always on top of things. Poor little girl, she likely cried herself to sleep that night."

"Well, we will plan her a surprise party and make it all right. Can you get in touch with her best friends and let them know somehow? I'd imagine Facebook would be the best way, private message, of course!"

"Yep, that won't be a problem, Mom. Just let me know when and where. Let's get the show on the road!"

"Now, Jamie, you came here to talk to me and I've distracted you with the party issue. Tell me, Son, what is going on and how can I help?"

Chewing his chicken slowly, Jamie took his time answering. "I don't know, Mom, it's hard to explain. Last night when I got back to my apartment, I started thinking about all the years as a pastor's kid, the pro's and the con's, I guess. Some of it was really good, and some of it was pretty tough. If it hadn't been for Adam, I don't think I could have made it through some of it. Dad was gone a lot in my teenage years, you know. It seemed he was always off to some speaking event or another, and there were times when I was pretty angry about that."

Shrugging, Jamie continued, "Then, I got to remembering all the special times, like my own sixteenth birthday. Remember, that was the time Dad took me to Scotland, just the two of us. We went fly fishing in the burns, stayed in a real castle, ate all kinds of strange foods, and I had the best time of my life. Anyway, I don't know, I guess it really hit me last night and this morning how that part of our life is gone. It will never again be the same."

Tears welled up in his eyes as he battled the strong emotions gripping him. "It's never going to be the same for you either, is it?"

Fighting her own tears, Suzanne slowly responded. "No, Darling, it isn't. But then again, it hasn't been the same for quite a long while now. Your dad started changing with the Alzheimer's nearly four or five years ago now. You kids didn't see it as much right at first because you were so busy with your own lives; school, college, and so on. But even before he was diagnosed, I knew something was dreadfully wrong. I had prayed and prayed it was something that could be fixed, but that clearly was not the Lord's plan."

Sipping her iced tea, Suzanne continued, "Jamie, life is full of changes. Nothing ever stays the same very long. You really begin to realize this as you grow a little older and see your own children growing and changing before your very eyes. I suppose it also happens to people in their middle years when they begin to see their parents getting older. To them it may seem it happens quickly, but in reality they have been growing older all along. The important thing is, Son, to learn to live each day as God would have you. To know without a doubt, at the end of the day, that you have done the best you could for God, and for those He's placed in your care. If you know of a certainty that you have done that, then all the other stuff will work out."

"Mom, changing the subject, but do you think you will marry Peter? I know he hasn't asked you yet, but if he does, do you think you will do that? I mean, Dad's been gone nearly a year now, it wouldn't be that awful if you had thought about it."

"I honestly don't know, Jamie. I do think about it sometimes, and Peter and I have grown very fond of one another over the past six months or so. However, I don't think I'm quite ready to take that step just yet. I need to know that Autumn is doing alright. I've loved living in Dallas for the last twenty-five years. If marrying Peter entailed moving, that might be very difficult. I certainly don't want to leave you and Adam's family behind. The adjustment to small town living would be a huge thing. It's a tough question."

Sighing deeply, she continued, "On the other hand, it would also be hard to live the rest of my life alone. I do think Peter is a good man, and I know he loves me deeply. If I wanted to marry again he would certainly be who I would consider. I guess I'm not sure my heart is free to love again just yet. I still have so many feelings for your father, so many memories to digest and try to hold on to. I don't want to lose any of that for the love of another. Does that make any sense?"

With wisdom beyond his years, Jamie replied. "It does make sense, Mother, but Dad is gone now. You, we all, must go on with our lives. You grieving yourself to death, not eating enough to keep a bird alive and rarely sleeping, is not going to help anyone. Dad will always be in our hearts and lives. He will continue on in Sandi, in the other children we kids will have, and in our traditions."

"And that is one of the things I wanted to talk with you about! What say we start a Scottish Christmas Tradition in memory of Dad? We could have one of our trees decorated with scotch plaid, play Scottish music, I don't know, lots of things. Oh and serve shortbread. I love their shortbread!"

"Oh, Jamie, that is an absolutely delightful idea! Last Christmas was such a sad affair, with all of us being thrown into mourning. It seemed no one really cared whether we had a tree or not."

Clapping her hands, Suzanne, exclaimed, "You and Autumn can pull it all together and we can have a special night to decorate the tree, with hot wassail and shortbread. I'll get Deborah to help me make some meat and cheese pies and we will have a feast!"

"Will you invite Peter?"

The question hung in the air like a hot air balloon about to explode.

Not sure how to answer, and certainly wanting to get Jamie's input and thoughts, Suzanne slowly replied, "Well, that's another thing to think about, now isn't it? I guess that would really be up to you children. If you think you might like him here then I would enjoy that, but if you want to have our getting ready for Christmas party all to ourselves then I certainly would understand that; as would Peter, I believe."

Looking down at his hands folded between his knees for a long moment, Jamie finally glanced back up at his mother.

"I would vote for having him here, if he wants to come. It feels right, and I think our family needs to begin to heal. What better way than to invite Peter to begin learning our celebrations?"

"Well, then! I suppose we will put the question to the others and see if all agree. If so, then yes, I would love to have him here. How can you know if you want to spend the rest of your life with someone if you never spend any time together? He especially needs to spend time with us as a family to make sure he feels comfortable with us. You do realize that he would have a much bigger adjustment integrating into this crazy family than we would have in accepting him."

Laughing, they both began talking at once, laying out the plan for the upcoming holiday season. Suzanne relaxed for the first time in days, glad to have the laughter of her son surrounding her, warming her heart from the inside out.

Deciding to take a dip in the pool, Jamie excused himself and ambled out into the fading sunlight. The little pool house was always ready for family and guests, with swimming trunks, towels, and anything they could possibly need.

Jamie swam for about an hour while Suzanne did up the dishes and a load of laundry. It was quiet in the house with Autumn gone. She usually kept a steady stream of chatter going during and after a meal. But this evening, Suzanne was enjoying the quiet more than usual. The visit with Jamie had soothed her soul. All of a sudden it came to her that she would like for him to move back home for a few months, if he would.

"That would be so nice, to have my son home with me for a little while longer. And Autumn would love it too, I'm sure." Suzanne hummed to herself as she put the towels away.

Ambling out to the pool, she sat down in a lounge chair next to the one Jamie had taken up residence in.

"Jamie, I had a thought just now. What would you think about moving back into the house for a few months. It would be so good to have you here while we are planning for the Thanksgiving and Christmas season. I'd love to have you home for a little while before you find a girl and settle down."

"Mom. . . Mom," Jamie interrupted. "You don't have to try and convince me. I'd actually thought about the same thing while swimming. Yes, I'd love to move home. The lease on my apartment is actually due for renewal in a week. It would be perfect timing. Are you sure you and Autumn wouldn't mind having me around for a while?"

Leaping from her chair, Suzanne did a little dance of joy. "Oh, my Darling, it would make me the happiest mother in the world. And I know without a doubt that your sister would love it! Yes! It will be wonderful!"

They chatted and visited for a little longer, after Jamie showered and changed back into his jeans and shirt. Assuring his mother that he would begin moving his things back in within the week, he gave Suzanne a hug and said goodnight.

After locking the door and setting the alarm, she climbed the stairs to her room. The house felt huge and lonely with Autumn gone overnight. She knew without a doubt that she would love having Jamie living at home.

"If Peter and I do decide to marry, the kids will be perfectly fine. This house could hold an army and have room to spare, providing we decided to live here of course."

She knew that Jamie's returning home was temporary at best. Still, it would be good to have two of her children home for a while longer. Sighing, she settled in for the night.

Tomorrow would surely come soon enough.

CHAPTER 24

AND SO TIME went by, one day at a time. The hourglass slowly dropped its sand one grain after another, ever counting down the hours. Life was evolving into a pattern of peace and calm for Suzanne and her children. Daniel was never forgotten, but was becoming a beautiful memory to be cherished.

It seemed that as Suzanne's grief subsided, her love for her family, and for Peter grew. He made a few short trips back and forth to visit in the ensuing months, always staying at the Marriott just down the road. She knew her home was amply large enough to accommodate him staying there. However, Suzanne appreciated that he was always so careful to respect her and her family by not expecting to. That would most likely have been considered by some as inappropriate. She marveled at his consideration.

Their relationship grew steadily as she found her way through her grief. It seemed that almost in spite of herself, Suzanne was drawn more and more to Peter. She would call to run things by him; not that she needed anyone's approval, she assured herself. It was good to have a second opinion in some of the more critical decisions facing her.

Of course, she had Adam and Jamie to give her input on things. However, Peter's sound business mind and calm wisdom gave her strength to make necessary decisions concerning some of Daniel's financial and legal matters.

They found time to be together when she made a trip or two back to her mother's home. Those were precious times of waiting on the Lord, and of healing from all the stress and worry that had been hers. She found solace in the home she had grown up in. Somehow the pain of loss seemed less there.

Peter took her to lunch or dinner and teased her from time to time about her being his special girl. However, he assured her that he was not pressing her for any kind of commitment, yet.

As to staying at her home, when he came to Dallas to visit, his response to being invited, as time went by, was simply put, "Suzanne, I am scared to death of the spotlight that hangs so close to your head. You know, the one that goes with the whole fishbowl thing! Seriously, I would never put your reputation, and my own temptation, to the test in such a manner. There will be time enough for us to be together under the same roof once we are married."

He was so certain that she would say yes to marriage that it sometimes frightened her. If she could not yet be entirely certain of her feelings for him, how could he possibly be so sure?

Without fail, on the first Saturday of each month, a single long-stemmed white rose was delivered to Suzanne's door. There was always a card; a card she never shared with her mother or her children. They all knew the rose was from Peter, but they refrained from asking questions. This was a romance that was unfolding, one petal at a time.

It was clear that no one in the family was opposed to the two of them forming a long-term, loving relationship. Her sons, and Autumn, all seemed to sense that their mother was giving herself time to heal; time to mourn the husband and father they all had lost.

Adam in particular respected his mother for the time she was allowing them all to find the peace and healing they so desperately needed. If anything, Adam and Suzanne grew closer still as they shared the burdens of decision making for the family as a whole. She would often tell him what she and Peter had discussed. They would then decide if it was the best for all concerned. Things moved along with a simple ease, as together they sorted out the financial and household matters.

As promised, Jamie and Suzanne put together a surprise birthday party for Autumn. Jamie contacted all of Autumn's best friends and enlisted their help with decorating and food. They decided on a poolside party with a Japanese theme.

Autumn had said for years that one day she was going to travel to Japan and study there. She was enthralled with anything from that culture. Her friends made sure there were colored paper lanterns, Japanese music playing in the background and several dishes of Japanese food. A few of the girls decided to serve as hostesses and wore costumes to compliment the theme.

Adam and Deborah took responsibility for finding just the right big gift. They searched high and low until they found a little yellow convertible that was in Suzanne's budget. They put a huge silver bow on top and hid it in Adam's garage until the day of the party.

Suzanne arranged to take Autumn to the movies, giving the others time to get the party all set up and ready for them on their return. The sun was hanging low on the horizon as they pulled into the drive. Autumn asked if she might take her bike and ride to her best friend's house if her mom didn't mind.

"I won't be gone long, Mom. Would that be alright?"

"Well, Sweetheart, I need you to help me first, if you don't mind. I have a large potted plant on the back patio that I'd like to move a little closer to the pool. It's on rollers, but is just awkward enough that I can't quite get a grip on it to move it by myself. Would you help me with that first?"

"Sure, Mom! Let's go do this thing, and then I'll go see Amber."

Laughing and talking a mile a minute to keep her daughter distracted, they walked around the side of the house to the tall wooden fence. Suzanne had already texted Jamie, letting him know they were arriving. All was quiet and peaceful until she unlatched the gate and swung it wide.

At that moment, the entire backyard erupted in shouts of, 'Surprise', and 'Happy Birthday, Autumn'. She was so taken off guard that she stopped and put her hands to her cheeks. When it dawned on her that it was her very own surprise sixteenth birthday party, she began to blubber and cry like a baby.

"Mom! How did you know I wanted exactly this for a party? I was so sad that my birthday was forgotten, but never would I have said anything!"

"I know, Darling. And I am so sorry that we all clearly forgot about your birthday last month. This is just a small attempt to make up for that terrible oversight."

Immediately Autumn was surrounded by laughing friends. The party was a huge success. When it came time for the last gift, Autumn and her friends were all totally surprised by the car. Adam drove it in through the back yard gate, and parked it catty-angled to the pool. Autumn immediately fell in love with the beautiful little black and yellow beauty. Screaming her excitement, she ran to her big brother and threw her arms around him.

"Oh, Adam, you found just the car that I've always wanted! I love it, and I love you, all of you!"

Twirling around in her excitement, she lost her balance and fell head-long into the pool. Coming up spluttering, she shouted with laughter, "Come on in everyone, the water is great!"

Soon the pool was filled with crazy teenagers, clothes and all. Suzanne and her boys stood by, watching in amazement. Clearly, they were all having the time of their lives.

After a few laps back and forth across the pool, Autumn climbed out and skipped back over to the car. Clasping her hands above her head, she did a little dance of excitement barely contained. Turning to Adam and Peter she exclaimed, "Oh my gosh, I can hardly wait to drive this baby to school!"

Of course, her brothers both cautioned her over, and over again about speeding, to which she just laughed.

"And you guys are such great examples of perfect driving, right?"

Her impudence did nothing to assure them that she would be careful, but she was more than cautious. It was not in her nature to be otherwise.

After all the excitement of the evening was over, Autumn settled in her room and called her cousin, Brenda. Knowing that she would want to hear every tiny detail of the amazing party, especially about the convertible, Autumn told her mom she would be on the phone for a while.

Suzanne took advantage of Autumn being preoccupied to call Peter and tell him all about the party as well. He had been invited, of course, but had several obligations that kept him from flying over to be there for the excitement. He asked how Autumn liked his gift, a year of car washes and detailing at one of the local vendors. Suzanne assured him that Autumn was thrilled.

They talked for a while, and then said goodnight. Peter told her he loved her, and Suzanne replied back with her usual reply, "Hmm, well time will tell on that, my dear."

Laughing, they hung up the phone, each rather wishing the other was there.

As soon as Brenda picked up the phone to answer Autumn's call, she squealed with excitement. "Oh my gosh! You got a convertible! A yellow convertible! I am so jealous. . ."

Of course, they both knew she was only jealous in the sense of being excited for her cousin and best friend in the entire world. The girls talked for a long while as Autumn told Brenda how thrilled she was and how totally surprised she had been.

"Initially, I really was devastated that my mom and everyone forgot my birthday this year, but I tried really hard to understand that it came right when Mom was at her breaking point in her grief. I would not have added to that for anything. Somehow, it may even be better that they all forgot, because this was totally the best birthday of my life! If I'd known about it, or thought it was going to happen it would not have been nearly as fun."

"I know what you mean about breaking points," Brenda interjected. "I haven't called to tell you about what's been happening with my mom, but it is pretty huge. I wanted to wait long enough before telling anyone to make sure that it was truly a life change."

Taking a deep breath, Brenda continued, "About a year ago now, shortly after Aunt Suzanne and you were here for that visit when your dad got so ill, Mom had a complete breakthrough. I think her yelling at Aunt Suzanne, and then thinking about that and a lot of other things kind of just brought her to her knees. One day, after your mom had stopped by to see her, she decided of her own accord to toss all her prescriptions and pour all her alcohol down the drain. I was there, helping her, and even I couldn't believe it."

"What did you think?" Autumn breathed.

"Honestly, I didn't know what to think, I didn't believe she would follow through with it for a long, long time. The first two weeks were horrible. I was on school break, and I stayed home with her all day every day for all that time. My little brother was at Dad's house and I was so glad. Mom lay in bed in her sweaty pajamas for two full days, shaking and crying. Then finally, she asked me to get her up and help her get a hot shower. I did that, then she ate a little chicken soup and went back to bed. We repeated this over and over again every day for the next ten days. Finally, after what seemed like forever, she was able to sit up for most of the day and began eating light meals. I saw her slowly getting better."

Brenda sniffed as she held back tears, "It was really hard, Autumn, it felt like I was the mother and she was the child. But you know, I think that because she really wanted to change; it wasn't Grandma or some doctor telling her to do this, it was purely the Lord, I think that is why it has worked. Mom has been completely drug and alcohol free for almost twelve months now. Every month we celebrate with a candlelight dinner on the anniversary of when she made her decision. She is the healthiest I have ever seen her. She has gained some weight, and goes to Bible study faithfully, and keeps the house clean. She is a real mom for the first time in my life. My little brother and I are both still in a state of shock, I think, but we are so very grateful to God."

"How has your dad responded to the new Karen?"

"Well, he is the same as always, poking fun at her for being skinny as a rail, and not really believing she will stick with the plan. It seems the more he torments her, the more determined she is to succeed. I have seen Mom treat him a lot differently though. She actually bakes cakes or brownies to send over with us when we go for our weekends, and always tells us to wish him a good weekend. Kinda strange after all her years of hating him."

"Do you think they will ever get back together?" Autumn inquired.

"No, I don't think so. He would have to do a lot of changing, and quite honestly, I just don't think they would be good together anyway. I do wish God would bring someone into Mom's life though, someone like Peter. She deserves a little happiness. Who knows, maybe one day she will find her knight in shining armor like Aunt Suzanne has!"

"Well," Autumn responded, "while we all do like Peter, and he and Mom seem to be getting closer, it hasn't quite moved toward marriage; at least not yet."

"Would you mind if it did?" Brenda wondered aloud.

"I don't think so. It doesn't feel as weird to think about it now that Dad's been gone a while, but I just don't know if Mom is ready to marry again. She seems very happy just being here at home and kind of finding herself again. Now that Jamie has moved back in, she is very happy, as am I. We laugh, watch movies, eat real meals together, all those things that we used to do before Daddy became so ill. Most people don't realize it, but it's been more than two years now since we had any kind of real family life. I must say, I really am enjoying it. If Mom and Peter do marry, I hope that doesn't change."

"Honestly," Brenda responded, "I don't think it will. Peter seems to want to have a family more than anyone I know, almost too much sometimes! He might drive you crazy with wanting to do things together."

"Well," Autumn sighed, "I guess time will tell on that. I think I'm okay with all of it, but I don't want to move, that's for sure. At least not right away. I love our home and all of my friends are here, except for you. Again, I guess that's something that we will all have to work out over time."

Chatting for a little longer, Autumn asked Brenda if she would mind if she told her mother about the transformation in Karen's life. Brenda assured her it would be fine. Both girls agreed to pray for a reconciliation between their mothers. Closing off the conversation, the two cousins wished each other a goodnight.

They both knew that the other was only a phone call away if needed.

CHAPTER 25

PETER CLIFTON STOOD on the high bluff overlooking the Buffalo River. The sun reflected off the windows of the magnificent home behind him, glinting on the water as it cascaded its way to the ocean.

Lifting his face toward the sun, he stood lost in thought for a long time. Finally, he turned and walked back up the path to the veranda where his cool drink awaited him. It had been several weeks since he had been to visit Suzanne, and he had only called her occasionally during that time. He'd felt, somehow, that she, and he, needed some alone time; time to reflect on their futures, separately and perhaps together; time to pray and seek God's heart.

With everything in him, Peter knew that he loved Suzanne and wanted to marry her. Yet, he wanted a wife who could love him for himself, not as a replacement for the husband she had lost.

"Is that possible, Lord?" he wondered as he stood in the shade of the wisteria covered arbor. *"Can she love me, putting Daniel aside, so to speak? Or will I forever have to live in the shadow of his ghost, trying to measure up to the man she, they all, believe he was and remember him as being?"*

Hearing a car in the drive, he sauntered around the side of the house; putting his worries behind him for the time being. He was more than a little surprised to see his dad behind the wheel and all alone. He must have had a good doctor's visit the day before if he was allowed to drive himself. Peter knew that his mother had kept a tight rein on her husband since the heart attack several months back.

Walking briskly toward the car, Peter greeted his father, "Hey there, Pops! Look at you, driving yourself for a change."

His father smiled as he climbed out of the driver's side, "Yep, I am good to go again. Doc says my heart checked out real well for an old man."

"Well, I'm glad you stopped by. I have a frosty mug of lemonade waiting for me on the veranda, would you like to join me?"

"I sure would, Son. Let's have at it."

Together they ambled back around the house. As his father stood looking at the river view, Peter hurried inside to get a second glass and the pitcher of ice cold lemonade. He poured his father a frosty mug full; he'd learned years ago to store his mugs in the freezer to use on warm days such as this.

"Son, this is the most beautiful place on earth, I do declare. I tried many years ago to get your mother to build a house right here on this spot, but she wanted to be closer to civilization. I've regretted it many times over. It thrills me to my very soul to know that you, too, fell in love with this spot and built your home here; and what a house it is. I could never have dreamed up such a place as this."

Settling comfortably in the cushioned bamboo chairs, father and son sat in quiet contentment, sipping their drinks.

After a while, Peter shifted in his chair, turning slightly toward his father. "Dad, what would you think if I should ask Suzanne to be my wife? It's been over a year now since her husband passed on, do you think it's too soon?"

Mr. Clifton slowly sat his mug on the table beside him. "Well, Son, that's partly why I decided to come by today; that and just the pure joy of being able to drive myself again," he chuckled.

"Your mother and I have talked a lot about this, and we both feel that this appears to be the genuine thing for you. Now, how Suzanne feels, that is yet to be seen. Son, I've felt for a long while now that I needed to apologize to you for putting up hurdles so many years ago. I realize that I was wrong. And yet, had I not, you would not be the man you are today, nor would Suzanne be the woman she is."

Clearing his voice, which had suddenly become choked up, he continued, "Still, I do realize that my opinion swayed you greatly; keeping you from possibly marrying the girl of your dreams, from having the children you've always wanted. For that, I am deeply sorry. Can you find it in yourself to forgive me?"

Reaching across the small table to grasp his father's hand, Peter squeezed his aging fingers gently.

"Dad, I forgave you long ago. Yes, I resented your interference for many years, but since finding the Lord and getting my heart right, I find it's useless to hold onto old grudges."

Looking his father deeply in the eyes, Peter squeezed his fingers one last time before letting go.

Settling back in his seat, he continued, "I see this opportunity before me as possibly a grace gift from the Lord. Suzanne and I likely will never have a child of our own, it's a little late for that; so if I can share her children with her, be a part of all their lives, it will be enough. I will have a family after you and Mom are gone. I will have children and grandchildren to enjoy and do things for. Isn't that what this life is largely about? I honestly don't think it will matter all that much if they aren't my biological children and grandchildren, they are grace gifts at just the right time. I will simply build on that."

With tears in his eyes, Peter's father replied, "Son, you are the biggest hearted man I know. You have the heart of a warrior. I am glad to call you my own. If there is any way your mother and I can help, any way at all, you know you've only to ask."

With a teasing look and a wink, he continued, "We would also love to be invited to the big event, when it occurs."

Seeing the look of caution on his son's face, he raised his hand to ward off the remark dangling on the tip of Peter's tongue.

"Oh, I've no doubt a wedding is in the making. I have no doubt that Suzanne is going to realize that she is as much in love with you as she ever was with Daniel, and maybe even a little more. You see, we tend to appreciate genuine love even more when we've lost what we had the first time. Besides, I've seen her eyes when she looks at you here lately, in her visits back and forth. She is a woman in love, all she needs is to realize it."

Peter knew his father had been married when very young and his first wife had died from a brain tumor after only a year of marriage. He'd heard the story from his mom when he was younger. She had always said her husband loved her even more from having lost his first wife. Perhaps it was true that Suzanne would come to love him as deeply as he already loved her.

He and his father visited the afternoon away, the first real visit they'd had in a long, long time. Peter was so glad to see his father acting more like his old self, instead of the invalid he had been for the past months. He hoped and prayed he would have both of his parents around for many years to come.

Telling his father about his plans to fly to Dallas to visit with each of Suzanne's children, he mentioned that he hoped her mother would be there visiting.

"I went by her place yesterday, thinking I might talk with her before talking with the kids, but she was gone. It looks like her place is all closed up, so I am assuming she is visiting with them in Dallas."

"Yeah, your mother said Velma had taken off a few days ago, 'gallivanting all over the country' is the way she put it."

Chuckling, he continued, "I think she is more than a little jealous that Velma gets to go to live the grand city life from time to time. Perhaps, once you and Suzanne are married, your mother can have the joy of a little trip once in a while."

Peter laughed and assured his father that both his parents would always be welcome, "When Suzanne and I are married. . .," he said with a wink.

"Well, we should know soon enough," Peter continued. "I am leaving day after tomorrow to fly out there to see if she will have me. I have to admit, it's about the scariest thing I've ever done. I have no idea what I will do if she refuses me."

"You worry too much, Son. I'm telling you, the woman knows a good thing when she sees it. And if she does turn you down, then you just woo her a little more, until she sees she can't live without you. How do you think I won your mother's hand all those long years ago? The woman turned me down three separate times before she ever said yes."

With a glint in his eye, he murmured, "And I loved every minute of the chase."

CHAPTER 26

A ND SO IT happened that one beautiful fall evening, a little past the one year anniversary following Daniel's death, Peter made his most important trip to Dallas yet.

He prayed one last time as he pulled the rental car out of the airport parking garage.

"Father, guide me and go before me. I trust that if this is your will, you will open the door to all of their hearts. If not, then you will give me a peace beyond understanding. Amen."

Before he stopped by to see Suzanne, he called and asked to speak with her sons. Meeting them at Adam's home, he presented to Adam and Jamie his desire to marry their mother.

Always the impetuous one, Jamie's response came first. "I thought you would never ask," the young man cried. "Finally, we get to see Mom happy for the first time in a long while."

His reaction did not surprise Peter. While he appreciated the younger man's approval, he knew that Adam was the one who would either make or break the deal. Adam was by far the more influential in his mother's life, and he was also much more serious when it came to considering the future of them all.

Adam was studying to be an attorney, taking night classes while teaching during the day. By all appearances he would be a good one. He was never one to make a rash decision. Once made, however, he could be depended upon to stick by it.

As such, Adam was a little slower in his reply. "Peter, I know that you will be good to our mother, I have no doubt of that. However, you should know that if you ever cause her sadness or pain, you will have me to deal with. As long as you understand my position on this, then yes, you have my blessing to marry her."

Looking steadily at Suzanne's eldest son, Peter thanked him for his honesty. He assured Adam that he would cherish his mother for the remainder of his days.

"After all, I have waited a lifetime to have her as my wife," Peter smiled.

Peter took his leave to go ask the same question of the remaining family members. For some reason, he grew more nervous as the moments passed. Realizing how very much he wanted this, it almost scared him to think that any one of them might put up a resistance. He worried that he may have read the situation wrong all this time. What a fool he would look if he went through all the process of getting the approval of everyone only to find out that Suzanne had no true feelings for him. She had, at times, been more than a little reserved for these past many months.

Saying a prayer as he traveled from Adam's home to Suzanne's, he was glad he had learned that Velma was there visiting with them. At least he could get the input of the two most important ladies in Suzanne's life at the same time. Maybe then, he would feel a little more certain of what her answer might be.

"*Lord*," Peter prayed, "*if for any reason this is not your will, I ask that you show me ahead of time that I should stop this pursuit for her love. If I am trying to make something happen that isn't your will, then I ask that you would open my spiritual and emotional eyes to see your truth. I want only what is best for all of our lives. But, Father, if it is in your will for Suzanne and me to have a life together, then I pray that you will make the way clear. Thank you, heavenly Father. I love you and appreciate that you truly do lead and direct my path. Amen.*"

He arrived at Suzanne's home and pulled into the driveway. Resting his hands on the steering wheel for another moment, he closed his eyes, trusting the Lord to guide him as he stepped out in faith.

Going to the door, he was relieved when Velma opened it instead of Suzanne. With a broad smile, she welcomed him into the house. Peter had loved Suzanne's mother almost as long as he'd loved Suzanne. As a young boy, with no church home to call his own, Mrs. Brummell's kindness and genuine love for those in their little community had always touched him deeply.

He would always remember attending the annual fall festival at their tiny church and bobbing for apples until his entire head was wet. Most often, it was the pastor's wife who handed him a towel to dry his hair, and ensured that he had a crisp apple to carry home with him. Seeing her bright smile was like a ray of sunshine on this uncertain day.

Autumn came bounding down the stairs with a glad exclamation at seeing him.

"Peter, I was just wondering when you were going to come for your next visit! I was hoping it would be before Christmas. I need your help in deciding what to get Mom."

Peter gave them both a hug. This was something he loved about Suzanne's family. They were the biggest huggers in the world and it made him feel like part of their family to be embraced warmly each time he arrived.

He replied to Autumn that he would love to help her, "But, I'm here on a different mission this time. If we can talk about that later I would sure appreciate it, and will be glad to help however I can. Believe me, we will have plenty of time to go shopping for Christmas, Autumn, and I would really love that; but it's still over a month until Thanksgiving. Right now I need to have a quick talk with you and your grandmother about something entirely different."

Pulling Velma and Autumn into the living room, Peter quickly asked if Suzanne was likely to come into the room. He was assured that she was in the garden and would not be in for a while.

Telling them of his love for Suzanne, he asked for their blessings.

Autumn then leaned forward from where she sat by her grandmother's side on the sofa and with serious eyes, she asked him, "Peter, I know that you love my mother, and that you want to be with her for the rest of your life. However, do you think you can put up with all of our craziness and find a way to fit into our family events? We get pretty intense at times, and the holidays are of utmost importance to our mother and to us all. We have many traditions that you would have to get used to. At the same time, we would try to learn your ways and do what we could to make you feel comfortable and welcome."

Smiling at the girl who so clearly loved her mother dearly, he replied with all the seriousness the occasion called for.

"Autumn, not only do I love your mother, but I love you and your brothers and grandmother as if you were my very own. I can hardly wait to introduce you to my mother and father and for them to finally have a granddaughter and grandsons to call their own. If you will agree to be my daughter, I will love you, along with your mother. I will protect you, take care of you, and see to it that your every need is met from now until that time comes when you are out on your own or are married. I consider that in marrying your mother, I am indeed making you my own daughter. Please understand; I will never try to take the place of your father. I know that you had a very special and wonderful relationship with Daniel and I realize that I could never fill his shoes. But, I would be honored to be your father by marriage and to love you as my own daughter."

Blinking back the moisture that formed in his eyes, Peter continued, "I look forward to many years of holidays, traditions and all. I have waited a lifetime to experience this."

Autumn sat for a few moments, eyes shimmering with tears. Glancing over at her grandmother, she looked at her as if asking permission for something. Finally, at a slight nod from Velma, Autumn looked back at Peter.

"I would be glad to have you as my father. I will always love my Daddy, but he is in heaven now, and nothing can change that. If Mom accepts your request to marry her, I will be thrilled."

Smiling, she glanced back at her grandmother, "Grams, I know you approve too. So, I guess we are going to be planning a wedding!"

Velma smiled and nodded her head, "Peter, you are going to be a magnificent addition to our family. I could not be happier for you, and for my Suzanne. God has answered a lot of prayers, it seems."

He was relieved that both Autumn and Velma unreservedly, gave their wholehearted consent and welcomed him into their family.

With that, Velma stood up and told Peter, "I will go find Suzanne. When I last saw her, she was out back weeding her flowers beyond the pool. She may need a few moments to get cleaned up. Autumn, why don't you go get Peter a nice glass of iced tea, Honey. I feel sure he could use something to drink about now."

Autumn hurried to the kitchen, and filled a glass with ice and fresh mint tea. Returning to the living room, she carefully set it on the table beside Peter. Seeing him sitting there in the big leather recliner where her father once sat, head leaned back and eyes closed as if tired out, it crossed her mind that he looked like a natural fit to their home; much as if he was meant to be there. Touching his hand with her fingertips, she whispered softly, telling him that the tea was there.

"Peter, I will leave you to rest for a few moments until Mom gets here," the girl said with a deeper sensitivity than many people twice her age might have shown. "You probably want a few moments alone."

"I honestly don't know what her answer will be, but please know that I will be praying for you both. Mom has been a bit melancholy these last few days; I think she misses Daddy quite badly at times. I also think she has been waiting for you to come. Sometimes she looks out the front window with a look of yearning on her face, as if waiting for your car to pull into the driveway."

"If you need anything," Autumn continued, "please let me know. I will be just down the hallway in the sun-room reading. Oh, and I will be saying a prayer for you and Mom. I think you might need it." With a wink and a flip of her ponytail, the girl vanished from sight.

Peter was grateful for the quiet moments allowed him. He was indeed very tired. The meetings with Suzanne's family members had been more exhausting than he expected. To top that off, he had stopped by to see his parents the evening before to remind them of his plans to fly to Dallas to ask Suzanne to marry him. He was glad to have received their blessings, and to realize that Suzanne and her family would be welcomed by his.

Velma found Suzanne in the back corner of the huge yard working in the shade of the giant oak tree. Telling her that Peter had arrived and wished to speak with her, Velma suggested that her daughter might wish to run in and freshen up before going to speak with the man.

"He seems to have something on his mind," Velma murmured. "If I were you, I would want to be a little more presentable."

Hurrying back toward the house and going inside before Suzanne could question her further, Velma quickly made her way to her own room. She knelt beside her bed to pray for the couple and the entire family.

Suzanne hurried inside and washed her hands and face. She brushed on a light coating of powder and lipstick. Changing into a fresh sundress, she felt a flutter of anticipation. There could be only one reason for Peter showing up like this; especially at just a little after the twelfth month of losing Daniel.

Feeling somewhat nervous, and yet excited, she hurried to find the man who had come seeking her attention. Looking into the sun-room, she inquired of Autumn why everyone was being so secretive. Autumn stared at her with wide-eyed innocence, "Mom, you will need to speak with Peter. I am sure he can better explain than I ever could."

Realizing that she was getting nowhere with her daughter, she went into the living room. Seeing Peter laying back against the leather recliner, sound asleep, her heart nearly stopped. In the lamplight, he looked so tired, so vulnerable, and so desirable.

Reaching over, Suzanne touched Peter's cheek. Jerking awake, he was embarrassed to realize that he had actually fallen asleep. Laughing, she sat down on the arm of the chair, handing him his glass of cold tea.

"Here, you sleepyhead, maybe this will wake you up."

"Thank you. I feel rather foolish just falling asleep like an old man while waiting. Guess I was more tired than I realized. I hope I wasn't drooling all over myself!"

Drawing in a deep drink of the cool liquid, he looked at the beautiful woman from under his lashes. Slowly setting the glass down on the coaster, he rose from the chair, lifting Suzanne with him. Standing for a moment, he looked deeply into her eyes as he held her hand in his, kissing the back of it gently. His green eyes seemed a deeper green than Suzanne could remember them ever being. Wondering if this was an indication of his feelings, she watched him openly.

Glancing down to hide his intensely emotional state, Peter smiled crookedly. A tiny part of him was terrified that she might actually reject his proposal. He had no earthly idea how he would handle that. Pulling her along with him toward the patio door, he wrapped his arm snugly around her. He asked Suzanne to walk with him, teasing her into compliance.

In the cool evening air, with the perfume of flowers all around them, they walked on the paving stones toward the backside of the garden. They soon approached a beautiful gazebo with a white wicker swing and big soft cushions in muted colors. Settling into the swing, Peter drew Suzanne closer still. Sitting there together, as the sun sank to the west; they swung in silence for a long while. Somehow, they both were content simply to sit; no conversation needed.

As the moon made its way high into the sky, Suzanne looked up at him with a glimmer of a smile and murmured, "Is there anything in particular you wanted, Peter? Or, did you just come for an evening swing in my garden?"

Chuckling, Peter sat up straighter and smiled down at her. "Hmm, well, now that you mention it, I did have something I wanted to ask you. Give me just a moment, if you will."

Taking her in his arms, he kissed her with a passion she had almost forgotten existed. Drowning in the emotions washing over her, Suzanne pulled back a bit and searched the strong face across from her. She realized that she truly was coming to love this tenderhearted man.

She wondered briefly if it was too soon after losing Daniel, and then she pushed aside the doubts that tried to swarm her thoughts once again. Remembering her visit with Pastor David, the precious letters from Daniel, and the afternoon walks in the garden, she trusted in the peace of knowing that God and Daniel both were rooting for her.

Getting up from the swing, Peter steadied it until it was still. He turned and knelt before her on one knee while taking a small velvet box from his pocket.

As he opened it, he smiled nervously, "Suzanne, with the blessing of each of your children, and of your mother, I ask you to please accept me as your husband and give me the honor of being my wife. I love you with all of my heart, and have for more years than I can remember. Can you find it in your heart to love me, too?"

As the moonlight glistened off the beautiful square diamond, Suzanne felt her eyes drawn to Peter's hopeful green gaze. Tears of joy filled her eyes. With a sharply indrawn breath, she suddenly knew, without a doubt, that new love was truly possible in the wake of a terrible loss.

"Yes," she whispered. "Yes, my love, I will be your wife. I love you and can't wait to begin our life together."

After slipping the ring on her finger, Peter rose from his position on his knee. Settling in beside Suzanne on the welcoming swing once again, he pulled her close to his heart.

"Sweetheart, you have no idea how long I've waited to hear you say those words. I promise you, I will do everything in my power to make you happy and to give you all the delights you deserve. I also vow to love your family as my own and am thrilled to be getting a beautiful daughter and two sons. Little Sandi and Deborah are the icing on the cake. My dear, you may never realize how I have longed for a family just like the one you are bringing to me. I can hardly wait for our first run of holidays together."

As he paused for a breath, Suzanne couldn't help but tease him a little, "So, are you marrying me for my family, or for my money, or just because you are a tad bit bored?"

Peter started to become a bit defensive. Glancing her way, he saw the moonlight reflecting off the twinkle in her eyes and the tiny quirk of a smile at the corner of her mouth.

With a deep chuckle, in a true southern drawl, he replied, "Why, Darlin', I was most sincerely considerin' marryin' you for your good looks alone."

They both burst into laughter. They then spent the next hour whispering and sharing dreams of the future. Peter felt he could never get enough of being with this beautiful woman. He knew that he was blessed beyond anything he'd ever imagined.

Suzanne was simply in awe of the goodness of the Lord to bring such joy into her life once again.

CHAPTER 27

T HEY ALL SPENT the next several weeks preparing for the holidays and the wedding. Neither the bride nor the groom wanted to wait any longer than was necessary. Theirs was a love set in the foundation of a lifetime of waiting.

With both Daniel's and the family's blessing, they knew it was going to be alright to make a life together. Suzanne wanted a small Christmas Eve wedding, one that was filled with the wonder of new birth. She knew that theirs would forever be a special anniversary day, for as long as they both should live.

Suzanne was determined to involve her children in the wedding process as much as possible. As far as she was concerned, they were marrying Peter right along with her. Thus, she felt they needed to feel every bit a part of the ceremony.

She and Autumn went shopping for the clothes they would wear, but for Suzanne it was more than just the shopping that was important. She took every opportunity to allow the teenager to talk about her father, and to remember the life they had shared with Daniel. Suzanne wanted to reassure herself that her child knew without a doubt she was not trying to replace her father in any way.

At first, Autumn was reluctant to discuss her grief for the father she had so adored. However, as the days flew by, she talked more and more of how much she had loved him. She shared how she wished so much he could be there for her own wedding day, and other important things like graduations and birthdays. On several occasions, they cried together and held each other as they allowed their tears to wash away some of the pain of loss.

Suzanne had struggled to decide what to do with both her and Daniel's wedding rings. Adam had given Joanna's wedding ring set to Deborah and, of course, he wore his father's matching ring from his parents' marriage.

After talking with Jamie and Autumn, it was agreed that Suzanne would save her and Daniel's rings for when Jamie became engaged. If his fiancé was the kind of person who would treasure and enjoy wearing the lovely pieces, then they would be passed on to Jamie and her. If not, then perhaps Autumn and her fellow would one day want to wear them.

It was amazing to Suzanne how having such a simple little decision handled gave her a feeling of relief. It was somehow as if Daniel was looking down on them all, guiding them in some of these difficult issues.

Removing her wedding rings was an emotional moment. Placing them carefully inside their velvet lined boxes, she put her lovely Scottish engagement ring and hers and Daniel's wedding bands in the wall safe; until they should be needed again.

With a sigh of relief mixed with a touch of sorrow, Suzanne turned to the future. A new day was coming and while she would forever love her Daniel, he was gone. A future with Peter awaited her and she was not going to let the past destroy the beauty of the life ahead.

Jamie had agreed to be his sister's escort for the upcoming ceremony and Adam was chosen to walk their mother down the aisle. Suzanne had coffee with Deborah and Adam one morning to discuss the final details of the upcoming event. They all agreed that little Sandi was much too young to be included in the ceremony.

While she would never have said so, Suzanne was quite relieved. She wanted a small, intimate wedding with as little drama attached as possible. Having a tiny little flower girl in the mix could have led to a disastrous conclusion.

She loved her granddaughter, and had Sandi been a little older, she would have welcomed the opportunity to involve her. It was a blessing that Deborah was a very kind and sensitive young woman. Suzanne knew she could not have asked for a better daughter-in-law. Adam had chosen well.

Before they realized it, Thanksgiving arrived. Jamie and Autumn had drawn up the plan for their Thanksgiving table décor and they decided to use that special day to introduce the Scottish theme that would be carried out throughout Christmas. They ordered a huge centerpiece filled with pheasant feathers, gilded fruit and candles, and with pieces of Scottish plaid woven all through it.

Suzanne and Deborah concocted the most amazing dinner any of them could ever remember having. The turkey seemed to fairly shout with glory as it lay in golden splendor on the platter, surrounded with garnish and glazed mushrooms. The side dishes of mashed potatoes and gravy, corn casserole, green beans and homemade yeast bread were amazing. They ended the meal with a dessert called Cranachan, a simple Scottish dish comprised of fresh raspberries, whipped cream, honey and toasted oats.

Peter was there as well. He had dreaded leaving his parents at home alone on the holiday. However, that worry was resolved when they informed him they were going on an island cruise.

"Is your father in good enough health to make a trip like that?" Suzanne inquired.

"Apparently. Mom said they ran it by his heart doctor and it's just what the doctor ordered. I think they will have the time of their lives."

"Oh, I do hope so," Suzanne noted. "Nadine sure deserves a break. Taking care of a sick husband is exhausting, especially when it involves months on end. I look forward to hearing their stories when they get back."

Following the meal, Jamie orchestrated everyone's help in putting up their memory tree. Deborah and little Sandi were encouraged to put the plaid bows on the tree after the lights were on. Autumn opened box after box of special ornaments they had scoured the internet for, all with a theme of their father's beloved Scotland. There were even a couple of shaggy little ponies to add to the mix.

It was with much laughter and love that they all spent that very special evening together. It was so very different from holidays past, especially the year before. This celebration was filled with the promise of many more to come.

And so the Thanksgiving holiday was spent, partially in sweet remembrances of the father and husband who was gone on to glory; as well as in building new and loving relationships.

Suzanne sat alone after everyone had gone to bed late that night. Peter had bowed to her wishes and agreed to stay in their home for the special holiday time. It was so much easier than rushing back and forth to a hotel room. He had gone upstairs when Jamie did to look at the new stereo system Jamie had installed in his room. Suzanne could hear them laughing and talking like old friends as their voices wafted down the staircase.

Smiling, she realized that the house was once again full; full of joy, full of laughter, full of peace. It was full of so many things that had been missing for so long.

"Thank you, Father, for bringing back the joy to our home," she whispered. *"I love that even as we are learning to live without Daniel, he is still very much a part of our lives. We may just make it yet, but only because of your amazing grace."*

Time flew by and with Peter living in another state, and so much to do, they hardly had time to see each other before the wedding date. He had his late hay crop to get in and needed to handle a multitude of details to ensure that everything was taken care of once they were married.

He arranged for a friend to care for his horses and cattle while he and Suzanne were gone on their honeymoon and was also trying to work out a long-term arrangement for afterward, as he was going to be living in Dallas for a while.

It didn't matter to Peter where he lived, as long as Suzanne and her family were a part of that life. However, there were some other practical matters that would have to be dealt with before the wedding.

He also had end of semester grades to get wrapped up.

Peter had applied for a teaching position at a small college not far from Suzanne's home and he was immediately accepted. They scheduled him to begin teaching with the January session. He and Suzanne were thrilled with the arrangement. This gave them the entire winter break to take their honeymoon and to get him settled in at the Dallas house before he began work.

With a deep sense of knowing that God was preparing the way, Peter submitted his resignation at the High School. The administrator assured him that when he and the family moved back to the farm, a job would be waiting for him if he wanted it.

Last, but not least, was the issue of his parents. Being an only child had its drawbacks in times like these. Thankfully, he had several close cousins who were more than willing to help with things as needed and could be trusted with his beloved mother and father. Knowing that they would not lack for anything was of utmost importance to Peter. Although he would be coming back and forth frequently, it was a good feeling to know that they would be looked in on from time to time.

Closing up his home for a while would not be a problem. He loved the big, rambling log structure that he'd built with his own hands. It would be there when they all returned eventually.

He would never forget the look on Suzanne's face when she first saw it. The place really was amazing. He'd built it high on a bluff that over-looked the Buffalo River. It had a certain elegance, with long windows and a huge fireplace, that set it apart from other homes he'd been in.

Peter was quite proud of the end result from his hard work. It had taken him nearly five years of hard labor and persistence to build the place. His home was as far removed from the beautiful home in the city where Suzanne had lived these past years as could be imagined. Yet, it had a magnificence that was breathtaking.

It was not at all unusual to see eagles soaring overhead, and other wildlife roaming freely on the grounds on a daily basis. Nighttime was just as thrilling, as the deer and other wildlife came right up to the house. Suzanne had been amazed at the beauty, elegance and peace of the home. The kitchen and dining area looked like he had plucked it right from the pages of some magazine. That had been a pleasant surprise for her. She immediately fell in love with the simple grandeur of the lovely home. She had told him that knowing this was where they would eventually settle to finish their lives gave her a great sense of peace.

Suzanne wanted to remain in her Dallas home for at least a few more years to allow Autumn to finish high school. They all had agreed that the little town would eventually become their home. For now, however, the house in Dallas would be their residence. Of course, Peter was thrilled to live with them in Dallas after he and Suzanne were married. The lovely log cabin would be there waiting for them to spend holidays and summers.

They finally got around to discussing the finances and how they would manage after their marriage.

"The Lord knows, I can provide quite well for us all with the proceeds from Daniel's life insurance, retirement fund, and book sales!" Suzanne exclaimed to Peter one evening as they were discussing the matter, never thinking that he might be offended.

Peter wasn't about to have any of that. He told her in no uncertain terms, that she could do what she wanted to with her money, give it to her children or grandchildren, he didn't care.

"I will provide for my wife, thank you very much, or have no wife at all!" he exclaimed.

"In fact, I have quite a bit of money put back from my years of teaching. There is no need for you to ever worry whether I can take care of you as you are accustomed to."

It was clear the man was wounded that she would think otherwise.

"Peter, I am sorry. Of course, you will. I had no intention of making you feel that you must live off mine and Daniel's money. It's just that there is so much of it! On the other hand, I never want you to think I am being selfish or stingy. We can pool our resources and will have more than we will ever need."

And so, they came to a compromise; for the moment at least.

Very shortly after Thanksgiving, Peter had set his mind to planning a honeymoon that would give him and Suzanne memories to last a lifetime. After talking to her children, he'd decided to take her on a trip to Paris. She had traveled the world with Daniel, yet somehow they had never found the time to make it to the city of love.

Not wanting to try and upstage any life experiences she may have shared with her deceased husband, Peter nevertheless wanted to give her something she had always wished for. He wanted to see the sparkle in her eyes as she wandered the cobblestone streets of the city she had only previously read about. He wanted to give her, them both, a wonderful beginning in a place that would be theirs and theirs alone.

Not telling Suzanne was the most difficult part. She wanted to know how to pack, what to take on the trip, and would she need her passport and visa. In spite of everything, Peter and Adam, with a little help from Autumn, managed to keep the location of their destination a secret the entire time up until the wedding day.

Overall, things worked out, step-by-step for the upcoming nuptials.

CHAPTER 28

BEFORE THEY KNEW it, the day had arrived. Everything was ready and the small chapel of the large church where Daniel and Suzanne had served so faithfully for so many years was decorated.

Suzanne was sitting quietly in the bridal chamber, waiting for her mother to bring her a hairpin when she heard the door open softly. Glancing upward in the gold framed mirror, she saw her older sister. Karen stood hesitantly just inside the door, her hazel eyes wide with anxiety.

Wondering what Karen could possibly want, Suzanne waited silently, eyes locked with those of her sister. Autumn had told her a little of the conversation she'd had about Karen's recovery from the drugs and alcohol. Suzanne had prayed for Karen, and hoped it was truly a life-changing experience she had undergone. She had wondered from time to time why Karen hadn't called her, but then life was so busy that she rarely gave it a second thought. Her mom mentioned Karen from time to time, albeit mostly that she seemed to be doing well.

However, as sisters, they had hardly said ten words to each other in the final months of Daniel's illness and the year following his death. Suzanne wondered, trying to remember if Karen had even offered her condolences at the funeral. Things had been such a blur, it was possible that she had and it had just been forgotten.

Slowly, Karen pushed the door shut and walked toward Suzanne. She wondered briefly if her niece, Autumn, had told her sister about her life transformation. It had made her wonder, as Suzanne had never called her to say anything. As soon as she thought them, she pushed the negative thoughts aside.

"*After all,*" she reminded herself, "*I haven't taken the time to call Suzanne, either.*"

Crossing the room and kneeling before her, Karen clasped both of Suzanne's hands between her own.

"Suzanne, I came to beg you to forgive me for the utterly foolish things I said to you back when Daniel was so ill. I have wanted so many times to come to you and ask you to let me explain. I have been so very foolish. You see, I allowed myself to become addicted to my prescription medication and alcohol. If you remember the day that you came by my house, that is the day that I finally made things right with the Lord, and decided on the spot to make the needed changes in my life."

Clearing her throat, Karen continued in a whisper, "I was so ashamed of how I treated you, even in my drugged mind, I knew that you were in the right. I fled to my back porch and bowed my heart to God and He heard me and helped me find healing. Brenda was there with me for the next two weeks while I cleansed my house and my body of every bad thing in me. It was awful, for me and for her. But we made it. I have found a new love for my daughter, and she has come to love and respect me after having had nothing to love or respect for so very long."

Bowing her head, and looking at her twisted fingers, Karen continued, "Suzie, I am not making excuses; I know that I acted badly that night at the gymnasium. If you will forgive me, I will promise not to act so foolishly again. With my doctor's help, and that of my daughter, I am finally painkiller free. I hope to never again use pills as a crutch. Beyond that, I've not had a drink in over a year. God has slowly healed me from head to toe. I needed to come today to see you, to let you know all that has gone on, and to ask you to forgive me. Will you forgive me? Please?"

Suzanne reached out and smoothed her sister's ever-unruly auburn hair.

"Oh, Karen, I am so glad you came to me today. I have missed our friendship so very much. You are, and have always been, so very special to me. This is a wedding gift I never expected. Thank you. I love you, and yes, of course, I forgive you. In fact, there was never anything to forgive. I do appreciate your humble heart and am so glad we can be sisters once again. I've missed you so."

With tears in both their eyes, the sisters embraced.

Velma arrived just then with the hairpin and a bottle of cool water, as well as a reminder that it was nearly time for the bridal march. Autumn and Brenda flew into the room behind their grandmother in their usual whirlwind fashion. Fussing over her a last little bit, they all declared that she was as beautiful as a bride could possibly be. Before she knew it, Suzanne found herself walking down the aisle to marry her bridegroom.

She was stunning in her soft cream-colored straight shift and cappuccino colored shoes. As the bride for a second time, she wore her hair in an upswept twist and a lovely wide-brimmed hat draped in coffee and cream Venetian lace. The flowers she carried were a bouquet of creamy white roses, tied with a deep red velvet ribbon, an inch or so wide.

Peter stood tall and proud in his deep brown tuxedo with its coffee and cream cummerbund and dress shirt. The old style neck cloth he'd chosen to wear gave him an air of rakish elegance that made Suzanne weak in the knees as she spotted him. It had a touch of the same lace as her attire; however, rather than appearing feminine, it emphasized his broad shoulders and masculinity.

His hair was slicked back in a twenty's fashion while the rose in his lapel was the same as in her bouquet. He captured every eye in the room. That is, until the bride entered and walked slowly down the aisle.

The backdrop to the ceremony was a collection of fresh green Christmas trees decorated in cream and cappuccino, with a touch of deep berry red added here and there. Their white lights shimmered softly as the bride and groom took their places. Her daughter, Autumn, the only attendant to the bride, wore a complimenting dress in a rich caramel brown with touches of cream lace at the neck and wrists.

With their family and closest friends gathered around them, Suzanne Brummell Parker and Peter Clifton said their vows. The young minister of the Laurel Oak Presbyterian Church performed the simple ceremony. He considered it an honor to do this for the woman he admired as his former pastor's wife.

Pastor David was gladdened to see the joy on her face, and to know that she had found her peace. Perhaps the time in his office praying and sharing with her had done more than he had hoped it might.

Suzanne had been a role model for both his wife and himself, for as long as he could remember, and he understood her better than most. After watching her walk through the valley of the shadow of death with Daniel, he felt he knew a little of the pain and sorrow she had experienced. He had wished so many times to be able to help her somehow overcome the sadness that had swamped her life. To see her smiling and happy on this beautiful afternoon brought him great joy.

After walking his mother down the aisle, Adam stepped over to stand beside Peter and serve as the best man. He gravely handed the rings to each of them as they shared the vows that would tie them together as man and wife. Jamie stood with Autumn, beaming on everyone as if this whole thing was entirely his idea.

At the end of the ceremony, Peter pulled Suzanne close. He kissed her softly on her cheek, whispering the words of so long ago, "Suzie, let's give 'em a show!"

Then claiming her lips in a long drawn-out kiss, he indeed made quite a show of it.

Suzanne laughed silently, her shoulders shaking, as their friends and family gave catcalls. Even Peter's mother and father got in on the excitement. Nadine waived her frilly white handkerchief and Mr. Clifton wiped a tear from his eyes with his large blue hanky. It was clear that they were thrilled to have Suzanne and her children as their very own.

Peter then drew her closer still and whispered to her alone, "Suzanne Claire Brummell Parker Clifton, I love you more than words can express. I promise that I will still respect you. . . and love you, in the morning, and for all the mornings to come."

Reaching toward the best man, his new son, Peter took from him a single long-stemmed white rose and presented it to his beloved.

He then stated firmly for all to hear, "This, my love, is the last of a full dozen white roses sent over the past year. They represent my seal of promise to you. The promise to love you from this day forward, and to cherish you as you deserve to be cherished until the day I die. As you accept this rose, you also seal your promise to be my wife from now until death should part us."

Somehow these words carried more meaning to everyone represented there than ever before. The very fact that Suzanne had lost her first love made this second chance at love even more precious.

Tears of joy glistened in her eyes.

"Peter Clifton," Suzanne whispered back. Her heart was in her eyes as she took hold of the rose, their fingers intertwined around the stem.

"The Lord has indeed turned my mourning into joy. I accept your rose, and I will love you and none other, from this day forward, until death itself should claim one or both of us."

There wasn't a dry eye in the place, as each one there rejoiced for the love that had found these two at just the right time. God surely was a God of healing and hope. He had brought joy even in the midst of the darkest of times.

Turning as one toward their guests, they greeted their friends and family for the very first time as Mr. and Mrs. Peter Clifton.

The End

About The Author

Lynette Chambers

AWARD-WINNING AUTHOR, *Lynette Chambers*, was born and raised in the small town of Evening Shade, Arkansas nestled in the beautiful Ozark Mountains.

The second oldest of a large family of children, she grew up reading novels by Grace Livingston Hill, Emilie Loring, Eugenia Price and others. The joy she received from their stories of love, hope, faith and redemption inspired her to begin putting her own thoughts on paper for others to read.

Lynette's books, poems and short stories encourage readers to deepen their walk with God. Her passion for history, experience with small town life and love of colorful characters uplifts even the most troubled heart.

When not writing, Lynette enjoys speaking, teaching and traveling with her husband, Dr. Jim Chambers, as well as spending time with her children and grandchildren. Lynette and Jim have two black cats who keep them entertained in numerous ways, so life is never dull at their little home in the Ozarks.

To contact Lynette regarding speaking engagements or other special events, email her directly at lynette@iolglobal.com. To view her books, blog or writings, visit www.lynettechambers.com.